The Amish of Seymour

Promised to Another

a novel

LAURA V. HILTON

WHITAKER
HOUSE

All Scripture quotations are taken from the King James Version of the Holy Bible.

PROMISED TO ANOTHER
The Amish of Seymour ~ Book Three

ISBN: 978-1-60374-257-3
Printed in the United States of America
© 2012 by Laura V. Hilton

Whitaker House
1030 Hunt Valley Circle
New Kensington, PA 15068
www.whitakerhouse.com

Library of Congress Cataloging-in-Publication Data

Hilton, Laura V., 1963–
    Promised to another / by Laura V. Hilton.
        pages cm. — (The Amish of Seymour ; book 3)
    ISBN 978-1-60374-257-3 (trade pbk.)
    1. Amish youth—Fiction. 2. Seymour (Mo.)—Fiction. I. Title.
    PS3608.I4665P76 2012
    813'.6—dc23
                        2011053420

2 3 4 5 6 7 8 9 10   **W**   18 17 16 15 14 13 12

Dedicated to:

Steve, *my best friend,*

Loundy, *my favorite song,*

Michael, *my adventurous one,*

Kristin, *my precious daughter,*

Jenna, *my sunshine,*

Kaeli, *my shower of blessing,*

And God, who has blessed me with these.

In loving memory of Allan and Janice Price, my parents; my grandmother, Mertie; and my uncle Loundy, each of whom has blessed me with some knowledge of our Pennsylvania Dutch ancestors.

Also, to Tamela, my agent, for not letting me give up and for giving sage advice.

Acknowledgments

I'd like to offer my heartfelt thanks to the following:

The residents of Seymour, for answering my questions and pointing me in the right directions.

My Sunday school class, for keeping me in prayer while I wrote.

The amazing team at Whitaker House—Christine, Courtney, and Cathy. You are wonderful.

My agent, for believing in me all these years.

My critique group—you know who you are. You are amazing and knew how to ask the right questions when more detail was needed. Also, thanks for the encouragement.

My husband, Steve, for being a tireless proofreader and cheering section. And my sons, Michael and Loundy, for taking over the kitchen duties when I was deep in the story.

And in memory of my parents, Allan and Janice, my uncle Loundy, and my grandmother, Mertie, all of whom talked about their Pennsylvania Dutch heritage.

Glossary of Amish Terms and Phrases

ach	oh
aent	aunt
"Ain't so?"	a phrase commonly used at the end of a sentence to invite agreement
boppli	baby or babies
bu	boy
buwe	boys
daed	dad
danki	thank you
dawdi-haus	a home built for grandparents to live in once they retire
Englischer	a non-Amish person
frau	wife
grossmammi	grandmother
gut	good
gut nacht	good night
haus	house
"Ich liebe dich"	"I love you"
jah	yes
kapp	prayer covering or cap
kinner	children
kum	come
maidal	an unmarried woman
mamm	mom
nein	no
onkel	uncle
Ordnung	the rules by which an Amish community lives
rumschpringe	"running around time," a period of adolescence after which Amish teens choose either to be baptized in the Amish church or to leave the community

ser gut	very good
verboden	forbidden
welkum	welcome
wunderbaar	wonderful

Chapter 1

"May I take you home from the singing?"

Annie Beiler's breath hitched, and her gaze shot from the dusty toes of her powder-blue tennis shoes to the drop-dead-gorgeous man standing not three feet in front of her. Unfortunately, his tentative smile wasn't aimed in her direction.

Nein, Joshua Esh's hazel eyes were locked on Rachel Lapp. Annie had to admit Rachel was cute, with her strawberry blonde hair and green dress that perfectly matched her eyes.

Joshua was what her Englisch friends called a "player," for sure. Everyone talked about how he never took the same girl home from singings twice. And Annie couldn't help hoping that he would eventually make his way to her.

Rachel's face lit up. "Danki, Joshua. I'd love a ride."

Annie scowled. If and when he got around to asking her, she'd turn him down. Someone should have the willpower to say nein. Just that evening, Rachel had been talking with Annie and some other girls about Joshua's flirtatious ways. It appeared that she'd merely been jealous since he hadn't asked to take her home.

Okay, to be honest, Annie did feel a bit envious, too. Make that more than a bit. And it wasn't just because of Joshua, although he had played a big part in it. The truth was, none of the buwe who'd come from Pennsylvania in the man swap had ever offered to give her a ride. Not a single one.

She didn't consider herself that unfortunate-looking.

Annie brushed past Joshua and Rachel and left the barn. Immediately, she regretted having gone outside, because she did need to find a way home—unless she rode along with another couple. But she didn't think she could stand there alone by the barn doors, hopeful, when all the buwe she noticed didn't seem to know she was alive.

Like Joshua Esh.

Especially Joshua Esh.

Annie kicked a rock and winced when it didn't budge.

"Annie? Is that you?" A familiar male voice sounded from out of the darkness ahead of her.

She jumped. She hadn't expected to hear that voice. Not in a month of singings. She frowned. "Luke?"

"Jah." He moved into the circle of light from the lanterns hanging around the barn.

Annie planted her fists on her hips. She wouldn't make the mistake of falling for Luke Schwartz twice—not that she'd really fallen for him the first time. It was just that he'd asked. And a bird in the hand is worth two in the bush, right? Okay, she'd realized he wasn't what she wanted—he wouldn't make her top-ten list of the dreamiest Amish men—but he was better than nothing. She pulled in a deep breath, steeling herself. "What are you doing here?"

"Ach, that's a wunderbaar way to welkum me. I've kum home."

She stilled, her hope building, despite her internal warnings. "For how long?" She didn't want to spend her life alone. Didn't want to rely on the kindness of other couples for rides. Didn't want to be the only girl left unattached, unaccepted, unwanted.

Unloved.

But, then again, she didn't want to settle for just anyone, either.

Luke didn't quite meet her eyes. "You wound me."

Ach. Not for gut, then. The pencil fell from behind her ear, and she stooped to pick it up, careful not to glance at him as she rose.

"Never without that ever-present pencil, I see."

She winced, hating that he mocked her. It wasn't common to take a pencil to singings, she knew, but what if she wanted to write something down? The name of a book she'd like to read, perhaps, or something she wanted to mention to her students the following week. Maybe even the initials of her number one dream guy, who stood somewhere nearby but didn't pay any attention to her. Who didn't know she was alive. "Sarcasm doesn't suit you."

He sighed. "May I give you a ride home? Looks like things are breaking up."

She took a deep breath. "I'm sorry, but I already have a ride. Maybe another time."

Luke laughed. "Right. I heard how popular you are. Having to beat the buwe off with a stick, ain't so?"

Annie stiffened. "So, you couldn't pay rent on that run-down trailer and ran home to your parents, jah?"

Someone moved up beside her, and she turned her head. Whoever it was didn't register. What she did notice was that others were gathering around her and Luke, watching their exchange.

She was in enough trouble already, having nearly gotten dismissed from her teaching post. The school board had permitted her to continue teaching, provided she was put on probation. All she needed was for one of these eavesdroppers to go home and tell his or her folks. She'd be out of a job so fast, a racing horse and buggy wouldn't be able to keep pace. She searched for something to say, something to defuse the situation.

Luke's glance slid from her to whoever had stepped up to offer wordless support. He sneered, then backed up a space. "Well, since you have a ride, I'll just catch you later, then. Gut to see you, Annie."

She forced a smile. "Glad you're back, Luke."

He turned and disappeared into the darkness.

Joshua stood beside Annie for a moment. Silent. Wishing he could say something to salve the hurt she must feel. He sensed the pain radiating from her as she watched the redheaded man walk away.

The whole situation confused him. He'd been attracted to Annie the moment he'd met her, but when he'd fished for more information about her, he'd found out she was taken. Off limits. All but engaged to Luke Schwartz, who had vowed to return for her someday. Apparently, that day was now.

Yet Annie hadn't been waiting with bated breath.

Joshua didn't know exactly what that meant.

He knew only what he wanted it to mean.

The crowd around them thinned as the pairs began to make their ways to their buggies. Joshua became conscious of Rachel standing on the other side of him, twisting her apron in her hand while she waited on him to do something. He wasn't sure what.

He swallowed the lump in his throat and turned to face the brunette schoolteacher. "Um, Annie. I'm going right past your haus. I can give you a ride, if you'd like."

The expression in her dark eyes could have withered a lesser man. "I couldn't possibly impose on a courting couple."

"Ach, you know gut and well Rachel and I aren't courting." He couldn't commit to anyone. Not when his attention had been caught and held by a certain Amish schoolteacher. But he wouldn't approach her— not until he knew for sure what was happening between her and Luke. Or until he could somehow catch her eye. Choosing a future frau was a serious thing. After all, he'd be spending the rest of his life with her.

It wasn't like God would point her out with a bright-neon light, one that he'd be sure to notice in this quiet, rural community. Then again, maybe He had. Joshua had certainly sat up and taken notice of Annie.

"I'm going right past your haus," he repeated, tucking his thumbs into his suspenders to keep from reaching out and touching her arm, grasping her hand, or otherwise physically imploring her to just hush up and come along.

The good Lord certainly hadn't made Annie Beiler into a submissive maidal. Not like Rachel Lapp, who still stood silently on his other side, waiting for him to finish. She'd probably be a docile, obedient frau. Unfortunately for her, he liked a bit of spunk.

Spunk was something that Annie Beiler possessed in abundance, if what he'd overheard during the school board meetings was true.

Ignoring him, Annie turned around and headed for the barn. He watched her go, torn whether to follow or not. Rachel still waited quietly by his side, so he straightened and faced her. "Shall we?"

She met his gaze, her green eyes wide. "Maybe we should wait to see if Annie needs a ride first. Her sister left with a beau, and her brother isn't here." She looked around. "Neither is her best friend."

"Jah." Joshua swallowed, then glanced back at the barn. "I'll ask again."

"Has Luke returned home for gut?" Rachel asked before he'd taken a step.

Joshua shrugged. "He was at the haus when we came back from church this afternoon, and he said he'd kum home."

"His parents must be so happy."

Joshua nodded, but the truth was, he didn't know. The Schwartzes had both seemed rather skeptical when they'd found Luke on the porch after church. Already, the whole community appeared to know about his homecoming. Who needed a phone when the grapevine was so effective? Annie had looked surprised to see him, however, so perhaps the news hadn't spread as quickly as Joshua had thought.

"I'll go see if I can find Annie. Be right back."

Rachel smiled. "I'll wait at your buggy."

Joshua gave a brief nod, then headed back inside the lantern-lit barn, where he breathed in the scents of animals, dust, and hay. He skirted the table, still laden with sandwiches, vegetables, and cookies left over from the singing, and walked toward a far corner where he thought he saw a brown dress in the shadows. Annie always wore brown, as if she wanted to go unnoticed. Hidden from view. Invisible.

Of course, given the recent conflicts with the school board, maybe flying low was the best thing for her.

With a sigh, Joshua paused, backtracked, and grabbed a couple of peanut butter cookies off the table. Taking a bite of one of the crumbly cookies, he retraced his steps toward the corner where he thought Annie was hiding. He swallowed. "Annie?"

No answer.

He rounded a pile of hay bales and saw her, crouched low. "Hey. You'll never find a ride hiding back here."

She jumped up and straightened her shoulders. "I wasn't hiding. I was...." She looked around and picked up a piece of straw, poking it back into the bale. "Cleaning. They missed this corner."

Joshua raised his eyebrows and silently watched her pick up more straw for several moments. Fighting a grin, he leaned against another bale of hay.

Annie balled her fists and planted them on her hips. "Aren't you going to go? Take Rachel home?"

"It's more fun watching you pick up straw. And I'm sure the Stoltzfuses will appreciate that you took so much time cleaning this part of their barn. By hand, no less. I'll be sure to tell Shanna."

"You're insufferable. Nein wonder your community swapped you out."

Her comment couldn't have been farther from the truth, but he didn't mind. That was just what he wanted everyone to believe—for now, at least. The temptation to grin won out. "Jah. I'll just be the thorn in your side, here. Now, quit being so stubborn and admit you need a ride home."

"I'll admit nein such thing."

She needed a ride, of course, but the thought of imposing on Joshua and Rachel—that wasn't right.

How could she? Besides, she didn't want a ride as an act of charity. Yet that was the only way she'd get one. She thought about walking, but she refused to give Luke and Joshua the pleasure of seeing her reduced to setting out on foot.

"I'll wait until you have a ride, then. Or till you accept one from me." Judging by the obstinate set of Joshua Esh's jaw, refusing was no longer an option.

She pulled in a deep breath and then nodded. "I guess I can let you drive me. Danki." It hurt to say that. If only he had asked her first, because he wanted to, instead of asking out of a sense of obligation.

Annie followed him outside and then climbed in the backseat of the buggy behind Rachel and Joshua. His was an open buggy, not one for courting, and the two sat with a good foot between them—a respectable distance. Annie reached for the folded quilt on the seat beside her and pulled it close, wanting the comfort. The security.

Joshua glanced over his shoulder at her. "Cold?"

"Nein." It was a bit breezy. The scent of autumn filled the air, though only a few leaves had started to turn. There was no good reason for wanting the quilt, other than her insecurity. She wrapped her arms around it, cuddling it like she would one of Mamm's quilted throw pillows when company came and she wanted to hide but had to be physically present. Not that the pillow hid her, but it made her feel more at ease. And this quilt certainly wouldn't hide her, either. She glanced down at it. Maple leaf pattern. It was beautiful.

Joshua turned around once more and studied her, open concern in his hazel eyes. The horse snorted and tossed its head, as if to show its impatience to be off. Annie squirmed, again wishing someone else had asked to take her home. Well, someone had. Luke. She winced, her stomach suddenly churning. An ex-beau or Joshua and his girl of the day: a lose-lose decision.

"I'll take Rachel home first, then you," Joshua said. He clicked his tongue to the horse.

"Nein, take me home first."

Joshua shook his head. "That doesn't make any sense. We'll kum to Rachel's haus before yours. If I take you home first, I'll have to backtrack to drop her off and then again on the way to the haus where I'm staying."

Annie frowned. "But—"

"I hate backtracking."

She pulled the quilt closer, crossing her arms over it.

Joshua glanced at Rachel before looking ahead at the road again. They hadn't spoken, but Annie was sure they'd communicated nonverbally. Probably a mutual acknowledgment of the unwelcome third party in the buggy. She'd never know.

"We got a lot done at the Kropfs' haus last week, ain't so?" Rachel turned sideways in the seat so that she faced Joshua and could see Annie. "You did a great job painting in the kitchen, Annie. It looks so much brighter with a fresh coat of white paint. Those brown water stains on the wall were nasty." She glanced at Joshua. "You were working upstairs, ain't so? Helping the other men put on a new roof?"

He nodded.

Annie sank into the backseat, glad that Rachel filled the silence with chatter. But still, she didn't need any more proof that her presence had put an awkward spin on things. What would she have to say to Joshua after Rachel was gone and they were alone? She supposed she could apologize for ruining their evening. She studied Joshua's profile when he glanced at Rachel, wishing for the thousandth time that he'd asked to take her home because he wanted to. She hugged the quilt even closer.

Rachel still babbled nonstop. "I heard that the floorboards upstairs were rotted, too."

"Jah. We had to be careful where we stepped. Should be as gut as new now."

"I think it's a shame that Amos Kropf let his haus fall into such a bad shape. Don't you?"

Joshua voiced appropriate responses to her comments, and, soon, their conversation was a vague drone in Annie's ears. Yet, all too soon, he pulled the buggy into the drive that led to Rachel's haus. It was a tidy stone place that looked hardly big enough to house her entire family. It didn't need to, of course, since all of her siblings but one were grown and married. Her younger brother, Esau, was fourteen, so this was the last year Annie would have him in class. He was one of the big buwe, but he hadn't caused her any trouble. He was as sweet as his sister. She'd actually miss him, she realized.

"I'll be right back." Joshua glanced at Annie, then vaulted out of the buggy and came around to walk Rachel to the door. They talked too quietly for Annie to make out what they said. All she heard was the muffled sound of voices.

The horse raised its tail and made a deposit. Annie glanced away, readjusting the quilt on her lap.

Too soon, Joshua was back. He climbed into the buggy and twisted around to look at her. "Move up here by me. I'm not a chauffeur."

"Jah, that's exactly what you are."

He hesitated, studying her. "Either that or a taxi service, jah?"

She smiled, in spite of herself. "Jah."

He grinned back. "Get up here."

After a moment, she laid the quilt where she'd found it, smoothing the wrinkles. Then, she climbed over the buggy seat, settling in next to him. Closer to him than Rachel had sat. "Danki for taking me home."

His grin liquefied her knees. Good thing she wasn't standing. Had he smiled at Rachel that way? He reached for the brake, released it, and clicked his tongue. Seconds later, they were back on the road.

"Did you have fun at the singing?"

"Jah." It had been okay, until Luke had shown up.

"Gut. You haven't kum to many singings in the past few weeks. Just on occasion."

He'd noticed her? Annie fought the urge to smile. "You're new in town. I go to all the singings. Well, almost all of them." She had missed a good number after Mamm's accident.

"I'm not that new. I've been here since the end of June. Four months. And I would have noticed if you were there all the time. Believe me."

He'd noticed her enough to miss her? Then, why hadn't he asked...?

"Sorry I tagged along on your ride with Rachel."

He glanced at her. "I don't mind giving you a ride. It's a pleasure. As for ruining the evening with Rachel, don't worry. I might decide to visit her later this week." He shrugged as if it didn't matter.

Annie's heart sank. She leaned back in the seat, shifting away from him as far as she could. Not that she'd been sitting indecently close. She did have a reputation to uphold. Such as it was.

He glanced at her again. "So, heard that you are meeting with the school board on Monday to discuss some things."

Tomorrow. She shut her eyes briefly. "News does get around."

"Heard you rented a van to take the students on a field trip to a Civil War battlefield. Without permission."

She fought the urge to bow her head in shame. Instead, she held steady, tightening her lips, glad that he didn't have any kinner in school and would have no reason to attend the meeting.

But then, he lived at the haus where the meeting would be held. With Luke's family.

Jah, he'd be there, to witness her humiliation firsthand.

Chapter 2

Joshua led the big draft horse pulling the wagon toward the field. Henry Schwartz had told him the horse's name was High Clyde—Hi-C, for short. Joshua's chore for the day was to start clearing rocks from the south pasture in preparation for planting next spring. The boulders had to be hauled away to another spot, where they would lie free for the taking. Someone would likely use them to build a stone haus or a fence. He worked alone, since Henry and Luke had gone to the leather shop, a place Joshua wasn't welcome. *The family business.* He didn't care much about leather, but it still galled him that he'd been excluded from the shop since his arrival in Seymour.

He didn't really need to find a job here, except for the desirability of having cash. After all, he was just killing time, unlike the ten other men who'd come to Missouri in the swap. But, to avoid suspicion, and to keep from appearing lazy, he'd figured he should probably do something productive.

The wagon wheels jolted over the rocks. Afraid of breaking a wheel, Joshua released the reins and started filling the wagon with rocks—a task that quickly appeared endless. It looked as if God had taken all of the rocks left over at the creation of the world and dumped them in the Ozark Mountains.

After he'd worked a couple of hours, he took off his straw hat and wiped a sleeve across his brow. Still morning, and already it promised to be a hot day. He wasn't used to the end of October being so warm. Sometimes, in Pennsylvania, they'd already had their first snow by now.

As he replaced his hat, he glanced across the field toward the south side of the neighboring farm. The Beilers'. Several men in unusual clothing worked around the odd-looking wooden boxes in the field, but there was no other sign of activity anywhere on the farm. He'd noticed the boxes before but had never seen anyone near them. He'd asked Henry about them once, and he'd told him what the boxes were called, but the term escaped him right now. Joshua hadn't wanted to appear dumb in front of his host, so he hadn't pressed for more information.

He figured Annie was at school right now. The schoolhaus wasn't visible from this vantage point, which was probably just as well. He'd be distracted by gawking at the pretty teacher. None of his teachers had been like Annie, as far as he could remember. Otherwise, he would have been a straight-A student, as well as the teacher's pet. He would have been more than happy to arrive early to help build the fire and to stay late to clean the chalkboards—anything to be in her presence.

The image came to mind of Annie gathering straw in the corner of the Stoltzfuses' barn last night. He chuckled at the memory. And then, she'd called him her chauffer...he sure had enjoyed their banter. Annie could give as good as she got. He gathered a few more rocks and carried them to the wagon.

As much as he wanted to ask Annie to go home with him after the next singing, he thought maybe he'd better wait. Keep an eye on her. With Luke back in the picture, there was always the chance he and Annie would pick up where they'd left off. After all, Annie had already been baptized into the church—the first step toward marriage. And, at the breakfast table this morning, the Schwartz family had talked as if Luke's prolonged absence hadn't changed anything. They'd even discussed how he could make up the membership classes he'd missed by joining another district and then marry Annie this wedding season, as originally planned. Of course, the bishop would have the final say.

Annie's feelings hadn't factored into the conversation. Maybe everyone assumed she would, of course, go along with their plans to resurrect the relationship. After all, she'd already agreed to marry Luke before he'd jumped the fence.

Joshua picked up a soccer-ball-sized rock and threw it harder than necessary into the back of the wagon. It landed with a satisfying thump. With a startled whinny, the horse took a couple of steps. Joshua drew in a deep breath. "Sorry, Hi-C." He turned and lifted another rock, then paused, again noticing the activity on the other field, where those strange-looking men worked.

Ach, his curiosity was getting the best of him. He was glad Hi-C was rein-trained, so that he could just drop the reins to the ground and the horse would stay. He was also glad he worked alone. He wouldn't have to feel guilty about abandoning his job and wandering off. He tossed the rock into the wagon and headed across the fields toward the activity at the Beilers' farm.

Joshua called out a greeting, but no one immediately responded. Maybe they hadn't heard him. A strange buzzing sound filled the air, like a bunch of miniature airplanes. Ach, beekeepers. That would explain the suits with the pant legs tucked into high boots, the heavy gloves, and the netted masks covering their heads.

He started to turn away, not wanting to interrupt their work or to risk getting stung, but the men looked up before he made his escape. Joshua took off his straw hat and waved away a few bees. "I don't mean to be nosy."

"Ach, nein problem, Joshua. We're beginning to collect the honey," the younger man said. "A bit late. It's normally done in September, but...." He shrugged.

"You're welkum to watch," the older man said. "There are extra coverings in the barn. We don't want you to get stung. Bees notice dark-colored clothing, not this light stuff." He turned to the younger man. "Aaron, take Joshua and get him set up. Danki."

Joshua nodded and then glanced back at the pasture where Hi-C was waiting. He suspected he'd been sent out there just to give him something to do. If the Schwartzes had been really serious about wanting to turn that pasture into a field, they would have been out there working, too. As long as he had something to show for his time, he'd be fine.

And this would be an opportunity to get to know the Beilers better. Maybe find out a bit more about what made Annie tick.

It certainly wouldn't hurt anything to get on her daed's good side.

Later that evening, Annie gulped and looked around at the expressions of condemnation on the faces of the parents whose children she taught. They'd each had a chance to shoot accusations that ranged from petty grievances, such as the rail breaking off of the stairs—even though no one had fallen, and the board was responsible for maintenance—to complaints that she'd allegedly given one of the scholars a meat pie for lunch but had not offered anyone else anything. Meanwhile, the little girl who'd taken the pie food hadn't had a bite to eat at the noon meal. So, of course, Annie had given her all she had—and gone hungry herself. Hardly grounds for dismissal. She'd explained away every issue as it was brought up, but she'd still felt the collective condemnation.

This next item on the table, though—she knew it could be serious. Her throat was dry, but she didn't dare reach for the pitcher of water on the table, afraid she might choke on even the smallest sip.

When every parent had voiced his or her complaint about the infamous field trip, the oldest member of the school board, Samuel Brunstettler, studied her with eyes narrowed.

"What have you to say for yourself, Annie Beiler? Why would you take the scholars on a field trip, and to see a Civil War battlefield, of all places?"

He made it sound as if another destination might have been acceptable. But the meat of the matter was, she'd taken the students without obtaining their parents' permission.

Annie shifted on the wooden chair but couldn't find a comfortable position. Out of the corner of her eye, she caught a movement in the doorway to the other room. Turning her head ever so slightly, she saw Joshua standing there, leaning against the doorframe. How long had he been watching? She hadn't noticed amid the barrage of accusations. Now, it was impossible not to notice that his gaze was locked on her.

She swallowed and looked at Samuel Brunstet-tler. "We were studying American history. Wars are a big part of that, but they're foreign to most of us, as conscientious objectors. I thought it would be worth-while for them to see a battlefield up close. Wilson's Creek isn't that far away, and the war museum there is really interesting. I think the scholars learned a lot."

"About fighting?" Samuel Brunstettler grunted. "About war?"

Annie shook her head. "The museum had some interactive displays about how both armies moved, but we mostly read about the generals and other of-ficers who served during the war. We also walked around the grounds of the haus that was turned into a field hospital for the injured solders."

"And you stressed what?" Seated across the ta-ble from Samuel Brunstettler, Bishop Sol fingered his beard and eyed her sternly. She wasn't sure why he was present. He wasn't on the school board. Maybe they figured she'd need some counseling after this.

They might not be wrong.

"I explained the two sides—the reasons they were fighting, why they believed what they did. We also discussed how they might have found an alternative way to deal with their differences instead of fighting and killing others. War, though we don't sanction it, is a part of history. Even Amish history. Timothy Hos-tler served as a conscientious objector in the Second World War. He worked in a field hospital." She dared a glance toward Joshua. He still stood in the doorway, looking as nonchalant as before. Still watching her.

"Are you planning any more of these field trips we should know about?"

Annie shook her head, still wondering what the verdict would be about the battlefield outing. This could cost her job. Why hadn't she considered that before she'd scheduled the trip?

"Nein. That was the only one." Well, almost. She'd harbored hopes of taking her scholars to the Bass Pro Shop and its Wonders of Wildlife facility, which was located near the battlefield. A driver had mentioned the popular store and museum in a casual conversation with Annie, and it had piqued her interest, especially when he mentioned that it showcased wildlife native to Missouri.

But how could she hope to justify a trip to a place these parents would surely consider too materialistic? She could hear their argument, even now: "Textbooks have perfectly adequate pictures of wildlife, so there's no reason to subject the children to such worldly notions as big bass boats and other equipment for outdoor adventures."

Annie had gone to the shop and museum with Luke while on her single trip to Springfield during her brief rumschpringe. On the same outing, she'd enjoyed a drink at the koffee shop—not koffee, though; she'd ordered chai—her first and, from all appearances, probably her last. Then, they'd gone to the Wildlife Facility and watched live fish and turtles swimming in a small pool. They'd even had some alligators there, like a real zoo, which she could observe without worry about them making her their next meal. She and Luke had leaned on the fence and sipped their drinks while they watched the bizarre scaly creatures.

Really, the whole shop and museum had been fascinating. But she'd never be able to take her scholars there. Unless she could come up with justification for making the trip.

Thomas Miller, the head of the school board, cleared his throat and glanced down the long wooden table. "Then, we will discuss this matter and pray over it. We'll let you know our decision, Annie Beiler."

At least none of the parents was clamoring for her immediate dismissal.

"But this trip, with you on probation...." Samuel Brunstettler shook his head, causing his long beard to flutter. "Things are not looking gut for you."

The lump settled back in her stomach. If she were fired, what would she do? Work as some mother's helper until she married?

With no one offering to take her home from singings, she didn't think she should get her hopes up about marriage, either.

Joshua straightened and slipped out of sight as the board meeting broke up. He had missed seeing the spunky Annie, but he acknowledged that she couldn't exactly act that way in front of the school board. Not with her job on the line.

He went out the front door and walked around the haus. Out back, he saw her heading, alone, toward her buggy. She was slumped, as if she carried the weight of the world on her shoulders. If only he could help her bear the burden.

"Annie."

She snapped straight before she turned around. "What?"

Joshua skirted another couple headed toward their buggy. He wanted to ask her to take a walk, or maybe offer to ride with her. But, with the board members still sitting inside and the parents taking their leave, that probably wasn't such a good idea. For now.

Instead, he pointed back to the south pasture where he'd worked—a little, at least—earlier that morning. He lowered his voice. "I'll be walking back there."

She raised her eyebrows. "Enjoy yourself."

Ah, there was a little bit of her spunk in that comment. Not much, but some.

He wasn't sure if she'd gotten the point. But she would. Eventually. "Ach, I will." He turned away as she clambered into her buggy.

"Giddyap," he heard her say to the horse.

It took longer to travel the roads by buggy than to walk across the fields to the Beilers', so Joshua beat her home. He waited outside the barn for her.

When she finally pulled up, he grinned. "Would have been faster to walk."

Her eyes widened with surprise for just a second. Then, she nodded listlessly. With her slouched shoulders, red, puffy eyes, and pouty frown, she looked like a whipped puppy. She must have cried all the way home. Sympathy flooded through him, but he reminded himself that Luke should be the one to comfort her, since he was her intended.

However, Luke wasn't around. He hadn't shown up to support Annie at the school board meeting. Joshua took hold of the horse's bridle and stepped nearer. "Let me help you. Are you free for a walk?" Maybe he could cheer her up.

Annie hesitated. Nodded. Then shook her head.

He quirked his eyebrows. "Which is it?"

"I shouldn't. Because...."

He could fill in the blank. Her reputation as a teacher was at stake. Had Amish teachers always had to toe such a straight and narrow line? It seemed that everything she did or said opened her life up to scrutiny. Not to mention, his place in the community would be at risk if his hosts caught him with Luke's girl. But it would soon be dusk—dark enough that no one would recognize them. "We could sit on the back porch."

She climbed out of the buggy, rubbing her forehead as if she had a headache. "Are you here to gloat, Joshua? My days as a schoolteacher are obviously numbered. I can accept that, if it's God's will."

"Gloating would be unkind." And unnecessary. Most of the faults they'd found with her had been so petty. He rubbed the mare's nose, and the mare nuzzled him in return, maybe looking for a sugar cube or a carrot. His horse back home always did that. She was especially fond of fruit. So much so that he'd named her Jonagold, after a kind of apple his friend Jacob raised in his family's orchard. "What's your horse's name?"

"Penny."

He cocked his head. The horse wasn't even remotely close to the color of copper.

Annie smiled fleetingly. "My friend Becky named her. It was the name of the horse in one of the books she read, and she thought it was nice. Since I was having trouble thinking of anything better, I used it. She named her own horse Shakespeare."

"Do you want Penny in the barn or in the pasture?"

Annie frowned. "In the stable."

"I'll take care of her, then."

"Danki." Annie took a couple of steps away, then stopped. "Do you want something to drink?"

He shrugged. "Jah. Sounds gut."

She nodded and headed toward the haus, her brown dress swaying.

I wonder what she looks like in blue, he mused. The traditional wedding color. He watched her for another moment, thoughts whirling, then looked down.

Chapter 3

Annie washed her face, hoping to remove all traces of her tears. Frowning at her reflection in the tiny mirror that hung on the bathroom wall, she tucked a loose lock of brown hair back inside the gauzy white fabric of her prayer kapp. For the first time, she wished she had another color to wear, something other than dull, boring brown. But, when Luke left, the life had gone out of her. She dressed to reflect the way she felt, like a plain, boring old house wren. Brown and drab.

The same as her life.

When she'd first met Joshua, she'd wanted him to notice her. She still did. But men like him didn't go for plain, brown girls from Seymour.

That didn't keep her from wishing she had a pretty, vibrantly colored dress—maroon, maybe, or lavender or green. Something, anything, to keep Joshua's attention on her, instead of on the other girls. Maybe she could borrow a dress from her sister, Cathy. After all, she'd given Cathy all of her old clothes. As quickly as the thought had come, though, Annie dismissed it. She wouldn't succumb to vanity for the purpose of impressing Joshua. Not that it would work. She could change her exterior as much as she wanted; on the inside, she would still be the same old Annie. Nobody interesting. Nobody worth staying around for.

And, apparently, nobody worth keeping on as teacher.

Tears burned her eyes.

She wiped them away, then washed her hands and face again, before going to the kitchen. Joshua would wonder what was keeping her. After all, how long did it take to get two drinks?

After Joshua finished brushing Penny down, he set the horse's brush on the shelf. Light footsteps sounded behind him, and he turned to see Annie approaching him. He pulled the gate shut and stepped out to meet her, wiping his hands on his pant legs.

She handed him a clear plastic bottle filled with water. One of those fancy filtered waters Englisch folk drank.

"It's spring water, but not store-bought," she explained, answering his unspoken question. "We refilled some bottles to keep in the refrigerator."

"Where'd you find the spring water?"

She pointed toward the woods. "We have a spring. Want to see?"

He glanced up at the sky. It was still plenty light enough, though pretty shades of blue, purple, pink, and red painted the horizon. "Jah, that'd be great."

Annie led the way to a rocky, uneven trail on the east side of their land. She started down into the woods a short way and then stopped. "Do you hear it?"

He listened closely. Jah, he could just make out the faint trickle of water. "Jah." He would have missed it if she hadn't said something.

A few minutes later, they pushed through some undergrowth and came out on a large boulder. "Right down there."

He looked down. Below them was a small pool formed by water bubbling out of some rocks.

"There's an easier way to get there, especially if we're filling the bottles. But this is the most scenic way. I like to kum here to be alone." Insecurity and embarrassment flashed across her face. Her cheeks reddened, and she dipped her head.

Joshua moistened his lips and stuck his free hand into his pocket to keep from touching her. Should he tell her he was flattered to be taken to her special spot? Or just let it go? He bent to set the bottle down and pick up a twig, then sat down on the smooth edge of the rock, his feet dangling over the side. It was still a good six-foot drop to the water. "How deep is it?"

"I don't know." Annie sat down beside him. Well, almost beside him. A large person easily could have occupied the space between them, with room to spare. "I've never gotten in. Everyone in my family comes here to fill the bottles, but they never get in the water or venture up to this boulder. I don't even know if they can see me up here. Unless I'm sitting like this, I guess."

"Do you kum here often?"

Her color deepened. "When I don't want to be around anyone."

He ached to put an arm around her and hug her. To assure her that everything would be all right. Surely, she wouldn't lose her job over a field trip. But then again, how many Amish kids could say they'd visited a Civil War battlefield? He certainly couldn't.

And he'd grown up in Pennsylvania, home to many battlefields, some dating back to the Revolutionary and French and Indian wars. He would have liked to have seen them. "So, Annie. This field trip?" He looked down at the clear water bubbling out of the rocks below. "You went to a battlefield, right? Would you take me?"

Annie's breath caught with a loud gasp. "What did you say?"

He shrugged, still studying the water below. "It just sounds like something I'd like to see."

"Really?" The shadows from the trees cast his face in darkness. She glanced at the sky, noticing that the colors had faded to dusk. It'd be dark soon. She scooted back and stood up. "If you're making fun of me, Joshua Esh...."

He stood, as well. "I'm not." He stepped closer but stopped before he entered her personal space. "Seriously, I would love to go. I've never seen a battleground. What are you doing Saturday?"

She should refuse. But then, he wasn't asking to court her. He was asking only for her to be his tour guide.

He ought to be able to manage a self-guided tour just fine.

"We'd go as friends, Annie."

They were hardly friends. He must have mistaken her silence as an indication that she wasn't interested in him. Either that or he wanted to emphasize his lack of interest in her. Most likely the latter.

"Nein promises, nein commitment. Just friends, for a day, jah?" He spread his arms out and shrugged.

Friends for a day? Then, they'd go back to be-ing...what? Casual acquaintances who virtually ig-nored each other? Moments ticked by while she con-sidered his proposal.

"Can't you handle that?" There was a touch of pique in his question.

She still couldn't see his expression in the shad-ows. After a moment, he sighed and moved away.

"Okay, never mind," he murmured. "I should probably get back." He pushed through the under-growth and started to walk off into the darkness.

"Wait." She shoved her way through the bushes and ran after him. "I'll go." Because they had no fu-ture, and this would be her one opportunity to be near him.

And maybe they'd become friends. Real friends. Instead of his simply being the object of her unre-quited affections.

Not expecting him to stop, she ran into him, and her hands came up against his chest. She heard his breath catch. When had he turned? She fingered the edge of his suspenders, her heart racing. His hands came out to steady her. For a second, they rested on her upper arms, and then he released her and moved away. Nothing improper about it at all. But the too-brief contact left her tingling, especially her arms, where his warmth lingered.

"Gut," he said quietly. "Danki." He didn't apolo-gize for his touch.

She didn't know whether to apologize for hers or not, though it had been far more inappropriate. "Ach, I'm sorry. I didn't mean to run into you."

"Quite all right. I won't tell." There was a hint of amusement in his voice. "I'll pray that you'll be able to keep your job, Annie."

"Danki." She paused at the edge of the woods and watched him move through the darkness toward the fields separating their homes. They'd left their water bottles on the boulder. She'd run back and get them, after she'd watched him go.

He paused and turned around, surveying her in silence for a moment. Then, he raised his hand in a brief wave. "See you Saturday, if not before."

"Saturday," she whispered. She couldn't wait for the weekend.

Just then, her excitement turned to a shade of dread. If they were spotted together on an outing, wouldn't that be a definite death knell for her job?

Chapter 4

Despite the late hour, the school board members were still in a heated discussion when Joshua came in to the meeting. He stopped to listen for a few minutes but wasn't sure which direction they were leaning. They seemed to be split equally. Some of them appeared to think Annie was the best choice to teach their children, despite her transgressions, while others favored asking Bishop Sol's granddaughter Ruth to teach, instead. Joshua wished he could voice his opinion, but since he had no children, much less school-age ones, he didn't know how Annie performed in the classroom. Nein, he knew only her caring spirit, which he'd first witnessed when he'd seen her comfort a child who had fallen and skinned his knee. He also knew how intently the children listened when she read them stories on church Sundays. And he knew Ruth King to be a silly, boy-crazy girl who giggled all the time.

As quietly as he could, he tiptoed up the stairs and slipped into the bedroom he shared with Luke and one of his brothers, Simon, and turned on the gas light. The room was empty—a blessing, since he wanted to read the latest letter from his parents without any distractions, away from the annoying presence of Luke and Simon. The younger buwe had gone to bed in their room, and he didn't know where either Luke or Simon had disappeared to after dinner. Truthfully, he didn't care.

He slid open a drawer and reached underneath his socks, pulling out the letter, which he'd received that day. He'd started to read it earlier, but Luke had come around, giving orders that he expected Joshua to obey right away. Joshua hated taking orders from his host's prodigal son, but didn't know what else to do. The son would be favored over the transplant. Henry Schwartz had made that more than clear from the beginning. "Nein transplant will be working in my business," he'd said.

Joshua walked over to the narrow cot and sank down onto the thin canvas, the metal bars biting into the backs of his legs. A wave of homesickness washed over him as he pulled the lined white paper out of the envelope, opened the tri-folded letter, and saw Mamm's familiar scrawl. He could almost smell the maple scent he associated with home. His mouth watered, remembering the taste of homemade maple syrup on his tongue. He loved every step of the sugar mapling process and longed to participate in it this year.

After he'd satisfied his wanderlust, he'd return home to Pennsylvania. Well, maybe he wouldn't even wait until then. His parents and he had agreed that he'd return before sugar season, in late February. As the only son—the only child—he was set to take over the family business and all of the sugar maple trees. But he'd wanted to see the world first, from Amish community to Amish community. He'd gone to Alaska with a bunch of Amish scouts, looking for land—an experience he'd relished, but the consensus had been that Alaska wouldn't be a good place for the Amish to settle. Disappointing, really. Now, he was in Missouri. He'd go home, as planned, before the start of sugar season, when they would harvest the sap from the trees.

It was a bit dishonest, maybe, as he was supposed to be part of the man swap meant to introduce fresh blood into the Amish community in Seymour. But as long as he chose a frau from here, he would fulfill his duty, right?

Annie's face flashed across his mind, and he frowned. He hadn't even taken her out. Though he'd wanted to. Desperately. Their friendship was tenuous, at best. So, why was she the single woman who'd made any lasting impression on him? The only woman he'd noticed? The only girl he really wanted to get to know? The one who came to mind when he thought of marriage?

Something bumped against the door, and Joshua looked up, bracing himself for an interruption.

The door opened slowly, and Luke peeked inside. "What's up?"

Joshua scowled. So much for reading in peace. He didn't care for the Englisch slang that permeated Luke's manner of speaking. He shrugged. "Not much." His fingers tightened around the edge of his letter. Maybe he could finish reading it in the barn or someplace else where he could be alone.

Luke opened the door the rest of the way, stepped inside, and sat down on his bed. The bed Joshua had slept in before Luke's return. A wave of body odor assaulted Joshua's nose. "What do you think of Annie?"

Luke seemed a bit defensive, judging by his set jaw. Had he been drinking? Joshua sniffed the air again. He did pick up a kind of yeasty smell. "Uh, Annie who? There are several around here." Might be best to play dumb.

"Annie Beiler. *My* Annie. I saw you talking with her." Luke balled his fists, though they remained at his sides. "Walking in the woods with her."

Joshua scooted away a bit, wondering if he should stand up or even make a hasty exit. He didn't need to fight with his host's eldest son. "Hmm. Did you?" Had Luke trailed them into the woods and seen their few moments of closeness? He hated the idea of someone observing that private moment, even though the entire scene was completely innocent. He hadn't even thought of anything happening—at least, not until he'd felt that unexpected spark when he'd touched her and heard her gasp. She'd noticed it, too.

She'd noticed it, too. He fought to keep his face stolid, in spite of the grin that threatened to form on his lips.

"She's my girl." Luke squirmed a bit, twisting to fully face him, anger coloring his voice. "Nein point in your meeting her outside the barn and going for a walk. She and I, we have an understanding. We're getting married."

"You were spying on us?" Joshua rose to his feet. "Any understanding you may have had was before you jumped the fence."

"I asked her to kum with me. She didn't want to leave her family."

Joshua refolded his letter and stuffed it back into the envelope. "Is that so?"

"Jah. And now that I'm home...well, you'll see."

Home? What did Luke mean by that? He'd returned to the faith? Or, he was just physically present once more?

Joshua scowled but refrained from pointing out that Annie had refused to allow Luke to take her home the night before. Instead, he walked over to the window closest to the bedroom door and opened it. He heard muffled voices as the school board members said their good-byes.

A decision might have been made. He wished he knew what it was. Henry Schwartz would know, but Joshua doubted he'd tell him.

He turned around and studied Luke. "So, you think they decided to let *your* Annie go?" Ach, it hurt to include that possessive pronoun.

Luke shrugged. "Who cares? If she isn't working there, she might be too ashamed to face the community and more willing to leave."

"You aren't planning on staying, then?" Joshua's eyes widened. If Luke left again, his parents would really be hurt. And if he were only toying with Annie, getting her hopes up...now it was Joshua's turn to ball his fists.

Luke pursed his lips and, without answering, got up and left the room.

Joshua slid the envelope back beneath his clean socks and shut the drawer. Luke had been warning him to stay away from Annie. He must have noticed something between them, too. His thoughts returned to the private moment at the spring.

A moment Luke might have witnessed.

Joshua sighed. Luke had a point. If Annie were fired, she might be more willing to leave the Amish. And that would give Luke the advantage. Not only that, but if the wedding were to go on as planned, or if she refused to leave this particular community, what was the point in even trying to win her?

She wouldn't be willing to leave with Joshua, either.

He shook his head.

Pointless.

❇

The next morning, Annie didn't know whether to go to the schoolhaus or not. She hadn't heard any news about the board's decision. She hoped they wouldn't show up when class was in session and humiliate her in front of her scholars. But, if they had decided to fire her, surely they would have the decency to come to the haus and let her know, instead of subjecting her to public humiliation.

Just in case they decided to come to the schoolhaus, maybe she should take the children on another field trip. One that was allowed, of course. Today would be a good day for a walk in the woods. They could collect different types of leaves to identity, or even use them for an art project. The youngest scholars could practice counting or naming colors or writing the letter *l*, for "leaf," and *t*, for "tree."

Her plan decided, Annie pulled on her brown dress and black apron, pinned her hair up, and covered it with her kapp, then headed downstairs to get started on her chores. Mamm stood by the stove, her walker in close proximity, as she stirred a kettle of oatmeal. "Gut morgen, Mamm."

"Morgen, Annie. If we get enough eggs, I'm thinking of making custard for dinner. Does that sound gut to you?"

"Jah." Annie grabbed her egg basket and went outside, but her stomach growled for breakfast.

"Gut morgen, Annie," Daed called to her from the barn. "Beautiful day."

"Jah. I thought I'd take the kinner for a nature walk this morgen. That way, we can enjoy this nice weather some." The egg basket banged against her knees.

"I need to work more with the bees, too. I'm way behind with the honey harvest since your mamm's accident. And I need to inoculate the bees before winter." Daed scratched his bearded chin. "Yesterday, that bu from Pennsylvania, Joshua—the one living at the Schwartzes'—suited up and helped. Surprised me. Guess he liked the bees better than he does picking up rocks from that field."

Her heart stuttered. Joshua had come to work with Daed? She forced her voice to remain neutral. "Is Henry Schwartz planning on doing something in that field?"

Daed chuckled. "If he were, I suspect it would've been done long ago. I think they just gave the bu something to keep him busy and out of the way until he found a job. Henry said he doesn't want a transplant messing with his leather. That's a family business."

"Too bad Joshua hasn't found a job." Did she sound as interested as she felt? She didn't want Daed knowing about her fascination with Joshua.

"Ach, I asked Joshua to kum work for me. Our Aaron doesn't care much for the bees, and he doesn't have a knack for tinkering with small machinery. Joshua didn't seem to mind either one. He got that Englischer's leaf blower fixed in nein time yesterday. Could free Aaron up to find his own place in life, since he wants to work with horses."

Joshua would be coming to work for Daed regularly? A thrill shot through Annie. She squelched it. "Too bad Aaron doesn't want to be in the family business."

Daed shook his head. "Just because I raise bees for honey doesn't mean he should. And just because I have a small engine repair shop doesn't mean it's a family business. If Joshua Esh wants to learn, great.

His family's business isn't going to be of much use down here. They raise sugar maple trees and make syrup. Not the right climate for that here. Besides, we don't have the right sort of trees."

"Maple sugar and honey...guess he's interested in sweeteners." No wonder Joshua was so sweet. She held back a dreamy sigh. "I need to gather the eggs. Mamm says if we have enough, she wants to make custard for dinner." She opened the gate to the chicken yard and went inside. Seconds later, she released the door to the coop and let out all of the fluttering, squawking birds before going inside to see how many eggs she could find.

When her task was complete, and her basket was filled with eggs, she set it down outside the door of the chicken coop, then went to get the feed and a bucket of water to replenish the dishes. That finished, she picked up the basket again and headed for the haus. She glanced over her shoulder a time or two, hoping to see Joshua crossing the field on his way to work for Daed, but she never saw him. He probably had chores of his own to finish first.

Funny how just the slightest hope of finding love put a spring in her step and a smile on her face. Annie tried to control it. After all, Joshua had asked to take Rachel home after the singing. And he'd mentioned he might visit her later this week. But he hadn't asked Annie for anything. Except for a walk, after the school board meeting. And a tour of Wilson's Creek Battlefield.

But still.... Possibly, if they had time, the driver could take them to the Bass Pro Shop, and they could go through the museum. Joshua might love it as much as she had. Perhaps, he'd enjoy a drink from the koffee shop, too. And as long as they didn't get caught....

Her mouth watered, and she quickened her steps toward the haus. A cup of chai, even if it was homemade on a gas stove, sounded wonderful right now.

Joshua carried another load of wood into the schoolhaus, then bent over to build a teepee of twigs and crumpled paper inside the wood stove, so that all Annie would need to do was light a match. He would have started the fire himself, but there was only a slight chill in the air, and it'd probably warm up enough by mid-morning to the point that a sweater would suffice.

After he finished, he turned to one of the desks and picked up the apple he'd lifted from the Schwartzes' fruit basket. He rubbed it against his shirt to polish it, then carried it over to the teacher's desk, where he set it down gently, front and center. Beside it, he placed the glass jar he'd filled with a bundle of colorful autumn leaves. It was the best bouquet he could come up with on short notice. Then, glancing out the window, he saw Annie crossing the field, carrying a lunch bag and a thermos.

He'd intended to keep this a secret. Just something to brighten her day.

Besides, he really did like her. A lot. And maybe a little pursuit wasn't pointless. He'd find out how things really stood between her and Luke.

He looked at the open front door, checked to make sure he still had the key in his pocket, and then, with hurried steps, he went to the back door and slipped out. He wished he could see her expression when she discovered the surprises he'd left, but that would be too risky.

Then, he hesitated. What if she thought Luke had been the one who'd left the gifts?

Nein, he couldn't wait. He'd promised her daed he'd be there to help with the bees, in the machine shop, or with whatever else was needed, as soon as he could.

A promise he intended to keep, if only to stay on her daed's good side.

Chapter 5

A nnie hesitated outside the schoolhaus when she saw that the door was ajar. She was positive she'd shut and locked it when she'd left yesterday. After all, she'd begged for a lock after vandals had broken in and destroyed her classroom several months ago. Her stomach roiled as she remembered the ruined books, shredded papers, overturned desks and chairs, and broken windows. *Ach, Lord. Please, don't let the school-haus have been ransacked again.*

With the barest touch, the door opened about twelve inches, and she peeked inside. The room appeared to be just as she'd left it.

But that didn't necessarily mean she wouldn't open her desk drawer to find a garter snake or a tarantula or something else equally unpleasant, planted there by a scholar who wanted to make her the butt of a bad joke. She'd had that happen before—firecrackers thrown in the wood stove, wild creatures stashed inside her desk, and even a tack positioned pointy-side-up on her chair.

That student, whoever it was, should have been more careful, because now she was on the alert. She pushed the door open wider and inched inside, looked around, and listened for any unusual sounds.

Hearing nothing, she walked toward her desk, but then she hesitated when she spotted the autumn

leaf bouquet and the shiny red delicious apple waiting for her. So, it hadn't been a vandal or a mischie-
vous student. Someone had wanted to cheer her up.
Still, to be sure, she yanked open one desk drawer
after another to check for anything that might jump
out at her. Instead, the items inside looked neatly arranged, just as she'd left them. And no tack waited on
her seat for her unsuspecting backend.

Annie slid the bouquet to the right edge of her
desk, checking for a note. But there was nothing.
Whoever had left her this surprise wanted to keep
the right hand from knowing what the left hand was
doing. Biblical. And sweet.

She went over to the wood stove to fill it with
firewood. Bending over, she gathered a few small
wood pieces, then opened the doors. Another surprise: kindling and crumpled papers had already
been arranged inside, tepee-style. Still, she checked
the pile for firecrackers, buried deep beneath the
kindling. Nothing.

A secret admirer? Joshua? For a second, her
heart lifted. Then, it crashed down to her toes. She
had no such admirer, secret or otherwise. Especially
not Joshua.

It must have been a student. She couldn't think of
anyone else who might have done this. And she must
have forgotten to lock the door on the previous school
day, or she hadn't shut it tight, as stressed as she'd
been by the imminent school board meeting. She would
make sure to close it and fasten the lock tonight.

Unless Luke had left the gifts. His daed was
on the board, and he would have access to a key.
But Luke had never done anything as sweet as this
before.

Her thoughts went back to Joshua. Living with
Luke's family, he would have access to the same key.

Her heart lifted again. But why would he...? Unless, maybe he'd noticed her in that way, too.

The school day went by without any unexpected visitors, and the kinner all went home with artwork they'd made with leaves, each type painstakingly identified and labeled. Even the littlest scholars had carefully traced all the letters.

With school finished, Annie swept the floor and washed the chalkboard. She was straightening the rows of desks when she heard heavy footfalls clomping up the front steps. She froze and straightened as the door opened. Samuel Brunstettler stood in the doorway, pulling at his long, grayish beard as he surveyed the room. Finally, his pale blue eyes rested on her. "Annie Beiler. We've reached a decision."

She waited, her heart now lodged in her throat. She was afraid to breathe, or even move, for what felt like an eternity.

Samuel Brunstettler didn't smile or do anything to ease her worry. He took a few more steps forward, his heavy work boots leaving dirt on her freshly swept floor. If she was about to be fired, she'd leave the dirt for the next teacher to clean up.

Okay, that wouldn't be very nice of her. She would clean it up, but only grudgingly.

Still not nice. *Lord, help my attitude.*

She swallowed hard but couldn't dislodge the lump.

Samuel Brunstettler cleared his throat. "We talked with Bishop Sol. He said to practice grace. So, we will allow you to stay on, under probation. With nein more field trips of any sort. If you want to take the scholars to see something special, you must notify the school board in advance about the trip, where you are going and what you plan to see, and we will decide if it is acceptable or not."

So, no more trips, even into the woods? Good thing she'd taken the class on an outing today, before knowing the verdict. She would have had a hard time convincing the school board of its instructional value. She was glad to be allowed to keep her job, but knowing that field trips were next to off-limits was almost too much to bear. Clutching the edge of her desk, she struggled to get oxygen into her lungs. She couldn't compel her voice box to cooperate enough to form even the simplest word. *Danki, Lord. Danki for grace.*

Samuel Brunstettler stared at her a few more seconds and then chortled. Annie jumped at the unexpected sound.

"A dumbstruck woman," he muttered to himself, still chuckling. "Never thought I'd see such a thing."

Still unable to respond, she simply watched him clomp back outside and down the steps to his buggy, chuckling all the way.

❁

Joshua's job that morning was to lift the honeycomb out of the hives and lower it into the blank frames. He was grateful for the thick layers of extra clothing that Annie's daed, Isaac, had given him to wear. The bees were riled, but he was protected from their angry stings—an occupational hazard he hadn't had to deal with in the sugar bush.

"This is usually done in late summer," Isaac said. He stood beside Joshua, supervising. "Now, we have to be careful to leave enough for the bees to feed on to make it through the winter, so we won't take as much honey as we normally would. Three strings per comb will be enough to secure it. Then, you put it in the box. You probably didn't know that the bees must visit two million flowers to produce just one pound of honey. They work hard, ain't so?"

Joshua nodded. "Interesting." He looked up and saw Annie crossing the fields on her way home from school. Did her way of walking betray her reaction to the school board's decision? Joshua was not yet aware of the conclusion they'd reached, but he'd seen Samuel Brunstettler driving his buggy toward the schoolhaus after the scholars had started for home, and he'd assumed he was going to deliver the news. Yet her posture told him nothing.

Beside him, he sensed Isaac stiffen. The older man put down the frame he'd been holding and looked in Joshua's direction, but their eyes didn't meet. "She's worried about her job."

Joshua nodded. "Jah."

"You were at the meeting last nacht?"

"Nein." He studied the ground at his feet. "Well, jah, I eavesdropped a little. Just long enough to find out what she'd done to get everyone so upset. None of my teachers was ever put on probation." Though some of them probably should have been.

"Ach. Silly stuff, really. People, they just like to complain about something, anything. Annie joined the church without taking much time for a rumschpringe. She knew she wanted to be a church member, so she passed up a lot of opportunities the other teens took advantage of. Her mamm and I were thrilled at the time. But, in hindsight, she should have taken a longer rumschpringe—experienced the world a little— because, when she went running around with her friends to Englisch places after joining the church, she disobeyed the Ordnung, and so she had to kneel and confess before the church. Some parents with school-age kinner were worried that such a 'worldly' teacher would be a bad influence. That field trip was not such a gut idea. You see how protective bees are of their honey. Parents are the same way with their young kinner."

"Have you ever been there? To the battlefield?"

Isaac shook his head. "Nein, but she told me about it."

Joshua turned to the haus and watched Annie climb the porch steps.

"Care for some tea or koffee?"

Joshua attempted a nonchalant shrug. "Jah. Sounds gut."

"We might even get something sweet. Think my frau mentioned wanting to make custard today."

Joshua's stomach rumbled in response, and the older man chuckled. "Let's finish up here so we can enjoy it."

🌸

Annie washed up at the kitchen sink and then got out five potatoes to peel for supper. Preparing for the evening meal had fallen on her shoulders ever since Mamm's accident in early September, when she'd been thrown from the buggy. Her recovery had been steady but slow, and she was still in a lot of pain and tired quickly, especially as the afternoons wore on. After working with the home therapists, nurses, and aide, usually right after lunch, Mamm took to her bed, worn out. She'd nap awhile, or sit in the living room and alternate between sleeping and sewing, mending, or reading.

In the mornings, Annie's sister, Cathy, did the laundry and helped with the baking before fixing herself a light lunch and going to work at the Amish grocery store for the afternoon. She came home about the time Annie was ready to serve dinner.

Annie spread out the daily newspaper on the countertop nearby and then reached for the peeler. She'd made just one cut in the first potato when the door opened. Daed and Joshua came in.

Annie stepped aside so that Daed and then Joshua could wash up at the sink. While Joshua scrubbed his hands, Daed cut two generous slices of the custard pie Mamm had made and set them on the table. "Care for a slice, Annie?" he asked.

"Nein, danki." She tried not to stare at Joshua. "You're going to ruin your appetite." She hoped neither one noticed the slight breathiness in her scolding voice.

Daed chuckled. "Ach, Joshua and I are just having dessert first, ain't so? Is there any hot water for tea?" He looked over his shoulder at Joshua. "Or do you prefer koffee?"

"Tea would be gut."

"I'll get it." Annie put the peeler down and pulled two mugs out of the cabinet, followed by a selection of tea bags and the sugar bowl, all of which she brought to the table. "Have a seat."

"You'll join us, ain't so?" Daed's chair scraped on the floor.

"I need to get supper ready."

"That'll wait a few minutes. Get a mug for yourself."

Annie shrugged and retrieved another one. With the other hand, she carried the teakettle. She filled each mug with steaming water, set the teakettle back on the stove, and returned to sit down.

Joshua and Daed had already selected their tea. Annie chose her favorite, a black tea flavored with ginger and peach, and ripped the package open. She dipped the teabag into the water and studied Daed. It was unusual for him to come inside the haus for a break, especially just before supper. "What's up?"

Daed leaned back in his chair. "Does something have to be 'up' for a man to have a slice of pie and a cup of tea?"

A grin played at the corner of Joshua's mouth. He pulled his teabag out of the darkened water in his mug and laid it on the edge of his plate.

Annie studied them both, confused. Then, she threw up her hands. "You saw Samuel Brunstettler drive by, jah? And you want to know what happened, ain't so?" When she lowered her arms, she hit the funny bone of her left arm on the edge of the chair. Her eyes watered from the sharp pain.

Daed shrugged and set his teabag on the side of his plate, too, then picked up his fork. "Ach, he came by?"

Annie rolled her eyes. "You know he did." She inhaled deeply and rubbed the tingling spot on her elbow. "I'm not allowed to take the scholars on any field trips without prior approval. I'm still under probation. They decided to show grace."

Daed nodded as he sliced into the flaky crust. "Gut. Glad to hear that."

"Me, too." Joshua followed her daed's example. He slid a piece of pie into his mouth and chewed thoughtfully for a few moments. Then, he swallowed and glanced at Annie. "Ser gut. Did you make this?"

She shook her head. "Mamm and Cathy do the baking in the mornings. Cathy makes a much better pie crust than I do."

"Ach, yours are okay," Daed said with a grin. "Cathy just bakes more than you do. You'll feel more confident when you have to do it regularly."

Annie shrugged. "Maybe so." She was conscious of Joshua's gaze resting on her. Did he think she couldn't cook? She took a sip of her tea, testing it, then stood. "I really do need to get supper started.

Are you going to join us tonight, Joshua?" She silently willed him to say "Jah."

He hesitated, glancing at Daed. "Nein, I think not."

Daed shook his head. "You're welkum to join us. You're earning it, anyway. I planned to give room and board to one of the men in the swap, until my frau was injured. What are your sleeping arrangements at the Schwartzes'? Do they have room for you now that Luke's come back?"

Annie stilled. Had Daed suspected her crush on Joshua? Did he think maybe having him under the same roof would bring them together? It had worked for Annie's best friend, Becky Troyer, after all. She'd be marrying Jacob Miller in five short weeks.

Joshua's eyes slid downward, and he studied the fork in his hand. "Ach, they emptied a drawer and provided a cot. That's gut enough."

"Can't be very comfortable. I can do better. I have a spare bed. A whole spare room, actually, now that I have only three kinner left at home. Just the two girls and Aaron."

And Aaron would be getting married in a few months. Daed didn't tell Joshua that.

Having Joshua under the same roof...would that make them kind of like siblings?

That was the last thing she wanted.

Chapter 6

J oshua stared at Isaac, speechless, before his gaze darted to Annie. She seemed frozen to the spot, her mouth gaping open, her eyes fixed on her daed. She didn't display enthusiasm about the prospect—but then, he didn't see signs of repulsion, either. The only clear emotion he could read on her face was shock.

The same expression he probably wore.

Living under the same roof as the girl he was most attracted to...that did appeal. But, on the other hand, so did the ability to keep an eye on Luke.

He'd rather keep his eye on the prize, not the competition.

But wouldn't it be better to keep his distance and not tempt things? If Annie did marry Luke—they had been promised to each other, after all—then it would mean heartbreak for him if he'd ended up falling in love with Annie.

On the other hand, living with the Beilers, he might be able to win her away from Luke.

Joshua drew in a breath and glanced back at Isaac. A smile played around the edges of the older man's mouth. And Joshua thought he saw a gleam in his eyes. *Ach, matchmaking.* A favorite pastime of the Amish. But Annie was taken. Or was she?

After what felt like an awkward period of silence, Joshua rubbed his chin, trying not to squirm under the scrutiny of Isaac and Annie. Did he really want to live with a blatant matchmaker? That would get uncomfortable. Fast.

Unless they were in agreement with each other.

Isaac looked away. Finally. "We can talk to the Schwartzes before we make a decision. But you're still welkum for dinner."

"Danki." But he wasn't sure whether to stay or not.

"What's for dinner, Annie?" Isaac picked up his mug and took a sip of his tea.

"Beef stew. I thought I'd make corn bread to go with it."

"Sounds gut." Isaac smiled at her, then finished off his pie. "About ready to get back to work, Joshua?"

"Jah." He swallowed the last of his tea and stood. "Stew sounds gut. Maybe I will stay for dinner."

"Gut." Isaac patted his shoulder. "Excuse me a moment. I'll be right back." He headed into the other room.

Annie sucked in a deep breath. "You can't stay."

Joshua raised his eyebrows at her. "Excuse me?" She was taking back Isaac's dinner invitation?

"Daed's offer for you to move in. You can't stay here."

"Ach, I'm sure he had his reasons for asking me." Joshua shrugged.

"Jah, sure he does. Aaron is getting married. Daed thinks he can't be without a bu at home." She tangled her hands in her apron. "It'd just be you and me and Cathy here, then, and I don't want you to be my brother." Her face turned a pretty shade of pink.

"We wouldn't be siblings." About the farthest thing from it.

"I also think Daed has matchmaking on his brain."

So, she'd caught that, too.

"Cathy is seeing someone," she went on. "And we both know you don't want me."

"We do?" Joshua frowned. The exact opposite was true. Thing was, he needed to figure out why she believed differently. And how she'd reached that conclusion. "And just how do we know that?"

She waved her hand dismissively. "Ach, I'm not going to spell out all the reasons. You know them better than I do, anyway."

❀

She didn't want to see him leave to go visit Rachel or whoever happened to be his girl-of-the-day. And, if they lived under the same roof, he'd never get around to asking her out again.

Not that she planned on accepting another ride home from singing, anyway.

She'd just like to be asked.

Joshua picked up his empty mug, glanced inside, and strode over to the stove. He lifted the teakettle and refilled it, then walked back to the table, picked up his used tea bag, and dunked it into the hot water. "Perhaps, you're the one who doesn't want me."

He thought he was a mind reader, did he? She gazed at his tea bag, floating on the surface of the water in his mug, and felt a sudden kinship with it. She was in hot water, too.

"After all, we both know that you're Luke's girl," Joshua added.

She couldn't identify the tone in his voice. Something dark. She shuddered. "I'm as much Luke's girl as I am yours." Translation: *Not at all.* She glanced up at Joshua, and something flashed across his face. Pain? He winced.

"And that's why the Schwartz family has your upcoming wedding all planned out, ain't so?"

The way he said it made it sound like impending doom. As if marrying Luke would prove fatal.

Maybe it would.

There was no "maybe" about it. Not with Luke's drinking. His sudden bouts of violence. His hot temper. Anybody else would be a better choice.

But no one else wanted her.

Joshua stepped nearer, just enough to cause her slight discomfort, but not close enough to be in her face. "Maybe that's why Luke felt the need to warn me to stay away from you."

Annie caught her breath. "But...but things have changed. Luke left. I have nein guarantee he'll stay. And I'm...I'm...." And she was attracted to Joshua.

"Maybe it'd do you both gut if I did move in here," Joshua mused. "Luke wouldn't presume to tell me where to go, what to do, who I can or can't see. And you would see that there are men other than Luke."

She knew there were other men. The problem was, they didn't notice her.

His comment the night of the singing about being "the thorn in her side" came to mind. He was more right than he knew. Anger flooded through her. "You just think you're God's gift to women, ain't so, Joshua Esh? Kum down here to Missouri, and you've got all the girls eating out of your hand—all except for me—and you just can't stand that. I wish you'd go back to Pennsylvania." Realizing she'd raised her voice, she snapped her mouth shut. Mamm was in the next room, and she wouldn't tolerate her being unkind.

His jaw clenched tight, and Annie could see he was trying hard not to bark back. After a moment, he spun on his heel, leaving his steeping tea on the table, and headed outside. "Tell your daed I'll be in the shop," he said without turning around.

Annie sighed. Her ugly attitude had surfaced, much to her chagrin. She had to face facts. She wanted Joshua to stay with her family—she liked his looks and enjoyed having him around—but, at the same time, she didn't want him here, since he wasn't for her. He'd been like a wasp invading a beehive right from the start.

She wished he'd get on the next bus out of town.

On second thought, she wished he'd come back inside and...what? Declare his undying love for her? After the showdown they'd just had, that was the last thing she ought to expect.

Tears burning her eyes, she reached down and picked up the wrapper from Joshua's tea bag. Vanilla coconut. So, he liked dessert teas? She thought she was the only one. She crumpled the bag in her fist, then smoothed it out again and slid it into her apron pocket.

She picked up his mug, inhaling the warm aromas of vanilla bean and coconut. With a glance toward the doorway to the next room, she made sure no one was coming, then raised the cup to her lips. The closest her mouth had ever come to Joshua's. Pathetic, she knew.

She closed her eyes, sipping the tea and savoring the moment. Seconds later, the door creaked open, and she lowered the mug—too late, she realized as Joshua crossed the room and took the mug out of her numb fingers.

With a smirk and a raised eyebrow, he walked out again, this time with the mug.

❧

The machine shop was quiet, the air heavy with the smells of gas, oil, turpentine, dust, hay, and fresh-cut grass. A faint musty odor also permeated the room. Joshua set his mug of tea on the counter and stepped back to survey it. Had Annie Beiler done what he thought she'd done? Jah, he knew what he'd seen, for certain.

She wasn't as indifferent as she wanted to seem. This could get very interesting.

His thoughts wandered back to Luke. He'd jumped the fence once, and she wouldn't be surprised if he left again. Did Annie feel the same way about wanting to stay here, close to her family? And would it be fair for Joshua to even begin a relationship with her that was doomed to fail from the start? He fully intended to return home to Pennsylvania in time to help with the sugar mapling. It was what he wanted, what he had always planned. And it was expected of him.

And Annie's daed would come to expect him to join him with the beekeeping, which Joshua found unusually fascinating, and in his small engine repair shop—a place that did provide an outlet for tinkering, something he enjoyed doing from time to time.

Was he wrong to spend time here, to want to be around Annie? To try to woo her? He wished he knew. If only she were open to leaving Seymour.

Joshua exhaled loudly and turned his attention to the older model gas riding lawn mower an Englischer had brought in sometime earlier. Isaac had said that the man had nursed it along all spring and summer and was about ready to give up on it and buy a new one unless Isaac could fix it.

With another sigh, he gathered a few tools and an old newspaper before he lowered himself to the dirty floor next to the mower. At least he got to start with the fun part: taking it apart.

But Annie kept intruding into his thoughts. That first time he'd seen her, on a church Sunday, he'd thought she looked like the kindest person he'd ever met, watching her as she comforted a small child. So encouraging. And all the little kinner had gathered around her to listen, completely engaged as she told them a story. She was beautiful, caught up in the story, in the kinner, in life. Jah, she'd caught his attention. But when he'd casually asked the other buwe about her, everyone had told him the same thing.

She was not available.

"Not available" had to be two of the most discouraging words.

The door opened, and Isaac came in, his gaze going to the partially disassembled engine beside Joshua. "Ach, gut. You've started on that. Let me know if you need any help. I'll start work on the riding mower that came in yesterday." Gesturing at Joshua's project, he added, "I'm told that with a bag on the back, it collects leaves and grinds them up for mulch." He shook his head, as if trying to understand the luxury of not having to rake leaves. "The owner is pretty anxious to get it back."

Joshua nodded, trying to wrap his mind around the concept, as well. In his community in Pennsylvania, they were allowed to use push lawn mowers, but they weren't gas. His family had an old model with a rotating blade. An antique, was what he'd been told by some awestruck Englischer. A gas lawn mower seemed a luxury to Joshua. And riding one...well, he could see where it might be handy. If it picked up leaves, all the better. He smiled and lifted his gaze to Isaac. "Should we give it a test run as soon as I get it fixed?"

Isaac grinned back. "It'd be remiss of us not to, ain't so?"

Chapter 7

Annie went through the supper preparations in a daze. Before she knew it, the beef stew simmered on the back of the stove; on the counter beside it sat the corn bread, baked to a nice golden-brown; and the table was set. Everything was ready for whenever Daed and Joshua came inside from working in the shop. Aaron would spend the evening with his future in-laws, and Cathy wasn't home yet. Annie glanced at the clock. Her sister was half an hour late.

The only thing that wasn't quite ready was the molasses pie she'd made to replace the custard pie, which the men had nearly polished off this afternoon. She'd made the crust herself, and while it wouldn't be as flaky as Cathy's, at least it wouldn't be burned. Well, she hoped not. She checked the time and peeked inside the oven to check on it. Not quite done. Yet, even when it was, she wouldn't be ready. It would take a million years for her to feel even remotely capable of facing this moment: Joshua, eating a meal with her—a meal prepared *by* her. She fought to keep an excited grin under control.

She wiped her sweaty hands on her apron, then turned and went into the other room. Mamm looked up from her mending. "It smells delicious, Annie. I'm sorry I couldn't help."

Annie forced a smile. "It's okay. You just get better."

Mamm nodded. "As fast as the Lord wills." She stuck the needle into the toe of the sock she was darning and laid her project across the arm of her wheelchair. "Your daed said he invited one of the Pennsylvania buwe to eat with us tonight."

Annie swallowed a dreamy sigh to keep it from coming out. "Jah."

"You met him, ain't so? What is this bu like? I miss so much, not being able to go out." Tears gathered in Mamm's eyes. "I feel like a prisoner in my own home."

"Ach, Mamm." Annie put her hand on Mamm's arm and squeezed. "Maybe with Joshua working for him, Daed will have time to build a wheelchair ramp."

"Maybe. Tell me about him, the bu from Pennsylvania. All your daed said is that he seems to be willing to work with the bees and in the shop." She gave a wry smile. "It disappoints him that Aaron doesn't want to, but he'll never say so."

"I know. And if I were a bu—"

"You aren't. And you mustn't think that way. But this bu from Pennsylvania?"

Annie swallowed. How could she describe Joshua without betraying every bit of longing she felt for him? Mamm would see right through her. "Ach, you'll see him soon enough." She waved dismissively. "Dinner's ready, so I expect they'll be walking in the door any moment."

Mamm shook her head. "Nein need to tell me how he looks."

"Um, he seems nice. I haven't spent much time with him." *Not nearly enough.* She couldn't say that. Nor would she say that he'd asked out every single girl. But he hadn't asked her, so maybe she would.

"He's what the Englisch call a 'player.'" She swallowed hard. Time for the basics. "He's gut-looking, and he knows it. Tall, dark blond hair, hazel eyes, with flecks of green, gray and blue, that seem to change color with the sky or his shirt."

So much for being objective or forgoing a physical description. Her face heated. Mamm stared up at her with her mouth partially open.

Annie struggled for something more to say. Other than that he was a dream come true.

Except for the "player" part.

"Someone special, then, jah?" Mamm said softly.

There was a noise behind Annie. She turned to see Joshua and Daed standing in the doorway. How much had they overheard?

❈

A player? Annie thought he was a player?

Joshua balled his fists in frustration. He could feel his lips tightening and a muscle start twitching in his jaw. How could she possibly think he was a player? He forced his fingers to uncurl and then shoved his hands in his pockets, not knowing what else to do with them. But then, he remembered the dirty job he'd been doing earlier and pulled them back out again. He didn't want to soil his clothes any worse than they already were. He and Isaac had cleaned up as best they could in the shop with some kind of soap called Goop, designed for removing grease, oil, and other grime. At least, that was what Isaac had said. It seemed to work fairly well, but the folds of his knuckles and his fingernails still bore traces of black grease.

He'd arrived in the doorway about the time Annie's mamm had asked about him, and now he didn't know where to look, other than at his hands. He glanced up, long enough to meet the older woman's gaze and nod at her, and then dropped his gaze again. He didn't dare look at Annie, afraid that all his hurt and dismay would show.

But he still wanted to know why she'd called him a player. His stomach churned.

She had noticed his eyes, and she'd called him "gut-looking."

That didn't even begin to negate the bad.

"Lydia, this is Joshua Esh, one of the Pennsylvania buwe," Isaac said. "He's been helping with the bees and in the machine shop. Joshua, this is my wife, Lydia."

"Really nice to meet you, Joshua." The woman smiled up at him from the wheelchair.

"Nice to meet you, too, Mrs. Beiler."

She waved her hand. "Call me Lydia."

Isaac glanced at Joshua and pointed toward the stairs. "Bathroom is the third door on the left, if you want to wash up more. Dinner is ready when you kum down." He turned to Annie. "Is Cathy home yet?"

"I haven't seen her." Annie sounded quiet. Subdued.

Joshua chanced a glance at her as he went by. Their eyes met, and the pretty pink coloring of her cheeks flushed a deeper red. He was pretty sure his own coloring had gone in the opposite direction—pasty white.

A player. The label was like a knife to the heart. How could she think that? He started up the stairs. And then, he remembered all the girls he'd taken home from singing—two at once the last time. Jah, he could see how that might look to a girl who was evidently interested. Did his attention to the other girls make her jealous? Hurt? Did everyone else in the community view him in the same way?

Even more important, did he have it in him to repair the reputation he'd made for himself, however unintentionally?

❀

Annie wheeled Mamm into the kitchen and helped her get situated at the table, then double-checked the place settings. Cathy rarely got home from work this late, so maybe she'd made dinner plans. Still, Annie had set a place for her. She wished she had dinner plans of her own. Maybe she could run down the street and eat with her best friend, Becky.

But as fast as that idea had come, she dismissed it. That wouldn't go over so well with Mamm and Daed. They'd figure out the truth soon enough, if they hadn't already. And then they'd talk to her about it. If she wanted her crush on Joshua Esh kept secret, she had to stay, smile, and...something. She didn't quite know what. Yet.

But she'd figure it out. She had to.

She grabbed a couple of potholders and carried the pot of stew over to the table, then went back for the cornbread. As she set it down on a trivet, Joshua came into the room.

"Is something burning?"

Annie stared up at him, and her eyes widened. "Ach, my pie!" She hurried over to the stove and opened the oven, letting out a blast of heat. Reaching inside, she pulled out the pie. The edges were a little black, but that was it. Still salvageable. How could she have gotten so sidetracked? With a grimace, she set it down on the thick towel she'd placed on the counter. So much for impressing Joshua with her baking skills.

She stepped back, still studying the pie, willing the burned areas to vanish. A light touch to her lower back made her jump. The contact, however casual, burned through her clothes. She hadn't realized he was so close.

"Ach, Annie. You baked." Joshua's voice held a slight mocking note. He leaned closer and lowered his voice to a whisper. "We need to talk."

His breath stirred the hairs hanging loosely around her ear, and she shivered.

Joshua stepped away and raised his voice a little. "Anything I can help with?"

"Um, nein. Danki."

"Okay." Joshua turned and strode toward the table, going directly to Mamm. He pulled out the chair next to her and sat down, then said something to her. But he spoke so quietly that Annie couldn't make it out.

Mamm laughed and then touched his hand as she leaned forward to respond. Annie could only stare. He charmed even Mamm, a frau. It wasn't right.

Every woman but her.

She swallowed her jealousy, pasted a sweet smile on her face, and walked over to the table. "Would you care for koffee or tea, Joshua? We have milk, too."

He looked up with a grin. "Whatever everyone else is having is fine."

She kept her smile in place. "Daed prefers tea with dinner."

Joshua shrugged one shoulder. "Tea is fine. I'm easy to please." Then, he leaned toward Mamm again and murmured something else.

Annie strained to hear as she went to fetch the basket of gourmet tea bags. Hopefully, she wasn't the main topic of this conversation. Nein, she needn't worry. She couldn't possibly be.

After Daed had come into the room and sat at his place, Annie set the basket of tea beside him, then went around the table to sit on the opposite side, across from Joshua. Not her usual seat. But that place was occupied by Joshua, so she sat in the place she'd set for him. She bowed her head for the silent prayer.

Seconds later, Annie lifted her head, picked up her spoon, and dipped it into her bowl. It tasted like sawdust, and it took all of her self-restraint to keep from spitting it out. Yet no one complained. Daed ate with his normal gusto. And Joshua even went for seconds. "Ser gut, Annie."

She finished her meal with great effort, then got up to serve the pies—what was left of the custard one and her slightly burned molasses one. Joshua took a small piece of each.

When dinner finally ended, Joshua bowed his head for the closing silent prayer and then stood. "I hate to eat and run, but I should get back before the Schwartzes wonder what happened to me. I didn't tell them I had dinner plans." He caught Annie's eye and nodded toward the door. Apparently, whatever he needed to discuss with her couldn't wait until tomorrow. Or Saturday.

Daed raised his eyebrows, and Annie wished she could give him a satisfactory explanation as to why Joshua wanted to talk to her alone. Something to prevent Daed from traveling mental rabbit trails of courtship and marriage. She didn't want him to get the wrong idea. Not that she knew the right one. But nothing came to mind. "I'll see Joshua out," was all she could think to say.

Joshua followed her to the door. "Thanks again for dinner. I'll see you tomorrow, Isaac. Really nice to meet you, Lydia."

Annie walked with him down the steps and into the dark yard. She wasn't sure what he wanted to say or why, just that he'd sounded so serious when he'd whispered those four infamous words: "We need to talk."

"Can we take a short walk, maybe?" Joshua glanced toward the woods, then looked up at the dark sky. "Down the road?"

"We could go in the barn," Annie suggested. She hugged herself, wanting whatever it was he needed to say over and done with. It couldn't be anything good. Maybe he'd picked up on her crush and wanted to tell her not to get her hopes up, that they'd never have a chance. Or maybe he wanted to back out of the trip they'd planned for Saturday. That might be a good thing. She couldn't think how they'd get away with it. Englisch drivers talked. Bishop Sol and the school board would find out.

She would be fired.

She gulped down the lump in her throat and tried to think of what they could do to keep their outing a secret, if he wasn't about to propose a cancellation.

Joshua glanced toward the road and then nodded. "Jah, the barn is fine. More private. Do you have a lantern in there?"

"Of course." A flashlight, too.

"Your daed, would he be done with his evening chores?"

"Nein, he'll be out directly." Annie sighed. "Maybe we could go up in a loft?"

"A loft is gut." Joshua allowed her to lead the way into the barn. She was careful not to let the dog, Bu, out. Daed had told her that the neighbors' dog was in heat, and they'd asked him to keep Bu home. They wanted to wait a couple of cycles before allowing their dog to whelp again.

Annie stopped long enough to grab the flashlight lantern, then quickly scampered up a ladder, going into the dark recesses of the loft, where Daed wouldn't see them or overhear them.

"What did you need to talk about?" She flipped the lantern on and set it atop a hay bale. The dim light left his face partially obscured. "If you want to cancel the trip to Springfield, I completely understand. It'd be best—"

"Nein. That's not it. I want to go." His expression turned serious. "You told your mamm I'm a player."

Annie slumped. He had heard that part of the conversation, after all. Still, she was surprised he had the courage to bring it up. She wouldn't have.

He waited a minute, as if giving her a chance to respond, and then frowned. "You and I, we haven't...I mean...." He sighed. "Ach, Annie."

Annie shrugged. "It's true. At least, it's what everybody thinks. Every week, you take a different girl home from singing. They talk...."

She shivered under his scrutiny in the semi-darkness. His frown deepened, but his steady gaze held hers. "I never meant...I only wanted...I wasn't sure about courting anyone, except...well, since...." He shook his head. "I thought inviting different girls would be a gut way to get to know people, and if I liked any of them enough to consider, I'd take her home again. Spend a bit more time with her."

"So, you haven't met the woman of your dreams?" She hoped that her smidgen of hopefulness hadn't come through in her tone. She really shouldn't have asked that.

After a long hesitation, Joshua chuckled—not a genuine laugh, really, but more of a forced sound, for lack of anything else to say. "I don't know. I think so, jah...but I'm not sure."

So, there was a chance he had? The flicker of hope died.

"Annie, I don't want a reputation of being a player. I didn't mean to mislead you—or anyone—that way."

She sucked in a breath. "I'm sorry for judging you."

"And just so there's nein more confusion, I won't take home another girl unless I'm reasonably sure about her."

"Ach, Joshua, that isn't fair to you. But you might get to know a girl better if you spent more than just a few minutes riding in a buggy with her." She didn't want him to have an unfavorable reputation. Maybe this would help improve it. Not that she wanted him to spend more time with other girls, of course. Especially not with whoever it was who'd inspired the "I think so" part of his answer.

The light from the lantern flickered and died. Time to replace the batteries. Joshua chuckled again, and, this time, it sounded real. To her shock, his hand grasped hers. Unexpected sparks shot up her arm. Could he feel them? "I'm looking forward to spending hours with you this weekend." He rubbed her knuckles with his thumb, leaving fire in its path, and then he pulled away.

Was he playing with her? Could he possibly be serious? She wished she could read his expression, but all she could see was a dark shadow turning away.

"I think we've been dismissed." Humor colored his wry comment. "I'll see you tomorrow, Annie Beiler. Gut nacht." He headed toward the ladder, apparently satisfied with the conversation they'd had.

Still trying to process his remarks and his touch, Annie hesitated a minute before grabbing the dead flashlight and scampering down the ladder. Joshua had left the door open, and she reached the ground level just in time to see Bu, the dog, dart outside, taking off for the woods.

Annie rushed outside. Daed would be angry if he found out she'd let Bu run off. "Kum here, Bu!" Annie shouted after the dog. "Now!"

The dog didn't listen, of course. But, to her horror, Joshua's steps stuttered, and he froze. After a moment, he slowly turned to look at her. "Were you talking to *me*?"

Chapter 8

Joshua opened the door to the Schwartzes' kitchen and slipped inside. Immediately, Luke shot up from a chair. Henry also rose, moving a cup of koffee closer to the center of the table as he did. It seemed that both men had been waiting for him. This didn't look good. Joshua hesitated, looking from one to the other. Luke had his hands in fists at his sides, and the anger that raged across his face colored it to nearly match his red hair.

"Where have you been?"

The question had come from the elder Schwartz. But it was rhetorical, really. Henry and Luke both knew the answer. Still, Joshua didn't appreciate the hard tone the man used, as if speaking to an errant child. Though he probably should have told them about his new job. "I was at Isaac Beiler's. He hired me on."

Henry nodded, his anger evidently dissipating. "All right, then. I wasn't aware of that. So long as you weren't there trying to court Luke's Annie. He said you'd been...well, never mind. My frau kept dinner warm for you." He gestured to the stove.

"Danki, but I ate there."

Luke's fists clenched even tighter, and his whole stance seemed ready to spring.

Joshua felt his own body tense in response.

Luke didn't even wait for his daed to leave the room. He took a menacing step toward Joshua. "I saw you and Annie talking tonight. You went into the barn together." The volume of his voice rose with every word.

Joshua surveyed him silently, calmly. He doubted Luke was looking for an explanation. And he certainly wasn't about to lie and say they'd been doing chores together.

"Annie is my girl." Luke moved even closer.

Henry paused in the doorway and turned back, maybe wanting to see how this would play out. Or to see that Joshua, the transplant, behaved himself.

"Did you miss that we're getting married this winter?"

Joshua shook his head. "You haven't even started membership classes with the other district, and there is nein way Bishop Sol will approve your marrying without them. Annie won't be marrying you until next year's wedding season." He tried to keep from smirking. "If then."

Luke shoved him. Hard. "I said, stay away from her."

Joshua staggered a couple of steps, then regained his balance. He sucked in a deep breath. "I think you're the one who should stay away," he muttered. "I heard her turn down your offer to take her home from singing. She won't even let you near her."

Luke's eyes bulged, as if they'd pop right out of their sockets.

Yet Joshua couldn't restrain himself. "I'm going to win her away from you," he added. Then, he gulped, shocked by his own spoken words. That was bold. Too bold. He certainly hadn't planned to say that. It had just slipped out. Now what? He'd probably lost his temporary home. A proverb Mamm always said surfaced in his memory: "*When you have spoken a word, it reigns over you. When it is unspoken, you reign over it.*" How true that was.

"How dare you!" Luke raised his fist and moved to strike, but Henry stepped in and stopped it mid-swing.

"Luke!" The man had anger etched in every line of his face, but Joshua could tell it wasn't directed at his son. He turned to Joshua. "I'm afraid having you stay here isn't going to work out. I have to ask you to leave. Get your things. You can spend the nacht in the barn. Tomorrow, we'll contact Bishop Sol."

Jah, Joshua had figured so. For a brief second, he considered apologizing, taking it back. But he couldn't, in good conscience. "I'll get out of your way, sir." Joshua headed for the stairs. "I'll be out of here in a moment."

When he remembered that Isaac Beiler had offered him a place to stay, he couldn't keep from smiling. Maybe he would sleep in the Schwartzes' barn tonight, as Henry had suggested, and approach Isaac in the morning. Or, maybe he'd just sleep in the Beilers' barn.

Danki, Lord, for giving me a place with the Beilers. Joshua would be glad to get away from Luke and his stereotypical redhead temper. If he had his way, Annie wouldn't end up with that bully. Joy bubbled up in his chest, producing another smile that couldn't be controlled.

Ten minutes later, Joshua had stuffed all of his belongings into two plastic grocery bags. With a nod to Henry Schwartz, he set out across the yard.

"Where're you going?" Luke sounded alarmed. "Where's he going?"

Wouldn't you like to know? Joshua kept the snarky comment unsaid.

"The barn. He's headed to the barn," Henry said firmly.

"You think?"

Grinning to himself, Joshua shifted his trajectory and strode past the barn, out into the dark fields toward the Beilers' farm. No one tried to stop him, which was surprising, since he was certain Luke watched his every step. He was a good spy. Ought to work for the CIA.

Even as he relished the thought of living with the Beilers, shame ate at Joshua for being kicked out of the Schwartzes' home. He shouldn't have goaded Luke the way he had.

Swallowing the lump in his throat, he climbed the steps to the Beilers' haus and opened the kitchen door a crack. "Hello?"

Annie stood at the sink, finishing up the dishes. She turned, a dishcloth and a plate in her hands. "Joshua?" Water dripped from the plate onto the floor, but she didn't pay it any attention. "What are you doing here?"

"Is your daed still awake?" Heat crawled up Joshua's neck. He held up his bags. "They kicked me out."

Her eyes widened. "Whatever for?"

Joshua shrugged, not wanting to explain. But it didn't matter. She'd learn the truth, sooner or later. Might as well be sooner. "Irreconcilable differences between their son and me."

Annie gave a little gasp. "Luke?"

He nodded, his temples throbbing—probably due to embarrassment, about both the way he'd acted at the Schwartzes' and having to face Annie in this homeless state. "He's determined to marry you this wedding season, and I was apparently encroaching on his territory."

"Marrying him? His territory? There is nein—" She turned abruptly and set the plate back in the dishpan. "So, they kicked you out and sent you here? That doesn't make sense."

When she swiveled to face him again, Joshua half smiled, feeling weary. He hated having to explain the situation. It was wrong in so many ways. "Nein. They kicked me out of the haus and told me to stay in the barn. They said they'd be contacting Bishop Sol in the morgen to find me a new home. But, since your daed offered to let me stay here, I thought that maybe just this once...if the offer's still open...?"

"The offer's still open."

Joshua turned around and saw Isaac standing on the porch. "Danki, sir."

The man gave a knowing smile. "Happened to look outside the barn as you were walking up. Annie will show you to your room, and then you can kum down to join us for family devotions. Aaron and I need to finish up the evening chores. We'll be in directly."

"Do you need help?" Joshua set his bags down on the porch. "I'd be more than glad to...."

Isaac had shifted his attention to the driveway, where the gravel crunched beneath buggy wheels. "Cathy's home." He looked back at Joshua. "You could help take care of the horse and buggy, if you would."

"Jah, I'd be happy to." Joshua nodded at him. "Danki again for taking me in for the nacht. I'll find a permanent place tomorrow."

Isaac clapped him on the shoulder. "Nonsense. This is your new home. I'll work it out with Bishop Sol. Glad to help." He looked past Joshua. "Annie, you take his things upstairs and make sure the room's ready for him." His gaze returned to Joshua. "You've met my daughter Cathy, ain't so?"

Annie stood in the kitchen for a minute or so, watching as Daed and Joshua met Cathy in the driveway and talked with her a bit, and then as Joshua unhitched Buttercup and led her by the reins to the barn.

Not wanting to be caught gawking, Annie grabbed Joshua's bags when Cathy headed for the haus, and hurried upstairs. The extra room up there used to be Mamm and Daed's, but they'd moved downstairs after Mamm's accident.

She opened the door to the empty bedroom and put Joshua's bags on top of the dresser. Then, she went to get some sheets and a quilt for the full-sized bed. She was tucking in the ends of the sheets when Cathy stormed into the room. Annie braced herself for the tirade. What had upset her this time?

"Daed told me Joshua's moving in. I wish he would have asked us first. With Mamm hurt, and everything else going on, it'll be more than awkward having a stranger living here. Not to mention more work."

Annie nodded. Work, she didn't care about. But "awkward" was an apt word to describe her relationship with Joshua and the emotions his presence stirred within her. She didn't know how to act around him. Should she treat him like a guest? There was no way she'd be able to act brotherly/sisterly with him. She didn't want to act like she knew Cathy would, either, all fluttery-eyed, not to mention willing to use any means available to spend more time with a man. When she'd had her eyes on Jacob Miller, she'd tried to drive a wedge between him and Becky Troyer by intercepting the letters he'd written to Becky while she'd been away at her sister's. And she certainly couldn't act all giggly, like the bishop's granddaughter Ruth did around men.

She'd drive herself insane.

"He'll just have to find somewhere else to live." Cathy shifted. "He has friends here...maybe one of them could take him in. Or his cousin Matthew Yoder, maybe?"

"Matthew's getting married in a few weeks. Probably wouldn't be gut for Joshua to go there."

"Whatever." Cathy waved her hand in dismissal. "He isn't welkum here, nein matter what Daed says. We'll just have to make that clear." She tilted her head. "Isn't that your quilt?"

Annie looked at the quilt she'd spread over Joshua's bed. It was the one she'd made for her hope chest— variegated green, with a double wedding ring pattern. She shouldn't have been so bold as to pick this particular one. Hopefully, Cathy wouldn't suspect her crush on Joshua. She decided to change the subject. "Well, if your David were homeless, you'd want Daed to take him in, ain't so?" Too late, she realized she'd just given Cathy enough to realize how she felt about Joshua. That is, if Cathy had been paying attention.

"My David?" Cathy blushed. "Well, that's hardly the same thing. Joshua isn't anybody's beau. He's a player, for sure and for certain. David might have been part of the swap, but he'll be all kinds of upset to find out Joshua's staying here." She glanced around and lowered her voice. "David asked me to be his steady girl. But don't tell anyone."

Annie forced a smile. "I won't." She gathered Cathy in a hug. "I'm really happy for you." As she released her and stepped back, she realized her sister very well might be marrying next fall. Then, she'd be the only one left at home. "But maybe Joshua isn't a player. Maybe his behavior is just misunderstood." Her discussion with him earlier that evening had suggested this was the case. But the way he'd touched her hand when they were alone in the loft...Annie still didn't know for sure.

Cathy headed for the door. "Well, we'll get rid of Joshua Esh in short matter. He won't want to stay where he's not wanted. Besides, I'm sure Luke will take issue with him staying here, too. Bishop Sol might even move him elsewhere."

Annie regretted allowing Luke to court her in the first place. "Luke has nein right to say anything. I wish everyone would quit bringing him up! We aren't getting married, contrary to what he's been saying. He left the Amish once already, and I can't trust him. Besides, I'm never leaving this community." And she no longer wanted to settle for just anyone. She might not be Joshua's choice, but, one day, maybe some good man would love her.

Cathy waved her hand again. "Still, everyone says you're Luke's girl. David told me that's why no one's asked to drive you home from singings. They all know you're taken."

Speechless, Annie watched her sister leave the room. Could that be true? Was that why Joshua had never asked? A flicker of hope reignited in her heart.

When the horse and buggy had been tended to, Joshua went to look for Isaac. He'd just extinguished a lantern. "Is there anything else I can help you with?"

"Nein, we're finished. Aaron's already gone to the haus. Danki for taking care of Cathy's horse. You'll be a real asset around here."

"I just appreciate your taking me in tonight."

Isaac clasped Joshua's shoulder. "I can guess what drove you away from the Schwartzes. And I'm not at all worried about Luke with you here." He basically spat the name of Joshua's rival. "She deserves better...much better than that bu. The way his eyes look sometimes, I wouldn't be at all surprised to find out he's using some sort of drugs. I know he drinks. And his temper...." Isaac shook his head. "Even if he joins the church, which I doubt he will, I want him to have nothing to do with my Annie."

Joshua scuffed his shoe in the dirt. So, he wasn't alone in his opinion. "I'll be glad to look out for her."

"Jah, I know you will. You're a gut bu. And I've been watching you. I...." Isaac frowned. "I'm not supposed to notice this, and I probably shouldn't say it, but I've seen the way you look at her. How you're always watching her. Not sure how you'll move past that reputation as a player, though." Isaac winked and then headed toward the barn. "Speaking of players, I do wish that dog would have kum home when Annie called him. Samuel Brunstettler isn't going to be happy with us. Not at all. And he's already upset enough with Annie."

Joshua shook his head sympathetically.

Isaac turned back and met his eyes. "But, just so you know, I don't want you playing with Annie's emotions, either. I will be here, watching."

"Of course." Joshua gulped. He was grateful for Isaac's blessing, but he realized now the gravity of the consequences that would ensue when the man found out that he intended to return to Pennsylvania.

He'd told Luke that he would win Annie away from him. But Annie refused to leave, and Joshua certainly had no plans to stay. The Lord alone knew how all this would work out.

Chapter 9

Annie positioned the final pillow on the bed in her parents' old room. There wasn't much else to do to get it ready for Joshua. She eyed the two grocery bags she'd set on the top of the dresser and thought about unpacking them. But she probably shouldn't take the liberty of going through his personal belongings. For once, she envied Cathy for her job of doing the laundry, since she would get to handle his clothes, touch them.

Annie thought again about what Cathy had said. If only she dared to ask Joshua if it was true that Luke's "claim" on her was the reason all the buwe avoided asking to drive her home from singings and frolics. The reason why nobody wanted to "date" her, as the Englisch would say. But she was afraid that asking would make her appear needy. Desperate. That, or he would contradict Cathy, and then Annie would know what she'd suspected all along: nobody liked her. Period. They all found her too plain. Too bossy. Too...what did Becky's Jacob always say? Obsessive-compulsive, whatever that meant. Annie had once asked Becky about the term, and she'd merely shrugged and said it had something to do with Annie's penchant for putting everything in alphabetical order.

As if that was something serious. The world was a much kinder, friendlier place when it was in alphabetical order. She could find things. She knew where to put them. She could tell at a glance when something needed to be replenished. And if someone wanted to know where something was, she could point him in the right direction. That was the way librarians organized their fiction sections. Alphabetically. Such a beautiful thing.

Not at all obsessive-compulsive.

Right?

She shrugged and decided to straighten the plastic bags of Joshua's belongings so that his clothes wouldn't wrinkle too much. Her thoughts returned to Luke and how he'd nearly ruined her prospects with the local buwe, staking his claim on her and presuming that she was his. And that was after he'd dated whomever he'd pleased, Amish and Englisch alike. Not fair. Why couldn't she?

She scowled when she realized she could. She'd simply refused to fully acknowledge her freedom.

But how could she get the word out that she was available without going around talking about it?

Annie stepped away from the dresser and surveyed the bedroom, double-checking each detail to make sure it would be perfect for its new occupant. Then, she hurried back to her own room to close up her hope chest. She didn't want anyone else to know that she'd made Joshua's bed with one of her marriage quilts. Aaron would tease her mercilessly, and then Joshua would be sure to find out. It was bad enough that Cathy knew. But, again, maybe she'd never make the connection.

What if Annie had made a serious error in judgment? It wasn't too late. She could go get another quilt and rescue hers, put it away, and save it for... nothing. Or, for a wedding with Luke, if she became desperate enough.

Sighing, she shook her head. Enough with the depressing thoughts. She straightened her shoulders. Tonight was a new night. Joshua was in her haus, and he would be staying awhile. He'd learn firsthand that Luke never came around. That his claims on Annie were just a bunch of baloney.

She decided to go retrieve her quilt and replace it with another. From the hall closet, she selected an old quilt of Mamm's, one that had been patched and sewn to a new backing. She carried it to Joshua's room—and froze in the doorway.

Joshua stood at the dresser, methodically transferring pair after pair of socks from one of his bags to the top drawer, where she could see them arranged in neat, color-coordinated rows. Impressive. He slid the drawer shut and looked up. "Danki, Annie." He came toward her and took the quilt, then laid it on the corner of the bed. "I think just one is fine for now, but it's awfully gut of you to look out for me this way. It might get cold."

Relief washed over her, even as she felt the rush of blood to her face. She frowned at her quilt lying on his bed. She couldn't take it back now. It was much too late. He'd already seen it, and there was no tactful way of saying she'd grabbed the wrong one. At least, none she could think of.

"Annie? Was there something else you needed?" Joshua studied her.

The way he'd said her name, with a hint of impatience, made her wonder if he'd said something else, and she'd failed to respond. Her face heated again. The last thing she needed was to look blatantly love-struck, standing there daydreaming like a fool. She shook her head abruptly. "Ach, nein."

Joshua smiled and took a step toward her. "Then, it might be wise if you found someplace else to be, other than my bedroom. It wouldn't look gut to anyone who happened to glance up at the window. The shade is up. And with my reputation and your probation.... Besides, we don't want to get your daed upset at me right away, ain't so?"

"Ach!" Another wave of heat washed over Annie, so intense that she wondered if she was having one of Mamm's hot flashes. She backed away. "Sorry. I wasn't thinking. It won't happen again."

He laughed. "Don't worry. Your daed said devotions will be in just a few minutes. I'll see you downstairs."

"Jah, downstairs." She turned and hurried back to her room, where she closed her hope chest and extinguished the lamp before joining her family in the living room. Daed sat in his wooden rocker, thumbing through the pages of the big family Bible, probably searching for a portion to read. Mamm still had her basket of mending right beside her, the yarn trailing her needle, while she darned a hole in one of Aaron's socks. Her brother came in, took his shoes off, and laid them by the door. Cathy wasn't there yet, but she was sure to be in directly.

A few seconds later, Joshua came into the room. Daed looked up at him. "You all settled?"

"Jah, didn't take long. I travel light. Annie did a nice job making up the room for me. Danki, Annie. Beautiful quilt she put on the bed, too. Double wedding ring. My grossmammi has one similar."

Annie held her breath and looked at Daed. He made a noncommittal grunt and turned his attention back to the Bible. Her attention slid to Mamm. She held the needle suspended in the air and stared at Annie, eyes wide.

Annie swallowed. Hard. But Mamm knew about her crush already. She wouldn't give it away, would she? Tomorrow, maybe Annie should go reclaim her quilt. Pack it away in the cedar trunk until she found someone who loved her.

Where was Cathy? She should have been down there already.

Joshua squirmed in his seat—a hard, straight-backed chair that became more uncomfortable by the minute—when Isaac read the Scripture that would serve as the theme of that evening's devotions. It was Hebrews 13:2: *"Be not forgetful to entertain strangers: for thereby some have entertained angels unawares."*

Joshua hoped Isaac wasn't trying to imply that he was an angel. He was about the farthest thing possible from angelic. In Missouri under false pretenses. In this home to woo the girl, under the guise of helping her daed. Not to mention picking arguments with the girl's presumed intended. He really ought to kneel and confess his dishonesty before the Lord and the church.

Jah, he was a huge sinner. "Angelic" didn't describe him even remotely. And it seemed that someone in this family knew it, for he heard a snort and turned to the left to discern the source. It had to have come from Aaron or Cathy, both of whom were seated to his left. Aaron looked rather preoccupied, and not at all focused on the Scripture reading. It must have been Cathy.

Maybe she, too, was of the opinion that he was a player. "It's what everybody thinks," Annie had said.

Shame gnawed at him. He'd had good intentions, but they hadn't been clear. Another verse came to mind, this one from Proverbs: *"There are many devices in a man's heart; nevertheless the counsel of the Lord, that shall stand."* He desperately needed to seek the Lord's counsel.

Seeing the family bow their heads for the silent prayer, Joshua followed suit. *Lord, please be with me here*, he prayed. *Help me to know if this girl—this place—is part of Your will.* He shouldn't have taken matters into his own hands as he had. He wasn't ready to confess before man yet. But God knew, so he would repent to Him, for now. *Forgive me for my dishonesty. Help me to follow Your plans instead of charging ahead on my own paths.*

After devotions, Joshua went upstairs to his room. He wanted to shower, but he didn't want to disturb his new host family. However, he knew he would sleep much better having washed away all of the filth and grime of the day's work. Decision made, he grabbed a towel and headed to the bathroom, but the door was shut, and he could hear water running. Apparently, someone else was of the same mind-set. How big was their hot water tank?

He returned to the bedroom and folded back the covers on the bed. The sight of an ugly black spider— the biggest he'd ever seen—made him jump, and it took all of his effort to contain the shout that wanted to erupt from his lungs. If there was one creature on God's great earth that he couldn't abide, it was spiders. He wasn't an arachnophobe, exactly, but probably borderline.

He narrowed his eyes and stepped a bit closer, studying the creature. It wasn't moving. It was...

dead? It must have been planted there, for no spider could have maneuvered on its own beneath that heavy quilt.

He opened a window, then grabbed a sock from the top dresser drawer and used it to pick up the creature by one lifeless leg and fling it outside, sock and all. "Ugh," he said, shuddering. Why on earth had Annie put a disgusting, dead spider in his bed? Was that her idea of a clever prank?

Or maybe she simply hadn't noticed the spider while she was making up the bed. But that was unlikely.

He shut the window firmly and closed his eyes. He wanted to march down the hall and give her a piece of his mind. If she thought she'd devised a humorous way to welcome him, she was wrong. He wasn't sure he could sleep on those sheets, knowing a creepy spider had touched them.

A door opened down the hall, and then another one shut. Joshua peeked out of his room. The bathroom was free. After coming into such close contact with a spider, he needed a shower now more than ever.

Tomorrow would be another day. And, hopefully, it wouldn't bring any more unpleasant surprises.

On his way to the bathroom, he glared at Annie's closed door. She was the last person he would have expected to pull such a prank. He shuddered again. At least he'd seen the spider before he'd gotten in bed with it.

Annie hurried through her morning chores in the barn but never saw Joshua, though she looked for him. When she returned to the haus, she helped Mamm and Cathy prepare a breakfast of fried potatoes, omelets, and crisp bacon, along with a stack of buttered toast. Then, she hurriedly set the table, finishing just as Daed, Aaron, and Joshua came inside to eat. Annie glanced up shyly. "Gut morgen, Joshua."

He took off his hat, hung it on a wall hook, and finally looked at her. The fury in his eyes almost made her reel back. "Annie. Nice of you to go to so much trouble to make me feel welkum."

She blinked. What had she done to anger him? In her mind, she reviewed the events of the previous night, then shrugged. She couldn't think of anything. Unless he'd somehow found out about her quilt and was upset about that. Her stomach roiled.

"So kind of you to consider that I might be lonely in that room all by myself," he added with an edge to his voice.

Daed turned sharply and stared at Annie, and Mamm's steps faltered, even though she held on to her walker.

Annie blinked back her tears and regarded Joshua just below his eyes, avoiding their icy anger, forgetting her family's shocked expressions. "Excuse me?"

"I found a grotesque arachnid in my bed, albeit a deceased one. It couldn't have gotten there without your help."

"A *what*?" She was just as surprised to hear him use such a scientific word for "spider." Her mouth dropped open, and she stared at him.

He shook his head and turned away. "Ach, don't think you can fool me. You know all about it."

Aaron chortled. "I doubt that. Annie wouldn't dream of touching a spider, alive or dead. Whenever she finds one, she screams, and then she yells for a 'dragon slayer,' all the while keeping an eye on it, so it doesn't escape."

Annie nodded her head vigorously.

Joshua turned back, his gaze softening. "Then, my mistake. I'm sorry I accused you. I just couldn't think how a dead spider would find its way into a freshly made bed, as tightly as you'd made it, without being planted there."

Annie shook her head again. "It wasn't there when I made the bed. I would have seen it. And—"

"She would have screamed," Aaron finished for her. "Jah, we all would have known it. In fact, based on past episodes, we would have heard her from the barn."

Annie's face heated. "Ach, nein need to tell him that."

Aaron laughed. "It's something he should know." He gave Joshua a light punch in the arm. "When you hear a bloodcurdling scream coming from the haus, rest assured, it's just Annie, face-to-face with a spider."

Annie huffed and looked around, trying to remember what she'd been doing before all of this unsettling talk about nasty creatures had begun. They'd been getting ready to eat breakfast. She plopped down in her wooden chair, so hard that it creaked, and bowed her head, hoping the rest of them would soon join her.

Within moments, she heard the scrapes of chair legs against the floor, followed by complete silence as everyone bowed in silent prayer. For a moment, Annie considered sneaking out while everyone's eyes were closed and minds were occupied.

But she needed breakfast before tackling another long day at school, and she'd need a lunch, too. Like it or not, she was stuck.

How could Joshua accuse her of such a thing? Her eyes popped open, and she glanced beside her at Cathy, who'd remained curiously silent throughout the entire exchange. She had her head bowed in prayer, but a smirk played at the corner of her mouth.

Cathy, who wasn't afraid of anything, especially spiders.

Cathy, who'd vowed to get rid of Joshua.

Annie clenched her folded hands together so tightly that her fingernails dug into her skin. She wouldn't go blaming Cathy out loud, for all to hear. But, somehow, she had to talk to her, try to get her to stop.

Before she did something even worse. More insidious. Possibly dangerous.

Chapter 10

O n Wednesday morning, Isaac came inside carrying Joshua's sock—the one he'd used to fling the spider outside. It was soaking wet and muddy from the rain. "You must have dropped this when you came in last nacht." He set it on the counter and turned to face him again. "There is another thing, though. I found your shoes and socks in the middle of the living room this morgen. We have to be careful not to leave things lying around, since my frau uses a walker or her wheelchair. So, when you take off your socks, please leave them in your room. I'm sure Annie left you a laundry basket to use as a hamper."

She had. And Joshua had thought he'd dropped his dirty socks in there, with the exception of the one he'd flung out the window. He wasn't completely sure. Tilting his head, he thought for a moment, and then he remembered: he'd worn his socks upstairs last night. He recalled sitting on the bed to take them off, all the while thinking about how glad he was not to have to share a room with Luke. He knew he'd tossed them into the laundry basket. And he knew his shoes hadn't been left in the middle of the floor. He'd left them by the door, neatly lined up with everyone else's footwear.

But he didn't dare contradict his new host. It would be childish to blame somebody else for messing with his belongings. So, he simply nodded and promised it wouldn't happen again. Meanwhile, he wondered how he would keep that promise, especially if someone else was responsible, as he suspected. Whoever had it in for him certainly seemed fearless, given his or her bravery with spiders and smelly footwear. Joshua shook his head. He still couldn't wrap his mind around the idea of someone ostensibly as kind as Annie doing things like this. But it had to be Annie.

Yet her entire family had teased her about her fear of spiders, and she was always busy, whether teaching school, grading papers, or doing household chores.

Joshua shook his head in confusion. Okay, maybe it wasn't Annie. But Aaron was so preoccupied with his bride-to-be, he probably wouldn't think of pulling pranks, and Cathy seemed innocent, except for her snort during the prayer last night. As far as he could tell, she was usually busy working, inside or outside the home, and spending time with the bu she was seeing.

He was pretty sure that bu was David Lapp, another man who'd come from Pennsylvania in the swap—and he hadn't been Joshua's friend. In fact, he and Joshua had seemed set against each other from the first day of school. Joshua couldn't remember all of the details, exactly, just that David had run out of the building in tears, climbed a tree in the school yard, and refused to come down until his older brother had shown up. David had blamed Joshua— for what, he couldn't recall. For taking David's pet bullfrog, maybe? Jah, that was it. And David had hated him ever since. Well, maybe "hated" was a little strong. But they certainly hadn't been friends.

An idea dawned in his head. If Cathy had been spending a lot of time with David, it was likely that he'd been filling her head with stories. Maybe he'd recruited her to target Joshua and help make his life miserable.

With another apology to Isaac about the socks, Joshua took all three of them upstairs. When he entered his bedroom, he stopped short. The double wedding ring quilt had disappeared from his bed. In its place was a nine-patch. It was a pretty pattern, too, but he was curious. Who would have switched his quilt after just one night? And why? It wasn't as if it needed to be laundered already.

When he returned to the kitchen, Isaac was gone, so Joshua headed for the barn. Sure enough, he found him there, setting up some sort of contraption.

"This is an extractor," Isaac said without looking up. "In a moment, I'll show you how to extract the honey from the frames."

Joshua remembered helping Isaac carry the frames from the hives into the honey room, which they kept tightly shut, so that the bees wouldn't rob the honey. *After we've robbed them of it*, Joshua thought with a smile.

When it was time to extract the honey, Cathy joined them in the honey room. She kept a fire going, and a pot of water boiling over it. Isaac explained that this was to keep the uncapping knife hot, which made it easier to remove the ends of the honeycomb.

Cathy wiped the steaming knife with a towel, then deftly removed the wax, setting it aside for later candle-making.

"Watch carefully," Isaac told him. "See how she moves gently from side to side, like slicing bread?

Start a quarter of the way from the bottom of the comb, slicing upward, and then complete it with a downward thrust of the knife, to uncap the cells on the lower part of the frame."

After the frame had been uncapped, Joshua lowered it vertically into the extractor with the others. Then, Isaac closed the lid and began cranking. "You start spinning slowly at first. Build the speed as you progress. Don't ever spin the frames at the maximum speed, because it might damage the delicate wax comb." After he'd spun the extractor for five or six minutes, he had Joshua turn all of the frames to expose the other sides to the outer wall of the extractor. Then, he let Joshua do the spinning.

"As the extractor fills with honey, it becomes difficult to turn the crank, so then we need to drain off some of the harvest." He opened a valve at the bottom of the extractor and let it filter through a honey strainer into the bottling bucket.

After that, they used the valve in the bottling bucket to fill the honey jars. "I'll let Annie label them later," Isaac explained. "One of her friends has a computer and a printer and can make these labels that we'll simply peel off and stick on."

The job took all morning and left him sticky, but Joshua had fun, anyway. They took a break for lunch around noon, and then Joshua spent the rest of the day working in the machine shop.

That evening, Joshua helped Isaac put the extracted frames on top of the hive, sandwiched between the top deep and the inner and outer covers. "We'll just leave them here for a few days and let the bees clean them up," he said. "They'll lick up every last drop of honey, making the frames dry and ready to store until next honey season." Honey extracting certainly made for easier cleanup than the sugar mapling process.

After dinner, Joshua asked to borrow a buggy but didn't explain why: he wanted to go to see Rachel, the girl he'd taken home from singing last Sunday. That night, he'd promised to come by and take her for a walk, but he hadn't yet. So, he headed for her haus, though his primary purpose in going was to break things off. He hardly knew Rachel, but he was sure she wasn't the one for him. Still, he didn't want to burn any bridges. He didn't return to the Beilers' until after Annie had gone to bed, so he'd barely seen her all day. He hated to imagine what she thought of him, spending so much time with another girl, especially after their conversation about him being a player. It certainly wouldn't look good.

And if Annie had been the prankster, she'd probably retaliate in some form. The first chance he got, he would tell her he'd ended things with Rachel.

On Thursday morning, when Joshua opened his bedroom door to go to the bathroom, he was showered with an aromatic white dust. Baby powder. Someone had sprinkled it heavily on the top of his door. Thankfully, no one was around to laugh at his sneezing fit, though he was fairly positive the perpetrator couldn't have gone far.

He proceeded to the shower, eager to rid himself of the smell he associated with babies' diapers. But another equally distinct scent—strawberry, he thought—emanated from the red-tinted water that gushed down on him. He quickly turned off the water, unscrewed the shower head, and found it filled with a mostly dissolved powdery pink substance. One peek inside the trash can next to the shower confirmed his suspicions: strawberry Jell-O. With water from the spigot in the tub, he cleaned the shower head of all traces of the powder, watching as clumps of gooey red whizzed down the drain.

All the while, he muttered to himself in disbelief. He'd had a warmer welcome at the Schwartzes', despite his problems with Luke. Given what he knew now, Joshua would gladly let Luke have Annie—again, assuming Annie was responsible. He couldn't rule out Aaron or Cathy. Heaving a sigh, he reattached the shower head and finally took a shower, hoping Isaac would show him mercy when he showed up tardy for morning chores. At this rate, he'd be lucky if he made it to breakfast.

All day long, Joshua was tempted to tell Isaac what was going on behind his back, but he decided to hold his tongue. Would it be a sin to retaliate once he'd determined for sure who was behind all of these pranks?

What would happen if he got kicked out of a second home? That wouldn't look so good on his record. Would he get sent back to Pennsylvania in disgrace?

He'd evidently been wrong to accuse Annie of planting that dead spider in his bed. But what about everything else that was happening in rapid succession? He would simply have to watch; to be on guard. Sooner or later, whoever was after him would get careless, and he'd catch her—or him.

After a day of work, he borrowed a buggy again and went to visit his cousin Matthew Yoder and his bride-to-be, Shanna Stoltzfus, at the haus they had purchased to live in after their wedding. There, he helped Matthew and their friend Jacob Miller shingle a portion of the roof. While they worked, Joshua shared a little bit about what had been going on at the Beilers'.

After he'd mentioned his suspicions of Annie, Matthew shook his head. "I can't imagine Annie doing any of those things. She's the schoolteacher, and isn't she under probation? I think she'd be too worried about her job to waste time playing practical jokes on someone."

Joshua shrugged. "I would have thought the same thing, but there has to be some explanation."

Jacob shook his head. "I agree with Matthew. Annie isn't the joking type. She's the one who wants to alphabetize the world. And, if she were going to play a trick, the farthest she'd go would be to organize your belongings in A, B, C order." He chuckled a moment, then frowned. "On the other hand, Cathy did some pretty unkind things to me and Bex. Maybe you should keep an eye on her."

"I don't know...Cathy usually seems to mind her own business." Joshua shook his head. "Annie's the one who told me I couldn't stay. She warned me outright. Maybe she's just making sure I get the message that I'm not welkum."

"It's not Annie. Just doesn't fit." Matthew picked up a nail and held it in place with one hand, raising his hammer with the other. "I agree with Jacob. It's probably Cathy. But no matter. You're welcome to stay here. There's room."

Joshua's face heated. "Nein, I'm not going to move in with you, when you're marrying your Shanna in mere weeks."

Matthew shrugged. "I promised to take her to Pennsylvania to meet my family. We'll be gone for a month, at least. Maybe more. And that should put us in the time frame for you to be going back home to your family to help out during sugar season, ain't so?"

Joshua frowned and shook his head sternly at Matthew, then at Jacob. "We can't mention that. No one knows, except you two."

Friday morning, the pranks were still just as time-consuming, but not as messy. Joshua's suspenders had gone missing in the middle of the night, which meant that someone had come into his room while he'd slept and had taken them. Highly inappropriate for a single girl. Was Aaron behind the pranks, after all? Or had one of his sisters enlisted his help?

Fuming, Joshua decided to take a shower and put off figuring out what to do about his lost suspenders. When he went to open his door, he was met with elastic resistance—his missing garment. He reached an arm through the opening and unfastened them from his doorknob, sending them sailing down the hall with a loud snap.

This was war.

That night, he rigged an aluminum canister filled with water above his door. If anyone opened it to enter his room during the night, he would know— and, more important, that person would be soaking wet and sorry.

Unfortunately for him, he forgot about the booby trap and fell victim to it himself on Saturday morning.

Early Saturday morning, Annie sprang out of bed and hurried to get dressed. Joshua had seemed to be avoiding her all week, after he'd accused her of placing a dead spider in his bed. She shuddered at the thought. He'd spent two of the evenings out, probably in the company of another girl. Most likely, it had been Rachel, though she didn't know that for sure. She'd tried to hide her envy from the rest of the family. With Aaron, it'd been easy, for his mind was consumed with thoughts about his future bride, as well as with his favorite activity: training former race horses to be buggy horses. And Cathy had made only one unkind remark about Joshua being a player before Daed had put a stern stop to it.

Not knowing if their weekend plans to visit the battlefield were still on, Annie hadn't called for a driver. She wanted to spend the time with Joshua, but she didn't know who she could call to drive them without the inevitable result of word getting back to Daed. He would probably be disappointed in her for disobeying the Ordnung by going off to see worldly attractions, but he wouldn't yell about it. And since she'd joined the church, she supposed her own guilty conscience would obligate her to kneel and confess before the church, even if no one caught them. And what would that mean, in regard to her teaching job?

It probably didn't matter, not with Joshua avoiding her and going off to visit Rachel or someone else, instead. She hesitated, then resumed pinning her dress shut. Would their trip be cancelled?

Probably so.

At least she'd rescued her quilt from Joshua's bed and packed it away again in her hope chest. Saving it for her future marriage, however small its prospects.

She shrugged, still hoping the act would help her to feel more indifferent, and then continued pinning the edges of the brown material together. If Joshua called off their trip to the battlefield, she would do her chores and then go see Becky. She didn't know what her friend had planned for the day, but even sitting together and hemming something would be more fun than drifting aimlessly around the haus, thinking of what might have been.

She went outside and did her chores, never seeing another soul. When she'd finished, she went back inside to help Cathy and Mamm get breakfast on the table.

After several minutes, Joshua came into the room, and her heart rate increased exponentially. Oddly, his hair was still wet, and it stood up in tufts, as if he'd towel-dried it but had neglected to comb it. The shoulders of his shirt were soaked, as well, as if he'd been caught in an unexpected downpour. Even though she'd been outside earlier, she glanced toward the window. It was still a beautiful autumn day; the sky was a brilliant blue, with not a cloud in sight.

Joshua nodded at her, his eyes icy, but didn't say a word. That wasn't unusual, considering their limited interactions this week. His personality had really seemed to change ever since Daed had welcomed him into their home. Maybe this was his normal temperament.

As he skirted the table, he caught her eye and lifted one side of her plate, sliding something underneath. Then, with a tiny nod, he looked away and smiled at Mamm. "Gut morgen, Lydia."

Mamm smiled back, the traitor. "Gut morgen, Joshua. Get caught in the line of fire?"

His grin flattened, and he glanced at Annie. "Something like that."

Was he really blaming her for whatever had gotten him wet?

Suddenly, Annie's anger was riled. He should have had the decency to greet her with more than just a glance and a nod. Well, she supposed she ought to be grateful for even that much. After all, she hadn't greeted him, either. She opened her mouth to rectify that, but then she shut it again, leaving the words unsaid.

She realized she ought to get over her crush. It was obviously unreciprocated. Two nights out with someone else, not to mention his attitude toward her lately...it hurt.

Added to that, the fact that he seemed to think her guilty of...what? Spraying him with the hose? Tossing a bucket of water on him? Whatever had happened, Annie certainly wasn't responsible. Tears burned her eyes. If only she could go to Daed about this. Surely, he'd know what to do.

During the silent prayer, she quietly lifted her plate, pulled out Joshua's note, and slipped it into her pocket. Immediately after breakfast, while Cathy washed the dishes, Annie hurried upstairs to her room to read it in private.

Annie,

I was tempted to slip this into the mail, the way things are supposed to be done. But this is the next best thing. If you are still free, meet me out by the low-water bridge at 9. A ride will be coming.

Joshua

He'd set something up. Their weekend plans were still on! Annie couldn't keep from smiling. Would it be wrong to pray for a good time, even though she felt guilty about going on this trip?

She glanced at the battery-operated clock on her dresser. It was barely six. She had plenty of time to do the rest of her chores before walking down to the bridge. Maybe she'd even get a chance to grade a few of the papers she'd brought home to check over the weekend.

Joshua was a bit early. He paced in the grass near the low-water bridge, keeping an eye out for Annie walking across the fields to meet him, as well as for the car that would be coming to pick them up. Of course, there was certainly no guarantee that Annie would show up. After everything that had happened this week, he was almost positive she wouldn't. Even if she wasn't to blame for all of the pranks aimed at him, she had to know about them. Sisters shared everything, ain't so? And she hadn't tried to stop them from happening. In his opinion, that spoke loud and clear of her lack of interest.

The pranks had been more than sufficient to get the message across. He wasn't wanted. To stand him up would be the crowning event.

Still, he couldn't quell his sense of anticipation. Hope. Belief that maybe Annie hadn't lied when she'd claimed ignorance about the pranks. That maybe the flicker of interest he'd sensed before had been real. That maybe, as his friends had suggested, Cathy was the one behind the unending tricks. He'd asked Annie to meet him half an hour before the ride was scheduled to come, so that they'd have time to talk. When and if she showed up, he'd try to find some nice, nonaggressive way of asking her about them. Give her an opportunity to tell him straight-out that she'd had nothing to do with the pranks. But she didn't come.

After what seemed like hours, he caught sight of her hurrying across the fields, just as a greenish-gold four-door car slowed to a stop nearby. The front passenger window rolled down. "Josh?"

He peeked inside and saw a young Englisch woman. She had alabaster-pale skin sprinkled liberally with freckles, and her red hair was pulled back in a ponytail. Behind the wheel was a young man—her boyfriend, maybe.

"Jah. I mean, yes. You are...." He hesitated, trying to remember the name of the friend Shanna had said would take them. "Belle?"

She smiled widely. "Yes. And this is my boyfriend, Harley. We've never been to the battlefield, so we decided this would be a great time to visit."

"Nice to meet you, Harley." Joshua put his hand on the top of the door. "Annie is coming. She's...." He straightened and turned. "Right there." Closer than he'd realized. She must have run. Their eyes met, and he forced a smile. At least she'd come.

Chapter 11

Annie stopped beside Joshua and checked out the two people in the car. They weren't the usual Amish drivers. *Danki, Lord.* She didn't have any idea who this couple was, or where Joshua had found them, but it seemed that their secret would be safe— for now. "Hi." Her voice was only a little louder than a hoarse whisper. She wondered if she should try again. She cleared her throat.

"Hi!" The young woman gave a friendly smile. "I'm Belle, and this is Harley. I go to school with Shanna Stoltzfus. Please, hop in!" She gestured to the backseat. "We'll stop by my apartment first and get you dressed in some other clothes, so that you won't stand out so much. Shanna said you'd want to keep this trip a secret so you wouldn't lose your job."

Shanna? When had Joshua enlisted her help with this outing? Annie gave him a curious glance.

Joshua shrugged, opened the back door, and gestured for Annie to get in.

"Wow. Shanna thought of everything." Did she sound as overwhelmed as she felt?

Joshua slid into the seat next to Annie, forcing her to scoot over. As she did, his leg pressed against hers, and the heat seemed to singe her through the fabric of her dress. She glanced over at him, wondering whether he'd be nice or continue giving her icy glares.

He didn't seem to be glaring, but the reason for that might have been as simple as the company they were with.

Belle turned around to look at Annie. "She said you wouldn't want to wear jeans, but I have a denim skirt you might feel comfortable in. I think it's almost as long as your dress."

Annie nodded. "Dank—Thank you."

"We have jeans for you, too, Josh, and a T-shirt. It looks like you might be about Harley's size. The shirt is plain, with no graphics. Shanna said that'd be best." Belle leaned over to look at the floor in the backseat. "As for your feet...oh, good. You're wearing tennis shoes. I'm sure we're in for a lot of walking. I wasn't sure if the Amish had to wear old-fashioned footwear or not."

Joshua snickered. "No rules about the types of shoes we can wear. Annie could have worn a pair of those spiky heels that are popular, if she wanted to." He caught Annie's eye and gave her a grin, as if he might like to see her in a pair of high heels. She was glad she was sitting down. Her knees turned to liquid.

Feeling her face grow warm with a blush, she turned away and looked out the window. "Jah, but those would last about ten minutes on a farm."

Harley checked the rearview mirror, then glanced over his shoulder as he backed the car onto the road. "Better buckle up. It's the law."

After they'd fastened their seat belts, Joshua slid his hand closer to Annie's. She didn't move away or resist, even when he wrapped his fingers around hers. She welcomed the sparks. Did he feel them, too? He tightened his grip a little, adjusting his hand so that it covered hers completely. "This'll be fun, ain't so?" he whispered.

She looked down at their clasped hands, knowing she ought to pull away but not at all wanting to. She glanced at him, hoping he wouldn't detect the longing in her eyes. Then, she looked away, out the window again. "An adventure. Seems you and Shanna thought of everything. When did you go see her?"

There was jealousy in her voice, for sure. Joshua resisted the urge to groan. "Thursday. Matthew had a work frolic."

Annie turned back to him, her eyes wide. "A work frolic? And the community didn't know?"

Joshua shook his head. "Just a few things needed to be done. Shanna and Becky painted the kitchen, and...."

Her breath hitched. "Becky was there, too?"

She sounded hurt that her best friend had known about it and she hadn't. He held her hand tighter, caressing the top of it gently with his thumb. "And Jacob. He was there, too." He should have invited Annie. Had thought about it. But, with everything that had been going on, and with him not knowing how she felt....

"Becky didn't tell me." She wriggled her hand a little, but not enough to free it from his grasp.

"Then, just so you know, they're painting the haus that Jacob built next weekend. You're welkum to kum with me."

"I love painting." Belle apparently decided she'd been left out of the conversation for too long. She twisted around in the front seat and sat sideways so that she could see them, painfully reminding Joshua that his conversation with Annie was not so private. He allowed her to pull her hand free.

Leaving Annie to carry on a conversation with Belle, Joshua turned and gazed out the window at the traffic rushing past. He adjusted his seatbelt and gripped the door handle, so tight that his fingers hurt. He hated the speed, the rush-rush-rush, of the Englisch world. Any sudden stop by the car immediately in front of them would mean instant death, he was sure. Why hadn't he considered the risks when he'd asked Annie to take him to the battlefield? He was jeopardizing her life due to his own selfishness. *Forgive me, Lord.*

Finally, Harley turned into the parking lot of an apartment complex on the west side of Springfield. He parked the car in between a pickup and a convertible, and then he and Belle opened their doors. "Come on up for a moment, and we'll show you what we found for you to wear, if you don't want to look Amish," Belle said.

Joshua shrugged. He didn't mind looking Amish. He was Amish, and would remain so. But Annie, as worried as she was about her job, and what would happen if they were to get caught, might feel more comfortable with a disguise of Englisch clothing. He certainly wouldn't condemn her for it. Although, if she were recognized in Englisch clothes, wouldn't that make things all the worse for her?

Annie hesitated a moment before opening her door and sliding out. Joshua did the same. They followed Belle and Harley up to a second-story apartment and waited while Belle opened the door, unlatching three separate locks.

The Amish didn't use any locks. It must really be unsafe in the Englisch world.

Belle swung the door open, and Annie stepped into a small room furnished with only a brown leather couch and a wooden koffee table. There was a giant television set mounted to the wall, along with some picture puzzles that had been glued together and framed. A galley kitchen took up the far wall, where a tiny metal table with a round glass top and two chairs sat in front of the stove.

Belle picked up a pile of folded clothes lying on a chair and handed them to Annie. "The bathroom is through that door."

Annie glanced at Joshua, panic on her face. Jah, she wanted to escape notice, but she hated the very idea of wearing Englisch clothes. A denim skirt? Well, Belle had said it was long; it might not be so bad.

But it was. When she'd put it on, the skirt hugged her legs all the way down to the hem, which was closer to her knees than her ankles. There was a slit in back, halfway up her thighs. And the shirt! She'd never worn anything so tight in her life.

Besides, she doubted the wisdom in wearing colors so bright. She would be hiding in plain sight, for sure and for certain.

She didn't want anyone to see her like this, but she didn't know what else to do. Everything was covered, except for the backs of her legs, which showed through the slit in the skirt. Yet, even with the relatively modest neckline of the shirt, she felt exposed.

Swallowing a wave of nausea, Annie opened the bathroom door. Immediately, everyone turned to look at her. She glanced at Joshua and caught the flicker of interest in his eyes as they traveled slowly down her body.

Chapter 12

Joshua studied Annie. She looked good. Real good. And if it weren't for the Amish kapp still on her head, she would have appeared as Englisch as Belle. But it looked as if she was going to be sick, the way the blood had drained from her face, leaving a greenish tint in its place. Of course, that might have been due to the clingy, peach-colored T-shirt she wore. The jean skirt hugged her hips and clung narrowly to her legs through the hem, just above her knees. It didn't look comfortable. Nor did it suit Annie, given her penchant for earth tones, not to mention much more loosely fitting Amish clothes.

Still, he could appreciate the new color scheme. And the curves. Definitely the curves.

Harley gave a wolf whistle, which caused the little of Annie's color that remained to vanish completely. She looked at him and then glanced back at Joshua, and he resisted the urge to give a whistle of his own. Instead, out of respect, he looked away, hoping Harley would have the decency to do the same. She couldn't go out in public like this. No man on the planet would be able to keep his eyes off of her. He swallowed. Hard. And turned to Belle. "Do you have anything else? Otherwise—"

Annie spoke at the same time. "Do you have anything else, maybe? I mean, I appreciate the effort, but...."

Belle tilted her head, considering her. "Hmm. I thought that skirt reached below the knees. You must have longer legs than I do." She went over to the closet and pulled out another skirt, this one longer, made of fabric the color of koffee with lots of cream. "Here, try this."

Annie took the skirt and disappeared back inside the bathroom.

"I suppose it might have been hard to hike in that," Belle conceded, "but that outfit looked better on her than it does on me." She closed the closet door. "I'd give it to her to keep, but she probably wouldn't be allowed to wear it."

There was no "probably" about it.

When Annie reemerged from the bathroom, she was dressed in her Amish clothes again. She handed the shirt and the two skirts back to Belle. "Thank you, but I'm going as myself. I just can't wear those things. I'd feel so...."

Her voice trailed off, maybe because she didn't want to hurt Belle's feelings. But Joshua could fill in the blanks. She'd feel sinful. Immodest. Exposed.

He cast her a knowing smile and then set down the jeans and T-shirt Harley had given him. "Jah. Me, too. It's for the best."

"But I thought you wanted to do this thing undercover." Belle's forehead scrunched.

"Not too many Amish will be at the battlefield, I'm thinking." Joshua took a couple of steps backward, toward the door. "And, if some of them happen to be there, they'll have some explaining of their own to do, ain't so?" He raised his eyebrows.

Annie shot him a look of total relief before turning back to Belle. "Thanks again, but...maybe we should just go."

Belle shrugged. "Okay, then. If you're sure."

"I'm sure." Annie maneuvered quickly toward the door, as if she was afraid that someone would catch her and force her to change back into the Englisch clothes. Her cheeks were flushed a hot-pink hue, a vestige of the embarrassment she must have experienced while wearing those too-revealing clothes.

Annie spent the half-hour car ride staring down at her hands, clenched tightly in her lap. This time, Joshua had the job of talking with the Englischers. Finally, they arrived at Wilson's Creek Battlefield, and Harley parked the car. He and Belle hesitated by the doors of the building, waiting for Joshua and Annie, but Joshua waved them on. "We'll catch up. I need to talk to Annie for a moment."

They hesitated a few seconds more, and then Harley took Belle's hand and led her inside the building. Annie looked at Joshua, her eyes widening. But she remained silent until the doors closed behind the other couple. "I'm sorry I embarrassed you with the clothing thing," she finally said. "I didn't know what to do, but I really wish I hadn't even shown myself wearing them. I can't believe you saw me like that." She shuddered.

Joshua reached out, thinking he would grasp her hand, but he merely brushed her skin and then drew back. "I feel bad that you were put in that situation. But it's not that. I wanted to talk to you about something else. It's...well, I seem to have become the target of a practical jokester."

Annie fidgeted with the front of her apron. "The spider, you mean?"

"Jah, but not only that. There have been several pranks. The worst, so far, has been the baby powder...

make that the strawberry Jell-O in the shower." He watched her face carefully for the tiniest hint of guilt. Any sign that she'd already known about the pranks. But all he could see was confusion.

After a moment's pause, during which she seemed to be processing his words, she narrowed her eyes pensively. "Does Jell-O taste different in the shower?" She shook her head. "Do I want to know?"

It hadn't been Annie. She was clueless. He wanted to kiss her. Pick her up and swing her around in circles. Or even wrap her in a bear hug.

He wanted to do all three.

But he did none of them.

Instead, he drew in a breath. "I'm sorry I thought it might have been you, or that you'd at least known about them. And I'm sorry I was unkind to you this week. Never again, Annie. My friends assured me it wasn't you."

Anger sparkled in her eyes. "You blamed me in front of your friends?"

"Nein, not blamed you, exactly. More like discussed the possibility of your being responsible."

"I can't believe you thought I might have played those tricks on you. There are others in the haus, you know."

"I know. My friends told me that Cathy was probably the perpetrator. And I believed them. But I thought you were at least aware of what she was doing. That you'd given your okay." He reached for her hands again, but she pulled them away and clasped them behind her back. "Ach, Annie. It isn't what you think."

"Then, tell me what it is."

He removed his hat, raked his fingers through his hair, and put it on again. Gulped down the lump that had formed in his throat. Swallowed again, for good measure.

"Fine. I like you, Annie. I thought you might like me. But I couldn't figure out the message behind the pranks. I still can't. What does Cathy have against me? And would it be possible for you to forgive me?"

He liked her. Annie struggled to keep a smile from spreading across her mouth, but she couldn't quite contain it. Totally inappropriate, especially with the question he'd just asked. Cathy was undoubtedly behind those unkind acts—after all, she had vowed to get rid of Joshua—but Annie hadn't heard about them until after the fact. Joshua had said there'd been several tricks, including one involving baby powder, another strawberry Jell-O in the shower. Annie shook her head. She couldn't begin to imagine where Cathy had gotten inspiration for her pranks.

She released her hands behind her back and, not knowing what else to do, folded her arms across her chest. Joshua liked her. What did that mean, exactly? She liked plenty of people who were mere acquaintances, who meant little else to her. Joshua, she more than liked. She swallowed. "I like you, too." *An understatement.* She dipped her chin slightly, hoping to hide any embarrassment that showed on her face. Or, maybe to hide the truth: she suffered from a serious case of puppy love. She lowered her arms and resumed fidgeting with her apron.

Joshua reached out and took her hand. The sparks that ignited in her fingertips made her breath catch. "Do you mind?" he asked as his fingers inter-twined with hers.

She ought to have minded. A good Amish girl didn't go holding hands with a bu unless they were courting under the cover of darkness. But, nein, she didn't mind at all.

Then again, would granting him that small liberty lower his respect for her? Would he lump her in with all of the other girls in the district, who were easily swayed by his considerable charm?

She shook her head slowly, then nodded.

He chuckled. "Well, which is it?"

Annie prayed for strength. "Nein."

He nodded, released her hand, and reached for the handle of the glass door leading into the visitors' center. Then, he let go of the door and turned to her again. "I am sorry, Annie. Ach, and you should know. I talked with Rachel. I won't be seeing her again."

She nodded, then repeated, "I like you, too." Her face heated. Now he knew. She might as well have admitted straight-out that she had a crush on him.

He chuckled and grasped the door handle again. "Allow me."

Belle and Harley were nowhere in sight. Perhaps, they were meandering through the cubicles that featured fascinating bits of trivia about the generals who had fought in the Civil War.

She'd browsed those panels on her last visit, but she couldn't get enough of them—or of anything pertaining to history: Amish history, American history, European history, linguistic history...any history at all, really.

Would Joshua be horrified if she stopped to peruse the display? Or, would he rather find their Englisch companions and then go out to the actual battlefield? He might be more interested in seeing the cabins and field hospitals, which were still standing. Or, the cannons, yet intact.

Well, she wanted to see that stuff, too.

Ever since her first visit, she'd wanted to come back during a reenactment. She smiled to think that, in her Amish clothes, she probably appeared to many visitors as a reenactor in costume, even though her attire differed vastly from true period fashion from the Civil War era.

"You can go find Harley and Belle, if you'd like." She hesitated at the beginning of the displays. "I won't be long."

Joshua looked around, as if wondering where she would go, if not with him, and then his eyes lit on the wall beside them. "I'll stay with you."

Lovely. All she needed was to have Joshua tell everybody how long she'd spent looking at the graven images of war heroes. Really, what they looked like didn't matter in the least to her. She cared only about what they'd done. After all, history was her favorite subject.

Maybe Joshua was interested in this, too. Coming here had been his idea, hadn't it?

Still, they shouldn't hang out in here too long. Belle and Harley had apparently whizzed through this area and gone straight for the model battlefield that someone had built to scale. They stood over it now, watching as it lit up to show the movement of the troops. Annie's students had found it fascinating.

So had she, to be honest.

But she hadn't expected Joshua to stay so close by her side. He was much closer than was necessary, really. It made it very hard to focus on the museum. Very easy to focus on the man.

And to wish, and hope, and dream, and pray....

As Harley drove the car through the battlefield, Joshua wished that he and Annie could lose their Englisch escorts and somehow obtain a horse and buggy to transport them, instead. Driving slowly through the fields with Annie close by his side, feeling the fresh breeze in their faces, would be so much more romantic than sitting in the stuffy backseat of a car and gazing out at the scenery through closed windows.

Harley never stopped the vehicle for them to get out, since the other buildings around the battlefield weren't open to the public that day. And the car maneuvered more quickly than a horse and buggy would have, meaning that their date was approaching its end much too rapidly.

There went any dreams Joshua had entertained of giving Annie a hug on the front porch of one of the cabins to thank her for giving him the opportunity to see it. To thank her for risking her job security—not that she had any, really—to take him there. And to thank her for spending time with him, despite the fact that he'd effectively ruined his reputation with the one girl he'd wanted to impress, both by coming across as a player and by acting irritated toward her about the pranks, in which she'd played not even a minor part.

He heaved a sigh as they drove away from the battlegrounds and back onto the highway toward Springfield. Back to Seymour. And back to the world where it seemed Annie was promised to Luke, not Joshua.

"Did you want to see anything else in town?" Harley glanced at his reflection in the rearview mirror.

Joshua shook his head. He didn't know anything about Springfield, so he had no idea what was there to see. Plus, he figured Harley and Belle had given up enough of their day catering to him and Annie.

But Annie nodded and glanced at Joshua. "Jah, if you don't mind. I'd love to go to the Bass Pro Shop. They have a museum there, and—"

"I think it's closed for remodeling." Belle looked back at them. "But there are some interesting things in the actual store. We could take you there for a little while. Pretty soon, though, I have to go to work, from two to ten." She looked at Harley. "We could have lunch there."

He nodded. "Sounds good."

Joshua settled back in his seat. He had no idea what a Bass Pro Shop might be. Well, he was familiar with the terms, of course, but not in that combination. If Annie wanted to go there, he figured it might be good.

She gave a contented sigh and smiled at him. S*miled at him.* A happy, I'm-glad-we're-having-this-time-together type of smile. His heart stuttered, and he couldn't help but turn slightly to study her as he wondered what, exactly, her look had meant.

Had she intended her declaration of "I like you, too" to be interpreted in the same way as he had wanted her to decipher his? He hoped so, especially since she'd repeated it. Maybe she really did want to spend more time with him, to get to know him better. Maybe even to court. And, maybe, she would one day be willing to leave her family in Seymour and move to Pennsylvania as his frau.

His gaze dropped to her lips. Were they as soft as they looked? Ach, he wanted to kiss her. Desperately.

Whoa, Joshua. He pulled back on the mental reins of his hopeful musings. "I like you, too" was a far cry from a promise. And it was certainly miles and miles from a lifetime commitment. But someday, maybe, if the good Lord willed it....

He looked away, then immediately wished he hadn't. They were back in the city, and the traffic seemed even worse than it had been that morning, if that were possible. Fortunately, it wasn't long before they reached the shop Annie had mentioned. The parking lot was so crowded that they had to park a distance away, almost to the road. Not that Joshua minded; he was used to walking. But anyplace with this many Englischers in it at once put him on edge.

He didn't care if he'd be perceived as unmanly; he wanted to hold Annie's hand for security. To make sure that she wouldn't get lost somewhere in the throng. How on earth would he ever find her in there if they were to get separated? He got out of the car and surveyed the humongous building, his stomach churning.

He'd never find her. And then, he'd face the mind-boggling task of facing her daed and admitting that he'd lost Annie. In the city. Someplace they weren't even supposed to be.

And then, to kneel and confess this major transgression—that would be a nightmare. Bile rose in his throat. *Lord, forgive me. Help me not to lose Annie. Protect us from temptation and the evil one....*

He reached out and took Annie's hand, entwining his fingers with hers. "I'm not letting go, so don't even ask."

Chapter 13

W as it sinful for Annie to take such pleasure in the feel of Joshua's palm pressed against hers? To relish the work-toughened roughness of his fingers? To bask in his attention, probably the way every other girl in the district did whenever he invited her home? Probably a greater sin was that this physical contact fueled her daydreams. And his gaze, lingering on her mouth, made her anticipate exceeding that stolen moment with the rim of his tea mug with actual kisses. Someday.

She didn't resist when he pulled her even closer to his side as they walked through the doors with a throng of other shoppers into the big retail store. Nor did she care what was on sale. Sure, she liked fishing with her friends, but only for the social aspect. As far as she was concerned, those fish could live to swim another day. Nein, she wasn't here for the gear. Right now, her top priority was the koffee shop—not their koffee, but their tea. If only the local McDonald's had chai tea on their menu, too.

Joshua looked around, his eyes wide. "This place is...overwhelming. Who needs all this stuff to go fishing?"

"Oh, they have more than just fishing gear. You can buy supplies for hunting, camping, and other outdoor stuff. They also have wildlife replicas: bears, moose, elk, reindeer, and other animals. They also have aquariums filled with turtles, fish, and maybe even some otters." She snapped her mouth shut, realizing she was rambling, and that his eyes were getting even bigger with information overload. "My favorite thing here, though, is the tea," she added. The koffee shop was right inside the door, so she pulled Joshua in that direction and got into line.

Annie had been dreaming of chai ever since Joshua had first mentioned the idea of going to the battlefield. At least that part of her dream was coming true with little effort.

The part about Joshua wanting to court her... well, that remained to be seen. But a girl could hope. And his behavior this morning was certainly fueling her hopes. She imagined Aaron moving in with his frau and her parents, and Joshua and her getting married and living in the haus, with Mamm and Daed moving into the dawdi-haus they'd build next door. Joshua would eventually take over Daed's machine repair business and beekeeping.

It would be a dream come true.

When they reached the counter, Annie placed her order and then turned to Joshua. He stared up at the menu, his face awash with a mix of confusion and panic. Then, his hand gripped hers more tightly. "Um, I'll have what she ordered."

"Chai?" Annie confirmed. "Have you had it before? It's tea, with milk and spices, and—"

"Tea's fine. I like tea." Doubt flashed across his face. "I've never had it with milk. And I've never heard it called 'chai.'"

"Two chais?" The woman behind the counter raised her eyebrows.

"It's gut," Annie assured him, then nodded to the cashier. "Two, yes. Please." She turned back to Joshua as he paid for the drinks. "Okay. We wait over there."

"How many times have you been here before?"

"Only once. We stopped here, at the koffee shop, and then visited the museum next door."

"The one that's closed?"

Annie smiled. "That'd be the one." They got into another line.

He angled his head. "'We'?"

Annie's face heated. She didn't want to admit she'd been here with Luke. "Ach, just some friends. During my rumschpringe."

Joshua shook his head and leaned closer to her. "This Englisch world is confusing," he whispered. His breath tickled the hair on her neck, and she shivered.

When they picked up their chais, Joshua took a sip of his and wrinkled his nose, but he continued to drink it without comment.

Annie felt more than a little uncomfortable, wandering around this fancy store. She was glad Joshua stayed so close to her, still holding her free hand.

Even if things between them went back to normal once they returned home—whatever "normal" was—at least they'd had this moment. This day.

In Joshua's eyes, the day with Annie ended way too soon. Before he knew it, he stood with her beside the low-water bridge, waving as Harley and Belle drove away. They were back in the world where they belonged, but also in the world where he couldn't hold her hand, couldn't whisper in her ear, and couldn't court her, unless the man who claimed she was promised to him somehow got out of the picture.

If only Luke would go back to the Englisch world.

Joshua immediately repented of that thought. He shouldn't wish Luke away from the fold. Luke needed to confess, needed to stay, for his own salvation. And he needed to find a new girl, so that Joshua could have Annie. Pure selfishness on Joshua's part, he knew, but he couldn't help it.

Joshua certainly had things of his own to repent of, starting with misleading the church leaders in Seymour and leading them to believe he planned to stay, when he had absolutely no intentions of doing so. Guilt gnawed at his conscience. Still, he couldn't go around announcing his agenda. That would end everything. He'd be sent home early, without any further chance of winning Annie's heart. Dishonest or not, he had to hold his peace. For now.

They started walking toward the Beiler farm.

"I had fun today, *Josh*." Annie grinned as she mimicked what the Englischers had called him.

When he smiled back at her, a faint blush colored her cheeks, and she averted her eyes shyly.

"Jah. Me, too." If only he could think of something to invite her to do with him next weekend. Or even tomorrow. Something. Anything. "Uh, you want to go to Jacob's work frolic this coming weekend? You could help with the painting and stuff. I'm not sure what all they'll need doing."

She nodded. "I'd love to. Danki for inviting me."

He sucked in a breath. "I'll give you a ride."

She arched an eyebrow. "Speaking of that, are you planning on buying your own horse and buggy? Or just borrowing Daed's for a while longer?"

Ouch. That was something else he hadn't thought of. There was no point in buying his own horse and buggy if he wouldn't be staying in Seymour.

And someone was sure to suspect him, sooner or later. After all, Matthew and Jacob, both of whom had come with him from Lancaster, had purchased their own this past summer. Joshua had gone along to the horse auction to help them pick good ones.

"Ach. I don't know yet. Eventually, I suppose." Evasive. But honest.

"Nein hurry, jah? Becky's haus is close enough for us to walk. It's just down the road a mile or so." Annie pointed to the right.

"Jah. So, we'll walk, then." Joshua smiled at her. When he heard the clip-clop of a horse coming up the hard-packed dirt road, he wondered if they should separate so that they wouldn't be seen together. He wasn't ashamed of being associated with Annie, but he didn't want to cause problems for her. And if she was ashamed to be seen with him, she could ask him to hide or to go on ahead of her.

But she didn't. Maybe whoever was driving the buggy wouldn't recognize them. Well, Annie was pretty unmistakable, dressed in her typical brown dress. Not too many other women dressed in brown around here. They preferred as much variety as possible in their wardrobes.

He doubted the driver would recognize him. In fact, he or she might think he was Luke.

Then again, it could be Luke in the buggy.

Joshua glanced over his shoulder to see. He raised his hand and narrowed his eyes to see whom he was waving to.

Luke.

Go figure.

Joshua stayed by Annie's side. Seeming not at all curious, she hadn't looked back to see who was going by. Perhaps she wasn't concerned, since they were almost home, or because she wasn't worried about Luke finding out.

Joshua was tempted to take her hand, but he didn't, not wanting to damage her reputation any. Instead, he leaned in closer to her. "Think maybe you'd like to go for a walk sometime?"

Joshua's question caught Annie off guard. "You mean to Becky's, right?" she asked. "Next week? I already agreed, ain't so?"

Joshua scratched behind his ear. "Um...well, actually, I was thinking along the lines of tomorrow. It's not a church Sunday. Or, I could take you on a buggy ride."

Annie's shoe caught in a rut in the ground, and she stumbled slightly. Joshua's hand immediately grasped her elbow, steadying her. She felt the sparks all the way to her toes.

He released her as soon as she'd gotten her footing again, but she tripped over something else, a tree root. Not on purpose. "Careful, there." Chuckling, he grabbed her by the elbow once more. He probably thought she'd tripped just so he'd hold on to her. She really needed to watch where she was walking instead of looking off expectantly toward the future, bright with the promise of love.

Perhaps "promise" was a bit presumptuous. After all, this was the man who'd taken almost every single girl in the district home from a singing or a frolic at least once. And going for one walk with him would hardly constitute courtship. It would merely make her like all the other girls.

She straightened her back, found her resolve, and told her head to shake from right to left. "I really appreciate the offer, Joshua, but I'm thinking nein."

He retracted his hand again and slackened his pace, allowing the distance between them to grow. But he didn't say a thing. Not one word. He simply gave a single nod of his head, confirming that he'd heard her and accepted her refusal, and that was the end of it.

She thought he could have at least tried to insist. After all, they'd spent a wonderful day together, acting like a courting couple during their rumschpringe. Couldn't he have asked her to reconsider?

She wished that he would. Because she hadn't planned on making "Nein" her final answer. And her heart sank with the realization that his quiet acceptance might very well be the death of her dream.

Chapter 14

Nein? After their enjoyable outing? Joshua was disappointed, hurt, and, most of all, confused. He'd assumed she would agree to take a walk with him, at the very least. Give their friendship a chance to grow into something more. But it appeared not.

Still, he wasn't prepared to give up just yet. There had to be more than one way to win Annie's heart. Maybe the simple act of sharing dinner at the same table, night after night, would earn him some favor. And he could offer to take her home from the next singing, if she didn't have a ride. If she refused, he wouldn't ask anyone else, for how else was he to topple his reputation as a player?

Besides, she'd already agreed to go with him to the work frolic at Jacob's. Surely, that was something to give him hope.

When they reached the end of the Beilers' driveway, Joshua sighed at the sight of Luke's buggy, parked in front of the haus. Beyond it was Luke, sitting on the front porch, like he belonged, nursing a glass of what appeared to be pink lemonade. It looked refreshing, despite the bright-pink color. Joshua wanted to make a beeline for the shop, the barn, or anyplace else that wouldn't require him to walk by Luke. Yet he'd seen Isaac through the front window, sitting in a chair reading a newspaper. Probably the

Budget. Being so new to the family, Joshua felt he should go inside, present himself, and see if there was anything Isaac wanted him to do.

What would happen, now that Luke would know for sure that Joshua had moved in with Annie's family? After boldly claiming that he would steal her away, he feared that nothing good could come of this.

Out of the corner of his eye, he saw Annie's shoulders slump. It shouldn't have, but it made him glad, because it reinforced his hope that she'd severed ties with Luke, that she was no longer his.

Luke stood up, his dark brown eyes narrowed in an angry glare at Joshua. He drained his glass of lemonade, set it on the porch rail, and took a step forward, never taking his eyes off of him. His mouth opened, and he drew in a sharp breath, as if he were about to yell.

"What are you doing here, Luke?" Annie demanded, her hands on her hips.

Luke shifted his gaze to her. "I came to see you. I told you, we need to talk."

"Jah, that was last Sunday. Almost a week ago. And I still have nothing to say to you."

Joshua winced at the sharpness of Annie's words. He didn't dare glance at Luke. His being there beside her was probably rubbing salt in Luke's open wound. *Lord, please bolster our self-restraint and help us to avoid fighting.* He went up the steps, intending to slip inside.

Luke glared at him again as he balled his fists. He'd taken a couple of steps toward Joshua when a knock sounded.

All three of them looked toward the window. There was Isaac, peering out.

Danki, Lord. Joshua opened the door and went inside. He hated leaving Annie alone with that man, but her daed was right inside, obviously watching. And Joshua would keep his eye on them, too.

Finding the pitcher of pink lemonade on the kitchen table, Joshua helped himself to a glass, then made his way into the living room. He saw that Isaac had opened the window a crack, maybe so that he could keep an ear tuned to the conversation outside.

Isaac looked up from his newspaper and nodded to the chair on the other side of the end table, so Joshua sat down, glancing out the window as he did. He couldn't hear a word of Luke and Annie's conversation. They'd probably walked away from the haus, out of earshot. Served him right for trying to eavesdrop.

He sipped his lemonade, wondering where everybody else had gone. Lydia might be napping. Aaron's upcoming marriage had been published, so he was probably over at his future in-laws' haus. And Cathy… she could be anywhere, which concerned him. How much mischief had she caused in his absence?

Isaac glanced at the window, then looked back at Joshua. "Did you have a gut morgen? You went with Annie…to that battlefield, I'm thinking?"

Joshua gawked at him. Isaac knew where they'd gone? If it hadn't been a secret to him, then would others in the community know, as well? Maybe Annie had told her daed. He forced himself to relax. "Jah. It was gut. Lots of traffic. And I'm not sure what I expected from a battlefield, but it was just a field. Nein crops, to be sure. Some buildings, but they weren't open for touring."

Isaac nodded. "Figured it'd be as such. Did you have lunch? Cathy prepared some extra sandwiches for you and Annie. We have some bags of chips and sliced raw vegetables, too. Cathy needed to go to work this afternoon because the girl who usually works on Saturdays traded days with her."

So, that explained Cathy's absence. Joshua eased back in the chair. "Jah, the couple who gave us a ride took us to a Bass Pro Shop. There are some restaurants there...on the third floor, I think." He hesitated, trying to remember the building layout. "We took a glass elevator up there and got something to eat, after we'd ordered drinks at the koffee shop there. Some kind of fancy tea...chai, I think it was called. Kind of spicy, but not too bad."

Isaac chuckled. "These places with fancy koffees are generating quite a following among our young people. Annie used to go to McDonald's for a free 'Frappe' almost every Friday when that promotion was going on. It's the only koffee she'll drink, as she's convinced tea is healthier. I'm not sure where she came up with that, but some of the tea she brings home isn't too bad. Not like the iced mint or lemongrass tea my frau makes by the gallon. Never did care for it, either. But I think that's what got Annie hooked on the stuff." He shrugged, set down his newspaper, and stood. "I came inside because that redheaded bu was here, and I wanted to keep an eye on things. But I guess he's taken Annie off somewhere, so I might as well go out and work a little in the shop. Need to get some of those leaf blowers fixed."

"I'll help." That would beat sitting around waiting on Annie to reappear, wondering what Luke had said to her, and whether she would fall for it. Joshua downed what was left of his drink, set the glass in the kitchen sink, and followed Isaac out to the shop.

❧

Annie kept a two-foot space between herself and Luke as they walked away from the haus, back toward the fields she'd just crossed with Joshua. She kept her eyes on the ground, not wanting to stumble. She didn't want Luke to touch her at all, not even to steady her. "What did you want to talk about?"

"Us." Luke grunted and spun to face her. "What were you doing, walking with that...that *transplant*?" He nearly spat.

Annie sighed. "Jah, we were coming home."

"From where?"

"We went to Springfield. Wilson's Creek Battlefield and then the Bass Pro Shop." She aimed a smirk in his direction, then belatedly realized she shouldn't have told him. His daed was on the school board. Ach, she might have just gotten herself fired.

He made no comment.

She wiped her suddenly sweaty hands on her apron. "We were just walking. There's no sin in strolling together."

"He was gripping your arm."

"I lost my footing, and he wanted to make sure I wouldn't fall."

"You know the reputation he has."

"Jah, I know. But it's unfounded." It had to be. At least, she wanted it to be, and so she would keep on believing what Joshua had told her to be true.

Luke huffed. "He told me straight-out that he'd win you away from me."

Her heart lurched, then landed with a dull thud somewhere near her big toe. "That was just talk." But it explained so much. His kind, caring, overly protective manner. The whispers. The invitation to take a walk or a buggy ride. He'd been treating her as some sort of trophy to be won, a heart he could hang on the wall, like the fish and buck mounts at the Bass Pro Shop. He didn't really like her; he just wanted to win. Tears burned her eyes, but she willed them not to spill over onto her cheeks. "That's not what we're talking about."

"I just wanted to warn you."

Annie nodded. "And you did." But she couldn't keep her voice from catching. She hoped Luke hadn't noticed. That he wouldn't guess she'd developed a crush on Joshua. That she was just another girl who'd fallen for him. She sucked in a breath. "But what about you? You jumped the fence, Luke. What made you kum back?" She studied him, noticing for the first time that his face looked soft, babyish, compared to Joshua's, which was stronger, with a more chiseled jaw. Handsomer.

Ach, Joshua. Why did he have to go and break her heart, just to prove that he could? Once more, she ordered herself not to cry.

"You."

She blinked, momentarily thrown off track. What had they been talking about? That's right—she'd asked him why he'd come back to the Amish. Talk about blunt. She'd never known Luke to be so transparent. "Me?" She didn't want to feel flattered, but she couldn't help it. At least Luke was up-front about his feelings toward her. In his eyes, she wasn't just some conquest to be won.

Joshua, on the other hand, was adept at playing games with her heart. She wouldn't dwell on that now. Maybe later, when she was alone and could think things through.

"I asked you to kum with me. You said nein. I can't marry you if I'm on the wrong side of the fence. And I intend to do that, Annie. I wanted it to be this wedding season, but I guess that won't work out. I talked to Bishop Sol, and he refused to let me start back into classes, even though I took at least half of them before I left. He says I need to think about things, make sure I'm coming back for the right reasons, before I take the instruction classes."

Annie nodded. "That seems wise." Bishop Sol had made some pretty controversial decisions recently, especially regarding Shanna Stoltzfus, whom he'd allowed back into the community after she'd left for college and earned a nursing degree. Apparently, the bishop wouldn't extend the same grace toward Luke. Annie wished she knew why.

And yet, Bishop Sol had also urged the school board to show leniency in her own discipline for taking the scholars on an unauthorized field trip.

Well, he wasn't likely to explain his reasons to a mere girl.

"I'll kum by tonight after dark to take you for a walk," Luke went on. "We can start courting again and then marry, just as we planned, only a year later. Next wedding season."

Luke spoke as if everything was settled. But it wasn't. Not by a long shot. Annie was just thankful he hadn't persisted in talking about her day with Joshua. He could have accused her of trying to recreate memories she'd made with him, and he could have threatened to expose her to the bishop, or to his daed, but he hadn't.

No matter. She would still be fired over this. Even if Luke had forgotten where she'd gone, he would remember eventually. And if he was displeased with her for not wanting to marry him, he would have no problem ratting her out.

Nein, she wouldn't settle for Luke. But how could she decline tactfully? "I don't know, Luke. I need…we need to pray about this, about us, before we jump into a relationship again. Bishop Sol is right. We need to be sure."

Oops. She realized she'd left room for a measure of hope—an indication that she might be willing to get back with him. So much for a tactful "Nein."

"I am sure!" Luke insisted loudly. He gripped her upper arms and gave her a hard shake. She cringed, and he released her, stepping back. "I just don't want you to be wooed away by that *transplant*." Again, he'd almost spat the last word.

"Don't worry." She rubbed her upper arms. She'd probably develop bruises there. "There's no chance of that happening." Especially since Joshua saw her merely as a trophy to be won. Then, he'd drop her. Cold.

"You're too levelheaded to fall for a jerk like him."

Annie held her breath for a moment. "Jah. Jah, I am." She hoped it sounded like she meant it. Because she knew she didn't, at least not completely. In fact, she was fairly positive she didn't mean it at all. Honestly, if Joshua came to her right now, and kept up his sweet act, she'd have just as strong a crush on him. The question was, which man was a bigger jerk? Luke had hurt her physically before. Not seriously, of course, but he'd never apologized. Not once.

Joshua had always treated her with nothing but kindness. And if she spent another day or two like this afternoon with him, her heart would be firmly within his grasp.

Never mind a day or two. It already was.

She loved Joshua Esh.

Joshua struggled to focus on the task at hand. He'd situated himself too close to the open shed door, and he couldn't stop himself from glancing out at the field where Annie and Luke stood, talking. They didn't appear to be arguing. And that didn't bode well for him.

Besides, he was a little scared that Luke would tell Annie about how he'd announced his intention to steal her away from him. If she found out about that, whatever would she think? She would conclude that all of his talk about waiting to court until he was sure had been hollow words. That he hadn't meant them. And that she'd be wise to stay away from him.

Isaac put down the equipment he'd been working on and walked over to the door to peek out at the couple. Maybe he was worried about Annie, too. Or maybe he was concerned because of how often Joshua was spying.

Moments later, Luke raised his hand, turned away from Annie, and set off at a run toward the Schwartzes'.

Isaac sighed. "He'll kum by again tonight."

Battling a wave of sadness, Joshua looked up at him. "You think so?"

"Jah. I'd hoped she'd say nein." Isaac turned away from the door and pulled out his pocket watch. "She'll be fixing supper soon. You have plans for the evening?"

Joshua forced a laugh. "Nein." Not since Annie had turned him down. And then gone and accepted Luke, two times in one day.

"Tomorrow?"

"It's not a church Sunday. Will you be at home or traveling around visiting family?"

Isaac frowned. "At home. My frau, she doesn't get out anymore, except for doctor's appointments. I have to hire a driver for those. Maybe family will stop by. Two weeks ago, Lydia's parents were the only ones who came. Her siblings and aents and onkels didn't bother. I know my frau is feeling secluded, but I don't know how to fix it. We could build a ramp to get her out of the haus without having to carry her, but she wouldn't be able to go any farther than the yard." He looked around, shaking his head. "Not sure how well a wheelchair would roll out here. And the ground is too rough for a walker."

Joshua thought for a moment. "They make portable ramps...I've seen them in Pennsylvania. They're metal, and you can fold them up to carry along in the back of a buggy. You could get her into other homes that way. Maybe, if you ask her therapists, they might know where to order one."

Isaac shook his head. "One of the conditions of home therapy is that she can't leave home for any reason except a doctor's appointment. They say she can't even go out for church. And Bishop Sol decided that, given Lydia's current condition, we shouldn't host church services until she's well. I understand why, but I know Lydia would enjoy seeing people. Though it would tire her out terribly."

Joshua rubbed his chin, feeling the roughness of a day's worth of stubble against his fingertips. He glanced out the door again at Annie, who was crouched down, picking up something from the ground. She stood up and tucked whatever it was behind her ear. Her pencil. It had gone all the way to Springfield with her, Joshua realized with a smile.

Quickly, his smile faded, as a lump formed in his throat. If only she'd notice him with her heart's eyes.

Chapter 15

Annie awoke suddenly and sat up in bed, listening for whatever it was that had roused her. Sure enough, her bedroom window was showered with what sounded like a handful of pebbles. She jumped out of the bed and peered outside, praying she wouldn't see Luke standing down there. She'd told him not to come, hadn't she?

But there he stood, holding a flashlight so that it illuminated his face, as he'd always done when they were courting.

With a groan, Annie opened the window and leaned her head out. "Jah?" she hissed.

"I told you I'd kum by tonight."

She must have imagined telling him not to come. "I'll be right down." She wanted to say, "I told you, I needed to pray about it first. Go home." But she was afraid of what he'd do if she rejected him then and there. She closed the window again, quickly dressed, and then hurried down the stairs, avoiding the squeaky step. She'd wait until she was outside, away from the haus, to tell him to go back home. Otherwise, his temper would probably wake her parents. And Joshua.

She stepped into the dark kitchen, wishing she'd taken the time to grab her own flashlight. Even the almost full moon didn't illuminate the haus very well.

She extended a hand to feel her way around the table and chairs. Two or three steps was all that it took for her to run into something. Hands gripped her upper arms, and she gasped.

"Easy there, Annie," Joshua said, his tone bemused. "Where are you off to in such a hurry?"

Heat flooded her body, and she stepped out of his arms. "Ach, just...um...." Well, this was awkward. How could she tell the man of her dreams that her former beau was waiting for her in the side yard? She cleared her throat. "What are you doing up?"

"I came down for a glass of water. I thought I heard something." He flicked on his small flashlight. "And I did. Hear something, I mean." He paused and, in the dim glow of his penlight, surveyed her with a serious look. She thought he looked almost passionate, like he wanted to kiss her. His gaze flickered over her lips.

Annie felt her heart leap to her throat. He did want to kiss her! Her, Annie Beiler. Worse, she wanted that kiss, with every cell in her body. She held her breath.

For the longest time, he stood there, studying her, as if attempting to memorize every inch of her face. But then, he suddenly blinked and stepped back. "Go on. Your beau is waiting."

"He's not my beau," Annie whispered. Tears welled in her eyes, and, this time, they spilled out, drenching her cheeks. Would she be turning her back on what her heart really wanted by going out to Luke?

"Ach, Annie. Maybe you should tell him that." Joshua sighed, then reached out with his right hand, his fingertips grazing her damp cheek. He swallowed hard, his Adam's apple bobbing, as a finger came to rest on her lips. It lingered there a moment before he dropped his hand. "Go. Before I do something I shouldn't."

He was right. He shouldn't kiss her, and she shouldn't want him to. At least he was man enough not to take advantage of a woman with little self-restraint. That spoke volumes of his character. Maybe it really wasn't as Luke had suggested. Maybe Joshua actually liked her for her, and not for the sake of his ego.

She blinked the tears from her eyes, wiped her face, and slipped past him, out the door.

Joshua stepped over to the kitchen window and watched Annie hurry to meet Luke. His heart ached, and his fingers curled into his palms, the nails digging into his skin. Luke said something to her as he gestured toward the road, and they started walking in that direction.

Good thing Joshua hadn't given in to the almost overwhelming temptation to kiss her.

Then again, maybe he should have. Because he was pretty sure she was getting kissed tonight, either by him or by Luke. And he wanted to be the one.

He took a step toward the door. He wanted to go after them, to keep an eye on things. But it would be wrong to slip out into the darkness to spy on a couple, even though he didn't trust Luke one bit.

He turned around and went back upstairs, dragging his feet all the way. He would go back to bed, though he doubted he'd sleep a wink until he heard Annie come back inside.

And maybe not even after that.

Instead, he stood at the window in his bedroom, watching them. Hoping Annie would tell Luke to leave her alone. Send him away. Tell him a firm "Nein."

What he would do if Luke kissed her, Joshua didn't know.

Annie kept her distance from Luke, as before, walking silently beside him as he talked about his plans for their future together. How he intended to build a small, one-bedroom haus on his daed's property, just to start with. How his job working for his daed would support them. He even promised to join the church. Annie listened, all the while thinking about what Joshua had said, as well as waiting for a chance to fit a word in edgewise.

Finally, Luke paused, and she spoke up. "We're not courting, Luke. Please don't build anything with me in mind." She moved further away from him, wishing she hadn't awakened and answered his summons. She should have stayed in the kitchen with Joshua, instead. Would he have kissed her if she hadn't been going to meet Luke? Did he really like her in that way? If so, her decision to meet Luke, anyway, certainly gave the wrong impression.

Luke said something else, but Annie didn't catch it. Oh, well. Hadn't his daed fired him once before, only to hire him back when he'd come home? She frowned, trying to recall whether that had been rumor or fact. Regardless, she didn't want to lead him on any longer.

"We aren't getting married." That had come out a bit harsher than she'd intended. No telling how Luke would take it.

He growled and stopped walking. She could feel the anger radiating from him. And she caught a whiff of his breath—whiskey? "You don't know your own mind, Annie. You *are* going to marry me," he insisted.

"Not if you don't treat me with some respect!" She hoped he didn't think that respectful treatment would change her mind, though. No matter what, she wouldn't settle for Luke—or for anyone else she didn't love. Much less anyone who didn't love her.

"I do respect you, Annie. How dare you say I don't? I haven't even tried to kiss you, other than that one time when I was drunk. I missed your mouth and kissed your cheek, instead, and then you slapped me."

"Jah, and I'll slap you again if you so much as touch me. Just leave me alone, please? I think you need to listen to Bishop Sol and think about why you want to join the church. If it's just so you can marry me, then you can forget it."

"I wouldn't be the first man to join the church for a girl. I bet half the men in the district joined because their future fraus wanted them to."

"But did any of them actually leave the community to go live in town?"

"Some of them did, jah." But there was a shadow of doubt in his voice, as if he couldn't provide particular names to prove his point.

Annie was tempted to ask for names, just to egg him on. Instead, she merely sighed. "Luke, I'm sorry, but I need to pray some more about this. I just don't feel secure about you. What if you decide you want to be Englisch someday?"

He hesitated. "You'd kum with me. You know that Bible verse that says, '*Whither thou goest, I will go*'? That's what a gut frau does. And you'd be a gut frau, Annie."

Now, she was angry. "But I don't want to go, Luke. I want to stay. Amish is who I am, who I'll always be."

He shrugged. "You can be anything. You could teach after you were married if you weren't Amish."

That wasn't true. Englisch schoolteachers had to go to college and earn a degree. They couldn't teach with only an eighth-grade education. But she knew from past experience that it was useless to try reasoning through anything with Luke. Especially after he'd been drinking. "You mean, you expect your frau to work? After you're married?"

"Lots of Amish fraus work; you know that. Most of them have their little cottage industries. Kind of hard to live on just one income these days, even for the Amish."

"Jah, but...." *"Sometimes, you're mean to me,"* she wanted to tell him. Like right now. He was controlling and stubborn. She bit her lip to keep the words from coming out. He'd only deny her accusation, just as he'd done countless times before. Granted, it had usually been after a spell of drinking, but she couldn't marry a man she feared. And she wouldn't marry the town drunk. She spun around. "I'm going home, Luke. Danki for coming by, but it's late. And maybe I'm mistaken, but it doesn't sound as if you intend to stay here in Seymour."

"You're right. You don't understand. I will stay. Really."

"Still, it's late." She hoped her voice sounded gentle and didn't reveal the frustration she felt. "Go home and pray about your reasons for wanting to join the church."

"Nein need to pray. I know exactly what I want."

Annie smiled sadly. "So do I." And it wasn't Luke. But how could she make him see that?

And would she regret turning him away if she found out that Joshua didn't want her?

She shook her head. She'd rather be a maidal. Spinsterhood was far preferable to marrying Luke Schwartz.

She wanted to say that out loud, but the stench of the whiskey, or whatever he'd been drinking, on his breath was overpowering. And he got mean when crossed. She winced, remembering the hard shake he'd given her earlier. When he'd been sober.

She turned and hurried back across the dark field toward home, never looking back to see whether Luke followed her. Normally, a bu would walk his girl back home, but she wasn't Luke's girl now. She was nobody's girl. And she needed to remember that.

She climbed the back steps and slipped into the kitchen. A couple of lit candles were arranged near the edge of the table, where Joshua sat, his Bible open before him. His forefinger hovered over the verse he'd just read.

Annie skidded to a stop. "Ach, you're still up?"

His smile was hesitant. Flickering. Kind of sad-looking. "I couldn't sleep. Decided to read and pray."

"Downstairs?"

"I forgot my water." He nodded toward the glass. "Did you have a gut walk?"

Annie shrugged. "Luke's full of plans. Talking about building a small haus and everything." She pulled out a chair and sat next to him. "What book are you reading from?"

"Psalms." Joshua slid a bookmark into the middle of the Bible and closed it. Then, he adjusted the two candles, sliding them a bit further away from him. Far enough from him to cast his face in shadows. "He's building you a haus, then, jah?"

"Me? Nein. I told him...I said that I think he needs to pray about why he wants to return to the Amish. That we need to pray about the relationship between us." She fidgeted. "Truthfully, I'd rather be a maidal than marry him."

"Did you say that?" Joshua leaned forward.

Annie shook her head. "I wanted to, but I was afraid. He has a temper. I mean, he's normally polite—harmless, really—and he was known to keep the Englisch parties under control during his rumschpringe. But whenever Luke drinks, his temper is easily riled, and he tends to get violent." She lowered her head. "I think he'd been drinking. I didn't want him to hurt me, given how much it hurt when he shook me earlier today, walking in the field." She rubbed her upper arms where he'd grabbed her.

"He hurt you?" Joshua's eyes widened. A muscle tensed in his jaw.

"Not severely." She didn't want to alarm him. "I may have some bruises, though, and it's a little sore."

"Annie. You need to stay away from him."

She nodded her head. "Jah."

He reached out his forefinger and gently lifted her chin, so that their gazes met. "There was an abusive man who lived near me in Pennsylvania. He was arrested for beating his frau in public. I was there. Scared me to death. I never want to see another woman go through that."

Tears burned her eyes. "Jah. There are some men like that around here, too."

"There's never a gut reason for a man to hurt a woman."

Whoever landed Joshua Esh would marry a good man. If only she could be the one he chose.

Well, if she allowed him to court her, maybe she would be.

He released her chin and leaned back in his chair. "I suppose we should try to get some sleep."

Annie took a deep breath and prayed for courage. Her cheeks warmed. "Joshua. When I said nein earlier today, I didn't mean it. I'd love to go on a walk or a buggy ride with you."

Chapter 16

Joshua tried to keep from smiling. "Ach, now, I don't know. You said nein. Not sure I want a wishy-washy woman keeping me company." He shook his head with mock seriousness. "Besides, you asking me is ever so bold. I'm not sure what my parents or yours would say if they heard that you'd asked me out." He stood and lifted one of the candles. "I need to get some sleep. Let me think on it overnight. Sweet dreams, Annie." He winked, hoping she would realize he was merely kidding with her. And, if she didn't, he figured she could use a taste of her own medicine.

He went off to bed, still smiling.

When he awoke the next morning, his smile was still in place.

After helping with the chores, Joshua went back inside the haus to wash up, then sat down at his place at the table. Cathy slid a plate with an omelet in front of him. Next, she added to the table a platter of bacon, a bowl of fried potatoes, and a tray of buttered toast. "Gut morgen, Joshua." She smiled sweetly.

Joshua raised his eyebrows. This was a switch. Cathy had been giving him the cold shoulder since his arrival, speaking to him only when necessary. Maybe his talk with Annie had cleared the air with all the Beilers, and there would be no more practical jokes at his expense. That would be a relief. "Gut morgen, Cathy. This omelet looks wunderbaar."

Her smile widened. "I'm sure you'll enjoy it. I made it especially for you, just the way you like it." She proceeded to set a plated omelet at each place around the table.

Annie came into the room, smiling shyly at him, and then set several jars of homemade jam on the table near the toast.

After everyone had gathered and paused for the silent prayer, Joshua took a helping of potatoes and a slice of bacon before passing each serving dish to Aaron. Then, he took a bite of his omelet. Immediately, his mouth started burning. He grabbed his glass of orange juice and gulped it down, then jumped up, rushed to the refrigerator, and poured his cup full of cold milk, which he proceeded to chug, as well. As he did, he ignored the stares of confusion aimed at him from almost every person at the table.

But he didn't fail to notice Cathy's smirk.

After draining his glass of milk, Joshua met Cathy's eyes. "Wow, Cathy. That is the spiciest omelet I've ever had. Is it a southwest version or something?"

"Do you like it?" Cathy's voice was saccharine sweet. "David told me how much you loved jalapeños. You add them to everything, he said. I wanted you to feel at home."

"He said that, did he?" Joshua wiped his mouth on his sleeve. "I'll be sure to thank him next time I see him."

"Catherine Grace." Isaac lowered his fork and knife onto his plate with a noisy clatter. "Step into the other room for a moment."

"What for, Daed? For trying to make Joshua feel welkum by fixing food the way he likes it? The hotter and spicier the better, I was told."

Isaac stood, his eyes narrowing. "Are you talking back to me, daughter?" He strode toward the door.

Cathy shrugged and then, casting Joshua a look of pure venom, followed her daed into the living room.

Now, Joshua had no doubt that Cathy had been behind all of the pranks. The question was, why? Had David put her up to it? Or did she have reasons of her own? Sighing, he poured himself another glass of milk. Then, he picked up his plate, scraped his omelet into the trash can, and returned to the table to eat the rest of his breakfast.

Aaron patted him on the back. "Sorry about that. I thought she'd done something like that to your egg salad sandwiches on Saturday. She told me not to eat them." Aaron bowed his head for another silent prayer, pushed away from the table, and went outside. Joshua was glad he and Annie had eaten at the Bass Pro Shop rather than sampling Cathy's fare.

Lydia shook her head. "Hardly a harmless practical joke, to be sure. And it wasn't very nice of this David to tell Cathy to do something like that."

Out of the corner of his eye, he saw Annie use her fork to lift the edge of her omelet and peek inside. Perhaps she wanted to make sure she hadn't received one that had been spiked with hot pepper, as well.

Lydia turned to Annie. "So, who is this David? Do you know him?" She twisted to look back at Joshua. "And how does he know that you don't like spicy foods?"

"He's one of the buwe who came down in the last bunch," Annie explained. "I think there were ten of you who came in June, right, Joshua?"

"Ten, jah. He's David Lapp. He's been seeing Cathy some, I think." Maybe he shouldn't have mentioned that, in case Lydia hadn't known. With his fork, Joshua moved some potatoes around on his plate. "We went to school together. He and I didn't get along so well."

Lydia set her silverware down on the edge of her plate. "And so, this feud between you is continuing here? And he's getting my daughter involved? Have you retaliated in any way?"

Joshua shook his head. "Nein. Only thing I've ever done was steal his bullfrog, back when we were just kinner. And I returned it with an apology." When his daed had made him. But at least he'd said he was sorry, even if he didn't mean it.

He'd also made fun of David for being a big baby multiple times over the years. He'd never apologized for that.

"Well, then. It is past time this thing gets settled, ain't so?" Lydia pierced him with a look that almost made him want to hide.

"Jah. Jah, it is." He lowered his head in shame. If only he hadn't taken David's bullfrog. Evidently, the prank had been far more serious in David's eyes than he'd anticipated.

"Annie, you and Cathy take Joshua and David out, maybe fishing," Lydia instructed her. "Today, if possible. Definitely the sooner, the better, I'm thinking. And, Joshua, you be the man here, if he won't."

Joshua nodded. Lydia's firm approach made him miss his mamm. This time, he'd apologize with sincerity.

Just then, he almost laughed. Had Lydia really just set him and Annie up on a date? He glanced at Annie, who stared at her omelet, a blush staining her cheeks.

He smiled. She'd asked him out last night, and it seemed as if her request would be granted, with or without his specific consent.

Annie stole a glance at Joshua. Considering the vague response he'd given last night to her retraction, she didn't know quite what to think about Mamm's arranging an outing for them. Joshua had basically said, "Let me pray about it," and everybody knew that was usually a nice way of saying "Nein." But fishing together ought to be okay. And they didn't have to go alone. She could ask Jacob and Becky to come with them, maybe. That way, she'd have someone to talk to.

She looked over at Mamm, regretting that she'd let her in on her crush. It had been clear enough, considering the way she'd described Joshua—and within earshot of him, no less.

And it hadn't helped matters when Joshua had revealed that Annie had covered his bed with her wedding quilt. Mamm had kept quiet about that, even after Annie had switched out that quilt for a nine-patch.

Of course, the walls of the haus were mighty thin. Mamm and Daed probably heard every word of their conversation last night, including the part when she'd asked him out.

And his refusal. Evidently, Mamm had decided not to take "Nein" as his final answer.

"Jah, I can do that," Joshua finally replied. "Annie, would you do me the honor of coming with me? If David says jah, that is?" Joshua nudged her foot with his. Touching her without Mamm knowing.

She nodded.

Mamm pushed her wheelchair away from the table. "I'll go have a talk with your daed and Cathy." She wheeled her way into the other room.

Joshua waited until Mamm was gone, and then he leaned toward her. "I'd love any chance to be out with you. But I'm sorry for the situation that's causing it."

Her heart nearly melted. Jah, she was in love with Joshua Esh, for sure and for certain. And he was acting as if he felt the same way about her. But, given the way she'd seen him act around every other girl in the district, how would she know for sure? He could merely be a master at sweet talk.

Annie really didn't know how to act around him. Nor did she know how to respond. She lowered her head. Who knew falling in love tied a stomach up in so many knots? Her friends had made it seem easy. Did it stay this hard, or did it get better as the relationship progressed? She wished she knew. At least she knew who to ask.

Annie stood up and followed Mamm into the other room, leaving Joshua to finish his breakfast at the table alone.

When Annie entered the living room, Cathy glared at her. "Why did you put them up to this insane idea? I don't want to spend any more time than necessary with Joshua. I want him out of our haus. He isn't welkum."

Annie sucked in a breath. She'd known how Cathy felt, but it hurt to hear her proclaim it out loud.

But then, Cathy didn't know how she felt about Joshua, did she?

Daed planted his fists on his hips. "Actually, this idea is not so insane. It is ser gut." He glanced toward the door. Annie turned around and saw Joshua standing there, closer to her than she'd expected. Just a tiny step forward, and she'd be in his arms. The thought made her catch her breath. She stepped away from him, figuring it best to eliminate the temptation.

Daed studied Joshua. "I don't know the situation between you and this David—"

"A bullfrog. I stole a bullfrog from him when we were kinner."

Daed shook his head. "I am not going to have this situation grow to include the members of this haus. It needs to be straightened out as soon as possible. Today is not a church Sunday. You can go visit him and get this worked out."

Joshua gave a single nod, his lips tight. He focused on Annie, and his gaze softened. "You'll kum with me, ain't so?" Then, he looked at Cathy. "And you, too, please? Since you and David are...." There was a long pause. Joshua probably didn't know whether they were officially courting, and he didn't want to expose Cathy to her parents. "Friends?"

Cathy huffed, considered him a moment, and then shrugged. "Fine. But I think it's a waste of time. You two have too much to work out; a simple apology over a stupid bullfrog is not going to settle things."

"What else do they have to work out?" Annie raised her eyebrows at Cathy. How could she say such a thing? And how dare she disrespect Mamm and Daed? Daed would have a private talk with her about this later, she was certain.

Joshua angled Cathy a look of surprise. "Excuse me?"

She spread her arms wide. "I'm just saying...."

Annie studied Joshua, wondering if he was hiding something else from them.

"What else could we possibly have to work out?" Joshua seemed as confused as Annie. Maybe he wasn't hiding anything.

Cathy shrugged again and turned on her heel. "We'd best finish up breakfast so that we can go. I think David's host family was expecting guests today. Aents, onkels, and cousins and such. David is missing his family. Might be gut for me to go. At least he'll have someone there who cares." She pushed her way past Joshua and returned to the kitchen.

Frowning, Daed glanced at Annie, then at Joshua, and shook his head. Then, he grasped the handles of Mamm's wheelchair and pushed her into the kitchen.

Leaving Annie alone with Joshua again. She sucked in a breath of suddenly charged air and moved to pass Joshua. Not to shove rudely past, as Cathy had done, but to give him as wide a berth as possible, lest she be tempted to do something inappropriate. She didn't want to even brush against him, as overwhelmed as she was by attraction to him.

But her efforts were in vain. As she walked by, Joshua reached out with both hands and pulled her gently into his arms. He held her against him for a long moment, his hands resting loosely on her waist, his chest rising and falling against hers as he inhaled and exhaled. She could have stepped away, but she didn't want to. She looked up, opening her mouth to say...she didn't know what.

He lowered his head, brushed her lips lightly with his, and then leaned back, his gaze searching hers. He must have sensed her desire, for his hands slid around to her back and drew her closer, his lips finding hers again. This time, he planted them there firmly, as though they belonged.

Joshua Esh, kissing her...Annie wondered if her heart could handle this delightful assault on her senses. She wanted to raise her arms and wrap them around his neck, but they made it only as far as his chest, stalling there, flattened against the roughness of his shirt. She heard his frantic intake of breath at her touch. She fingered the opening down the middle flap of the fabric, as well as the Velcro closure, and then gripped his suspenders and held on. She stood as still as she could, afraid to move, not wanting to destroy the moment.

"Relax. Just do what I do," he whispered against her mouth. His lips moved against hers, coaxing a response. Her first kisses ever, not counting the time Luke tried and missed, planting a peck on her cheek, instead. She attempted to mimic Joshua's moves. Was she doing it right? She released his suspenders, slid her arms up to his shoulders, and allowed herself to get lost in the moment, responding as he deepened the kiss.

What could have been hours later, but was probably only seconds, he stepped back, his hands falling away. He glanced over his shoulder toward the kitchen. As she tried to focus on breathing, sounds of the family in the next room seeped back into her consciousness.

"Joshua!" she whispered. "What was that for?" Did she sound as breathless as she felt? She wanted to ask if she'd done okay.

He met her gaze. "For courage. For good luck. And because I figured either Luke Schwartz or I would be kissing you, and I wanted to make sure it was me."

Annie mulled over his words for a few moments. Maybe too long. Shame washed over her. How could she have allowed him such liberties? They weren't even courting. Plus, even though she'd kissed him back, she didn't know if she'd done it right. He might compare her against others he'd kissed and find her wanting. That would make it worse. Her face heated. How many other girls had he taught to kiss? She moved out of reach and tried to find a frown. "Don't ever do that again, Joshua Esh."

Her warning didn't seem to faze him. She didn't see an ounce of repentance in his eyes. He just smiled. Shrugged. "Fine. The next time I kiss you, it'll be because you asked me to."

The next time? Pretty presumptuous, wasn't he?

He turned and walked out of the room, whistling one of the tunes that was popular at singings. And leaving her standing there, still feeling his kisses, torn between begging for more, right then and there, and calling after him that he shouldn't expect her to ask for any more, ever again.

Joshua surveyed the farmyard of the home where David Lapp was staying as he maneuvered the buggy, pulled by Annie's horse, Penny, onto the property. Almost a dozen other buggies were parked around the driveway. How long would he be able to hold out before they forced him to go buy his own?

He glanced at Annie, sitting stiffly beside him in the front seat, as if afraid to relax, in case accidentally touching him would cause her to lose all self-control. Or, maybe she simply didn't trust him. He looked over his shoulder at Cathy, minding her own business in the backseat. At least she'd finally stopped glowering at him. Maybe the prospect of seeing David Lapp had brightened her attitude.

He stopped the buggy in front of the porch and set the brakes. Then, he glanced at Annie again, his eyes darting to her soft lips. He wanted another kiss for courage. He hadn't expected her to be inexperienced with kissing, especially considering she'd been promised to Luke, but it pleased him. He'd been her first. He couldn't keep from grinning. He wanted to reach out to her, touch her, even if only her hand.

Instead, he vaulted out of the buggy and reached up to help Cathy. She ignored his offer and scrambled out on her own, while Annie climbed down on the other side, opting not to wait for him.

The front door of the haus opened, and David Lapp stepped out onto the porch with a wide smile. "Cathy Beiler. What brings you by? Kum on in. We were about to have some shoofly pie." He nodded at Annie. And his smile faltered and seemed to freeze as his gaze came to rest on Joshua.

Lord, give me the words to speak. Joshua slowly approached the porch. "David. Can we talk a moment?"

David studied him, and then his dark brown eyes darted to Cathy, his eyebrows arching. She shook her head.

He looked back at Joshua. "For a minute, jah. In private?"

"Jah, if you don't mind." Joshua wanted Annie by his side, but he would manage. It was probably better if neither she nor Cathy overheard their discussion.

David hesitated for a moment. "Jah." He turned away. "Cathy, Annie, go on in. Make yourselves at home."

The door opened again, and David's host mamm peeked out. Joshua couldn't remember her name, though he'd met her once. The Beilers lived in a different district, so the two families didn't attend the same church services. She held the door open wide. "Kum in, kum in."

David waved. "Jah, Joshua and I will be right in. Give us a moment."

Joshua stood by the buggy, waiting for David to join him.

He approached, stopping a good three feet away from Joshua. "What's on your mind?"

"I have a past wrong to make right."

David raised his eyebrows.

"Years ago, when I stole your bullfrog, Daed made me apologize. I feel I need to do so again, for real this time. And I never should have made fun of you afterwards. Please forgive me?" Joshua took off his straw hat and wiped the moisture off of his brow with his sleeve.

There was a very long silence. Joshua put his hat back on and shifted his weight uncomfortably.

Finally, David nodded. "Forgive as the Lord has forgiven." He paused for a moment. "But why now?"

"Because it's time we laid the past to rest. I'd like us to be friends. Especially since...." Joshua looked toward the haus.

David's eyes widened as Joshua's unspoken meaning became clear. "Since they're sisters?" he finished the sentence for him. "Jah, we should mend fences, then."

Since David had forgiven him so readily, Joshua figured that Cathy must have exaggerated the seriousness of their feud. That David hadn't been behind the spicy omelet, after all. That Cathy had lied. Should he warn David about his girl's devious ways?

Maybe later. Joshua grinned. "Gut. That's settled, then. Would you like to kum fishing with us? We have enough gear in the back of the buggy."

"Jah, that sounds gut. West Wildcat Creek isn't too far away. Just across the highway. I've caught white catfish and smallmouth bass there."

Joshua nodded. "Or, we could go to one of the stocked ponds around here. The Stoltzfuses won't mind if we fish at their place."

"We could, though I prefer fly-fishing in streams and rivers to stocked ponds," David said.

"I didn't bring a fly-fishing reel, just normal spinning reels." Joshua shrugged. "But that's fine. You can fish your way, and I'll fish mine. Do you make your own flies?"

"Jah, I learned how to tie up in Pennsylvania. I took up fly-tying to cut the costs of all the flies I left in bushes and trees everywhere I went. Discovered they sell pretty well, too. I'll get Cathy and Annie. Did you happen to think of a picnic lunch?"

"Cathy and Annie put one together." Joshua would pass on any parts Cathy had prepared, just in case she'd decided to give him another dose of jalapeño.

David went inside to summon the girls, and, before long, they were headed toward the creek David had mentioned. Annie sat beside Joshua, just as tense as before, perched almost on the edge of the seat. David and Cathy sat together in back, shoulder to shoulder. Joshua wished he could pull Annie closer. If only she'd relax. Trust him. For now, he would have to be patient. Though she must have realized how he felt about her when they'd kissed. Surely, she wouldn't think he went around kissing all the girls. With his reputation, though, she just might assume as much. He'd have to correct that impression. She hadn't been his first kiss, but she had been the first in Missouri. And he hoped she would be his last.

Joshua glanced over his shoulder at the couple in the back. He was glad that mending fences with David hadn't been so hard, after all. He should have done it a long time ago. Maybe a new friendship with David would go a long way toward patching up his relationship with Cathy. It'd be nice to have a good rapport with his potential future sister-in-law, even if they wouldn't cross paths too often, with David and Cathy in Missouri and he and Annie in Pennsylvania.

They reached the traffic light along the highway just as it turned red. Joshua braked to a stop. A pickup cut in front of an oncoming eighteen-wheeler. It blared its air horn, startling Penny. She reared and then bolted, right into the path of the semi.

Chapter 17

Annie woke up to mayhem. A horse screamed. Sirens wailed. People shouted. She ached all over. She opened her eyes, disoriented, and found herself face-to-face with a stranger. She struggled to sit up, even though the man tried to restrain her movements. He wore a uniform, but he didn't look like a police officer. Dizziness washed over her, and she grabbed her left wrist with her right hand. All of her pain seemed to be radiating from there. The stranger said something—she saw his mouth move—but she could hardly comprehend one word.

"Cathy? Joshua? Are they...okay?" She looked around, trying to get her bearings, but everything was blurry. "What happened?"

The man muttered more sounds she couldn't interpret, but they were quickly drowned out by a deafening siren. Annie twisted her head and spotted an ambulance, lights flashing, on the other side of the highway. What was she doing in the middle of the road?

A horse kept on screaming. Penny? She attempted to struggle to her feet, but the man pressed her back down again, gently yet firmly. The grave look he gave her deterred any further attempts to move, though she still couldn't make out his words.

A shot rang out, and she jumped, pain shooting through her afresh. The screaming had stopped. "M-my horse?" Tears filled her eyes. "What happened?" she asked, even though she knew the answer.

"Shh, shh." The man frowned with concern. "The horse was just put down. An act of mercy, really, as bad as it was hurt. It's a miracle you're alive. The buggy was destroyed." This time, she understood him. Maybe because it was quieter, calmer. Or possibly because he'd raised his voice.

Penny, dead? What about Cathy? Joshua? David? Tears flowed down her cheeks. She blinked them back and craned her neck to see the ambulance. To try to identify who the other people in uniform were tending to. "My sister...? My friends...?"

She was shushed again. "Everything will be okay. You'll be fine."

Maybe so, but what about the others? Her arm ached when she tried to move, but she struggled to get up again. He held her down. "Let me go. I have to know."

"I'll find out." The man got up, turned to someone else, and spoke, too quietly for Annie to hear. The other person walked off.

"What's your name?" the man asked.

Annie stared at him. Who cared what her name was? She certainly didn't see how that mattered. "My sister? Joshua? David? How are they? I need to know." Her stomach churned.

"They're checking. But you were knocked unconscious. I need to know if your memory is functioning. What's your name?"

She sighed. "My memory is just fine. I'm Annie May Beiler. Do you want my birthday? Do you want to see some ID? Perhaps you'd like to hear me recite the alphabet? A, B, C, D...."

The man smiled. "A feisty one, eh? No, that won't be necessary. Your memory appears to be fine."

Annie looked around again, but she couldn't see through the crowd of people, the traffic backup, the semi, to tell what was happening.

Someone must have been loaded into the ambulance, because it rolled away, lights flashing, siren screaming. Seconds later, another ambulance pulled into the same space. Another man, this one wearing an EMT badge, came to check on her. Evidently, her injuries weren't life-threatening, so she was left to await another ambulance. Meanwhile, the second ambulance pulled away as urgently as the first.

Time seemed to roll by in decades rather than minutes or seconds. No one came to tell her about Cathy or Joshua or David. But, if they'd been dead, surely they wouldn't have been taken away first, right? Live victims would get the top priority, she was sure. That was her only consolation.

She stared up at the sky, still sunny and blue. Not a cloud in sight. Ill-fitting weather for the tension that permeated the air. It should have been overcast, maybe drizzling.

A third ambulance arrived and then left a short time later. How would she get word of the accident to Daed? Tears again streamed down her face and dripped off her chin. Part of her didn't want him to find out. After what had happened to Mamm, how would he bear it?

※

Joshua was lucky to be alive. At least, that's what everyone kept telling him. He ached with what a nurse had called a bad case of road rash, but he hadn't broken any bones, miraculously. He racked his brain, trying to recall what had happened. The horse had bolted, and he'd managed to shove Annie out of the buggy just before vaulting out of it, himself. He must have hit his head, because the next thing he remembered was waking up in the emergency room. His nurse had told him that they'd decided to keep him overnight in the hospital for observation after the series of tests they'd performed on him, all because he'd been unconscious when the ambulance had brought him there.

He hadn't heard a word about the others. No one seemed to know anything. And so, still clueless, he lay awake in this tiny hospital room with green walls. There was a curtain dividing his room, and he knew that the bed on the other side of it was empty. He hoped it would stay that way.

His head throbbed, despite the pain medicine that undoubtedly was flowing in through the IV tube in his arm. He closed his eyes and managed a quick prayer. *Lord, please let everyone else be alive.*

When he awoke again, he saw figures moving in the semidarkness. There was a man with a beard, wearing a hat and black pants. Joshua sat up quickly, painfully, as recognition dawned. "Bishop Sol?" His voice sounded raspy.

"Jah." The man came to stand at Joshua's bedside and flicked on the lamp above his head. "Do you have need of water?"

Joshua nodded, wincing from the pain in his aching head. "That'd be gut." He watched as Bishop

Sol poured water from a pitcher into a plastic cup. Then, he held the cup to Joshua's mouth. "Drink up, then."

Joshua lifted his arms to take the cup, himself, but the bishop waved his hands away. He tilted the cup, and Joshua was surprised by how little of the liquid dripped down the front of his hospital gown as he sipped.

Once Joshua had drained the cup, the bishop moved it away. "Do you know anything about the others? Did they...um, did they live?" *Lord, let Annie be all right.* He gripped the bed rails, awaiting the verdict.

"Jah. They're alive. David Lapp is in the bed next to yours, in fact. He is sleeping now; they had to put him under to repair a badly broken arm. Multiple fractures. His host family is here visiting." He nodded toward the curtain. Joshua heard muted voices on the other side. "Cathy also broke a bone, but she was treated and released. They said you and Annie both would have died if you hadn't jumped out."

Except that Annie hadn't jumped. He'd shoved her out. He hoped that if she remembered that violent move, she'd forgive him in light of how it had saved her life.

"Annie is okay?"

"Sprained wrist. They have some sort of contraption on her hand. She'll be going home."

Danki, Lord.

There was no way Annie was going home, even with Daed insisting that she should, since she'd merely sprained her wrist. He'd already sent Cathy home with a driver, ordering her to go immediately to bed, and Cathy hadn't objected. Probably due to the pain medication they had administered.

But Annie hadn't heard a word about Joshua or David, and she wasn't about to leave until she found out something about their conditions.

So, she and her daed struck up a compromise: as long as she would allow him to push her in a wheelchair, despite her determination to walk, he would take her up to the third floor.

When they exited the elevator, Annie saw Bishop Sol step out of a room down the hall. Daed sped the wheelchair in his direction. "Are the buwe okay?" he called out.

"Jah, they'll live. They say Joshua has a concussion, so they are keeping him for observation. David's arm is broken in multiple places. He had to have surgery."

"May I see them?" Daed asked.

The bishop nodded. "David is sleeping, but Joshua is awake and already restless, squirming around in the bed. They're wise to keep him in the hospital for the nacht. I need to figure how to get ahold of the families of these buwe. They'll want to know, though Joshua could probably call and leave a message for his parents, and they could get the news to David's folks." He turned and went back inside the room.

"You'll wait out here." Daed pushed Annie's wheelchair up against the wall and secured the brakes, then disappeared through the doorway of Joshua's room after Bishop Sol.

If he thought she was about to stay put, he was crazy.

Annie tried to stand, but with the footrests in her way and her arm aching so, she couldn't push herself out of the chair. She reached down, disengaged one brake and then the other, and slowly turned the metal contraption on the wheel. She couldn't maneuver it too adeptly with just one arm, but she managed to wheel her way into the room.

Joshua was in the first bed. His face was a bit scraped up, but she figured hers was, too. And he looked a little pale. He turned toward her, and his eyes lit up, but she also read pain in them.

"Annie." His voice sounded kind of husky. He reached out a hand.

Daed turned in her direction, his gaze searing. "Didn't I tell you to stay out in the hallway?"

Bishop Sol had turned around, as well, shock in his eyes.

Oops. She hadn't been thinking. Entering a man's room, even if it was in a hospital setting, was verboden. And she had to go and do so in front of the bishop.

Chapter 18

Joshua wanted to protest when Isaac muttered something about impropriety and wheeled Annie back outside. It was a hospital room, for goodness' sake. But the way Bishop Sol's eyebrows had arched when Annie had entered gave him pause. He supposed that the mandate for each Amish schoolteacher to be above reproach in every way extended to hospital stays, with no exceptions, even if she were visiting the man who'd saved her life. No wonder she was so cautious about everything she did. If anyone had seen her at the battlefield or at the Bass Pro Shop, she'd be fired, for certain. And yet she'd risked it. For him.

And how had he rewarded her? By stealing kisses from her novice lips. Shame and regret gnawed at him. If the bishop found out, it would be yet another death knell for her career. They weren't even courting. Yet. Though her responses to him, her glances, her risk-taking, all indicated strongly that she would agree to let him court her. She might even come to love him, eventually.

He glanced at Bishop Sol, who fingered the cord of the phone on the bedside table. If he knew how to operate it, Joshua was sure the bishop would have already insisted he place a call to the phone shanty in his district and leave a message on the answering machine. Joshua had already tried to call out, before the bishop's arrival, and discovered that he needed a code to access an outside line. And he wasn't about to volunteer to ask a nurse what that code would be. No point in worrying his parents about this accident. He was fine. And Mamm would get so upset, she'd probably insist that Daed go out and buy him a bus ticket home. Immediately.

Joshua had no intentions of going home now. Though he thought it might be wise to call regarding David. He went to retrieve his cell phone from his pant pocket, only to remember that he'd been stripped of his clothes while unconscious and dressed in a hospital gown. The flimsy garment barely reached his knees, and one of the shoulders had slipped off, exposing more skin than was decent. His face heated. No wonder Isaac had shooed Annie out of the room. Joshua wasn't clothed appropriately to receive visitors of either sex. He yanked the gown up to cover himself better.

A groan came from the other side of the curtain. Bishop Sol stood up and peeked through the fabric at David. "Ach, gut. He's waking up." He disappeared to the other side.

"Are we allowed to open the curtain all the way?" Joshua glanced at Isaac.

Isaac shrugged. "Guess if we're not, they'll tell us." The metal rings clattered as he pushed it open so that Joshua could see his roommate.

Joshua swallowed. "Where's my stuff? Do you know?" He gave a cursory glance at David, still groaning. His arm was in a cast, and the other one was connected to an IV, just like Joshua's. David's host daed and mamm nodded briefly at Joshua before returning their attention to David.

Joshua looked at Isaac. "I could call the phone shanty."

Isaac nodded. "I think that'd be wise. They might have put your clothes in a bag in the closet. That's what they did with Lydia's after her accident." He pivoted and went to the small closet, opening it up. "Jah, there it is." He pulled out the small pile of clothes and set them on the foot of Joshua's bed.

Joshua fished his phone out of the pocket. "Could I have a moment?"

Isaac nodded and walked over to the other side of the room, next to Bishop Sol. Relief washed over Joshua. He didn't want them to know he was calling to report David's condition alone. He really didn't want to get into his reasons for doing that, either.

After a moment's consideration, he pressed the speed dial number for the phone shanty near his parents' farm. He'd left a message there only once before, to let his parents know he'd arrived safely in Missouri. When the generic message kicked on, he held his breath, listening. Then, at the beep, he spoke quietly. "This is Arthur Esh's Joshua, calling from Seymour, Missouri. There's been a buggy accident. Arlen Lapp's David has a couple of broken limbs. He'll be fine, but he's in the hospital." Not knowing how to conclude, he simply ended the call. Someone would get the message and notify David's folks.

Isaac looked up with a smirk when Joshua closed his phone. "Forgot to mention something, didn't you, son?"

Fuming, Annie fidgeted in the wheelchair for what seemed like hours before Daed and Bishop Sol finally exited Joshua's hospital room. She understood the rules, really; she knew that she wasn't allowed in a man's bedroom, but this was a hospital. A place of life and death. It seemed that those rules shouldn't apply here.

She wished Shanna Stoltzfus was around to sit with her awhile, but it was Sunday, so Shanna didn't have any clinical today. She'd be with her family, making visits around the district. But word must have spread about the accident. How else could Daed and Bishop Sol have learned about it?

Daed went behind her and began pushing her down the hall.

"It's a pure miracle those kinner survived." Bishop Sol's voice held some awe. "A pure miracle. The gut Lord has a purpose for someone, for sure. Maybe a future minister." There was a moment of silence. Annie could imagine Daed nodding his head in agreement, although he—and most of the men she knew—lived in fear of "the call." No one wanted the responsibility, but a man had to accept it if he was called of the Lord.

"Thank the Lord there were nein fatalities," Daed agreed.

"Want to go down and get a koffee before we head back to Seymour?" the bishop asked.

"Koffee? Maybe some tea for Annie and me. Sounds ser gut. But I'm not sure we'll be going back right away. I'll want to check in on Joshua and David once more before we go."

Annie sat up straighter, her hope renewed. Daed would give her some time with Joshua, after all! Just out from under the bishop's watchful eye. Of course, if that was his plan, it meant he knew far more than he was supposed to.

They weren't courting. They were developing a friendship. She needed to remember that. Even if he had given her the kissing lesson of a lifetime.

But Bishop Sol dismissed his words with a wave of his hand. "Nein point in wasting a ride. They'll be fine. I'll call for a driver. Just be ready to go when he arrives."

Annie tried not to slump in her seat, but the bishop's word was law. Daed wouldn't dare go against him.

"That bu is like a son to me." Daed's voice was quiet but forceful. "I need to say gut nacht and assure him I'll be by in the morrow to bring him home."

Bishop Sol exhaled. "Very well, then. I'll have the driver wait. A half hour should be long enough. And, while you're at it, call his parents. I don't care what his reasons are for withholding the fact of his own injuries, but if my son were in the hospital, I'd want to know. Even if it is just for observation. I don't see anyone observing anybody else. They're all going about, doing their own business."

Annie fought a grin as they entered the elevator. Daed had dared to cross the bishop. And won. Kind of.

Leaving the bishop to nurse a koffee and munch on a sandwich in the hospital cafeteria, Daed pushed Annie back toward the elevators to go visit Joshua and David. "We won't stay long, jah?"

"Jah," Annie agreed. "Will I need to stay in the hall this time?"

Daed chuckled. "Nein. You can go in. I didn't want you getting in trouble with our gut bishop over something so trivial. Just keep in mind that I'll be there as a chaperone. Nothing improper will happen, then, ain't so?"

Annie felt the heat rise to her cheeks. "Daed," she whispered, her voice tight with embarrassment, as he wheeled her into the empty elevator. Did he know about the kiss?

He chuckled.

Lord, don't let Bishop Sol come up and catch us. Daed would be in trouble, too, if he did. As for her, well, that would be the end.

Daed pushed her into the room and paused beside Joshua's bed. His eyes were closed, though, and he looked sound asleep, so they moved past him, coming to a stop at the foot of David's bed. "He had to have surgery to repair some really bad breaks," Daed told her. "You can give Cathy an update, since I'm not supposed to be aware of their relationship yet."

Annie looked up at him. "Why do you pretend not to know when you do?"

He shrugged. "It's the way things are done, the way they've always been done. And, occasionally, there are surprises in the district." He chuckled again. "I suppose I also need to pretend not to know about you and Joshua."

"There's nothing to pretend about," Annie whispered. How she wished there were. But she still wasn't sure, given his alleged history as a player, that she wasn't just the latest in his long line of victims.

Daed rolled her chair backward, away from David, and back over to Joshua's bedside. Then, he reached over and plucked Joshua's cell phone from the blankets.

"I'll be in the hall. I need to call his parents; they deserve to know. And then, we need to go back downstairs. Can't have Bishop Sol getting impatient and coming back up here to interrupt things."

Annie expelled a breath and watched as Daed studied the phone in his hand. Then, he turned and walked out of the room, pressing a series of buttons. When he was gone, Annie summoned her courage and reached for Joshua's hand. She grasped it, and he roused, his eyes opening and blinking before they focused on her.

A slow smile crossed his face, and he raised her hand to his lips. "You came back." His voice sounded husky. She trembled when his mouth caressed her skin.

"Just for a minute. Daed's in the hall, and Bishop Sol is downstairs, in the cafeteria. He said he'll call a driver."

"I'm glad you're okay. Cathy and David, too. I... I'm sorry about your horse."

Annie blinked back fresh tears. She'd miss Penny. "Jah." She wondered when Daed would go to a horse auction to buy a replacement.

"Can you kum closer?" Joshua's gaze dropped to her lips.

Maybe she had done it right that morning. He wouldn't want to kiss her again if she'd been a complete failure. Heat rose in her cheeks. "I can't get out of the wheelchair. I tried. There're footrests in the way, and...."

Joshua sat up in bed and twisted his torso, leaning over the side, toward her. He glanced down at her feet. "Can you fold up the footrests? Or put your feet down behind them and stand?"

It seemed her face was on fire. Carefully, she positioned her feet on the floor behind the footrests and then tried to move the contraptions out of the way with her toes. They swung out to the sides. She secured the brakes, not wanting the chair to move while she struggled to get up. Then, she pushed herself out with her good arm.

Joshua grinned. "Gut girl. Now, kum here." He patted the edge of the bed.

Her stomach fluttering, she gingerly sat down sideways, so that she was facing him. She'd have to jump up quickly if Daed came back into the room, but sitting here a minute shouldn't hurt. She wondered what Joshua had in mind. Hopefully, she'd guessed correctly that he wanted to kiss her.

But he merely sat there, looking at her, studying her, while his fingers caressed her hand. Reached out to touch the curve of her cheek. Traced the outline of her lips. Then, he groaned. "Aren't you going to ask me to kiss you?"

Annie gasped, and a shiver worked its way up her spine. "Ach...."

His fingers slid down her neck, along the exposed part of her collarbone. "Please?"

"I don't know how to.... I mean, I tried, but—"

"You did great." He smoothed some hair away from her face.

Unable to find the courage to ask, she scooted closer and leaned forward, until her chest touched the fabric of his hospital gown. His arms slid around her back, and he sighed contentedly as her lips hesitantly touched his. He raised one hand to the back of her head, pressing her in closer, deepening the kiss.

Someone coughed.

Annie jerked back and slid off of the bed, keeping her eyes on Joshua. His gaze was directed past her, showing shock. Fearing the worst, she turned around and looked into the stern face of Bishop Sol.

❋

"Annie Beiler. What is the meaning of this?" The bishop narrowed his eyes at her. "You, the school-teacher, not only in a man's room, unsupervised, but in bed with him. You should be ashamed. Where is your father?"

Annie shook her head. "I...I...um, I thought he had stepped into the hall for a minute. That's what he said, anyway."

"Hmm. He will be upset to learn of this behavior." He shook his head. "You will get married, of course."

Joshua sucked in a breath.

Bishop Sol exhaled loudly. "Not in two weeks. Now. I mean, tomorrow, after we obtain a license."

Annie swayed on her feet. Joshua grasped for her, but she sank back into the wheelchair. "What?"

"And you'll be dismissed from your job, of course. I was going to have to let you go anyway, I'm afraid. Someone mentioned you'd gone into Springfield on Saturday. To that battlefield."

Someone had seen them? Well, it could have been that one of the few people who'd known about their excursion had let it slip. Annie's family knew, for sure. Including Cathy. But why would she have tattled on her own sister?

"I'm sorry, Annie," Joshua whispered.

"So, Joshua, are you prepared to take this wom-an as your frau? To make this matter right?"

Annie looked up at the bishop and shook her head. "You can't force him to marry me."

"You dare question me, Annie Beiler?" Bishop Sol glared at her. "The way I see it, you lose your job, regardless. Either you lose it to marry, or you lose it in disgrace for your actions. And Joshua knows I won't tolerate this sort of behavior outside of marriage." He waved toward the bed.

"I'll marry her." Joshua hoped his voice sounded clear and strong. He'd never meant for this to happen, but he couldn't say he was disappointed. This would get Luke out of the picture, for good. Joshua would have the woman of his dreams. He'd lose his reputation as a player. This was a win-win situation. The only downfall was that Annie didn't seem to want it. Didn't love him.

At least, not yet.

Someday, she would—he hoped.

And, maybe with marriage forced upon them, she'd come to love him sooner rather than later.

The bishop nodded. "Gut. Don't get any ideas about leaving town."

Joshua thought he saw relief flitter across the older man's face. He must have imagined it, though. Nothing about this situation could bring him any measure of satisfaction.

"I wouldn't dream of it." Joshua glanced at the young woman sitting beside him, silent, her lips slightly parted, and longed to reassure her.

Annie would be his frau.

Chapter 19

Annie's heart was cradled in numbness when Daed finally reappeared. Once he learned of the imminent change in her marital status, he handed Joshua his cell phone and wheeled her out of the room without a word, his expression unreadable.

Tomorrow, Annie would need to move her things to Joshua's room. Or, he would move his things to hers.

How could this happen?

The community would look at her in judgment. Bundling was forbidden in their district, but they hadn't been doing that. Their behavior had been more...innocent.

But they'd been kissing.

He'd touched her face, her neck, her shoulders.

Far from innocent.

She pulled in a shaky breath, forcing her mind to forget his caresses, at least for the time being.

She'd been fired. If not for the kissing, then for taking Joshua in to see Wilson's Creek Battlefield.

Whatever happened to the grace that Bishop Sol had asked the school board members to show to her?

Luke had told. She should have known he would. In fact, she'd expected it. And she was to blame, blurting it out as she had. But she certainly hadn't expected her "punishment" to include marriage.

Joshua would resent her. He had to. Because, once married to her, no longer would he be able to get to know the other young women in the district. His bride would be none other than Annie Beiler.

Soon to be Annie Esh.

Till death do us part.

And she hadn't wanted to settle. She'd wanted a man who loved her.

Okay, she was hardly settling. She wanted Joshua. But not this way. She'd dreamed of an engagement similar to those of her friends. A romantic proposal, with declarations of love.

Now, she would have to tell her kinner that she and their father had been forced to marry. That no man had ever proposed to her.

Her eyes burned with tears as she slumped in the backseat of the van, next to Daed. The bishop sat in the front, next to Tony, the driver.

She wouldn't have a normal Amish wedding. No usual two-week waiting period, with the frantic preparations, the Thursday wedding while the kinner were in school. Nein, she would get married in haste. Tongues would wag.

Would they have to confess before the church? Bishop Sol hadn't said. She didn't want to ask. Maybe Daed would inquire privately.

She glanced at Daed again. He remained silent. With one hand, he tugged absently at his beard, but his gaze was locked on the back of Bishop Sol's head. If only she could read his thoughts. Did he resent the bishop for doing this? Was he angry at her and Joshua on account of their poor judgment? She should have known better.

How could she face her friends? And Mamm?

✿

When his nurse came to check on him, Joshua refused her offer of medicine to help him sleep. However, she changed out his IV bag, and he had no idea what might be in the liquid pumping through the thin line attached to the back of his hand.

She lowered the bed, pulled the chain over his head to turn off the lights, and then, with a cheery "Good night," slid the curtain shut that separated his bed from David's. The room wasn't completely dark—the light in the tiny entryway was still on—but it was dim enough to sleep.

If sleep would come.

Annie…. What had he done? Would she ever forgive him?

Joshua had no idea how long he tossed and turned. He needed to call his parents and let them know about his bride-to-be. He'd never even mentioned Annie to them in his letters. There'd been nothing to tell.

How would they take this earth-shattering news? And how was he to tell them? He couldn't just leave a recording on the answering machine for whoever checked it next to spread around. He could imagine the gossip, even now: "Did you hear? Joshua Esh got a girl in trouble in Seymour, Missouri. They were forced to wed!"

He closed his eyes. It sounded worse than it was, for there wasn't any illicit baby involved. But that was what people would say, anyway, both here and in Pennsylvania.

So much for clearing his reputation as a player.

Unless…. Maybe he could talk the bishop into allowing them to wait the customary two weeks before getting married. Maybe Isaac would support the idea. Give both him and Annie time to get used to the notion. Allow Joshua's parents ample time to travel to Missouri to witness the marriage of their only child.

Not to mention, give him and Annie time to heal. And give him time to court her properly, to win her love, before they both said "I do."

Joshua reached for his cell phone. He fingered it for a moment, then drew in a deep breath, turned it on, and dialed the number for the phone shanty back home. The answering machine clicked on. "This is Arthur Esh's Joshua. I need my daed to call me when he gets a chance." He snapped the phone shut, ending the call.

"Rough day, ain't so?"

Joshua jumped at the unexpected voice from the other side of the curtain. David. "Jah. At least we're all still alive." He eased himself out of bed. It hurt to move, probably due to his badly skinned knees, but he made his way around the curtain to the other side of the room, maneuvering his IV pole with him as he went. He lowered himself into the chair next to the window, at the end of the bed.

"You weren't hurt badly?" David asked.

Joshua shook his head. "The nurse said I have road rash. That seems to be what they call this type of thing." He held up his hand, palm facing out, to show David the raw skin. "It's on my legs, too. But I was unconscious for who knows how long. Longer than two minutes, for sure. They're keeping me overnight for observation."

"I broke my leg." David exhaled. "And my arm." He patted the white plaster on his left elbow.

"Jah. Badly, I think, since they did a surgery."

David shook his head. "Figures that you'd get off easier than me. You always had it easier." He snorted. "Sports, academics...you excelled at everything you put your hand to."

Joshua dipped his head. David was more of a quiet soul, the type who would enjoy spending hours making those fancy flies for fishing trips. "Ach, you're an artist, for sure. I remember the drawings you made in school. Such detail. My people always looked like stick figures. And I never could make those flies you make. I don't have the patience."

David chuckled. "Ach, I'm sure you'd do just fine. I'll teach you sometime, if you like." He grinned. Then, his smile suddenly vanished, and he grasped his chest, his mouth opening as he gasped for air.

"Are you all right?" Joshua struggled to his feet and lunged at the foot of the bed. "Do I need to call a nurse?"

David's eyes widened. He made a slight nod, his hands pressing tighter against his chest.

Joshua reached for the call button attached to David's bed and pushed it. The last time he'd done this, on his own bed, someone had answered on an intercom, asking him what he needed. This time, however, there was only silence. The nurses' station must have been unoccupied. Should he wait?

David gasped, his eyes bulging with sheer panic.

"I'll go find someone." Joshua hurried as fast as his sore legs and the IV pole would let him to the door and peeked out. No one was in sight. He looked around and spotted what had to be the nurses' station, down the hall to his left, and he headed, however haltingly, in that direction.

A woman was standing beside a large metal cart, onto which she was loading what looked to be empty dinner trays.

Joshua waved his arm at her. "Help! I need help."

She looked up from the cart, then averted her eyes, looking sheepish. "Sorry, but I'm just a dietary aide. I'm not allowed to help with patient care. You need to find a nurse."

Dietary aide? Joshua started to back up. "Do you know where I can find one?"

She shrugged. "You might try the nurses' station."

"I did. There's no one there. We need help." Joshua turned around and saw a tall man in black scrubs coming down the hall. He hurried toward him. "My roommate is having trouble breathing. Can you kum check?"

"Sure." The man followed Joshua down the hall into the room, took one look at David, and then reached behind him and slapped a button on the wall.

When Joshua looked at David, his heart constricted. He must have passed out. His skin was gray, his lips blue.

The male nurse steered Joshua and his IV pole toward the other side of the room. "You'll need to keep out of the way."

A moment later, an announcement came across the intercom. "Dr. Blue, report to room four thirty-five. Dr. Blue, room four thirty-five."

"Go on in, Annie." Daed shut the back of the van firmly, then stepped around to the other side. Both Tony and Bishop Sol met him over there, Bishop Sol saying something in a low voice.

Were they discussing her and her poor decisions? Of course, they were. What other reason did they have to talk? They were probably making arrangements for

Tony to take Joshua and her to the county courthaus tomorrow to obtain a marriage license. But Tony...he was an outsider. Surely, they wouldn't air her shame in front of him. She glanced back and saw Bishop Sol looking her way. So, she was the topic of conversation, as expected. She dragged herself up the porch stairs and into the haus, tears burning her eyes.

Mamm was in the kitchen, her hands folded over an open page of *Die Ernsthafte Christenpflicht*. Annie recognized the German prayer book and wished she could thumb through the pages herself. Maybe something in there would relate to her situation.

Mamm looked up and quickly wiped her tear-streaked face. Then, she lifted her arms and held them open. With a sob, Annie fell into them, collapsing to her knees beside the wheelchair. Mamm wrapped her arms around her, holding her tight. "Ach, you're all right. You're really all right."

"All right?" That statement was relative. Mamm didn't know everything. She'd heard only that Annie had survived. She figured now was as good a time as any to tell her the rest of the story.

Annie had just finished choking out the entire tale about her job loss and upcoming marriage when the door opened and Daed came in, still tugging at his beard. He looked older, more haggard. With a sigh, he went over to check the kettle on the stove, poured some hot water into a mug, and added a teabag. Then, he came over to the table and dropped into the chair next to them. Heaving another sigh, he picked up the teabag by the string, dipping it in and out, in and out.

"Isaac." Lydia smoothed her hands over Annie's kapp. "Is it true?"

"Jah. It's true." He shook his head. "It seems that our gut bishop has taken to heart the recent complaints about his leniency, and so he's decided to kum down harshly on our Annie. He says he'll kum by and talk to us about it later; that right now, he has to get home to his frau."

"But a forced marriage for kissing? That just seems...excessive." Mamm frowned. "Most of the teenagers in their rumschpringe experiment with... physical things."

Annie sniffed and got to her feet. "I'm sorry, Daed."

Daed waved her off. "I forgive you, Annie. And when I said that Joshua is like a son, I wasn't teasing. I just didn't expect...well, never you mind. It's over. Done. And, nein matter the bishop's reasons, it's final."

"But what will we tell people when they ask? They'll think that Annie's with child." Lydia closed her prayer book with a thump.

"Let them think what they will. It'll soon be proven false. There'll be nein boppli nine months after this wedding, ain't so?" Daed pulled the teabag out of the tea completely and dropped it into a small bowl. He grimaced. "But I see nein reason for them to marry tomorrow. I think it should be done the usual way—announced in church on Sunday, with the wedding two weeks later. In fact, I intend to speak to Bishop Sol about this. It's one thing to fire Annie. But any more than that...nein."

"I thought you were standing guard outside Joshua's room," Annie said quietly, not wanting Daed to think she was blaming him.

"A nurse came. She told me I had to use the phone down in this one special room, and she took me there. It was fancy, with a koffeepot and a television."

Annie pulled in a shaky breath. "Where will you want us? Joshua and me, I mean. In my room or his?"

"His. It's larger. And I expect we'll be putting his parents up as soon as they get wind of this." Daed looked at his watch. "An Englisch neighbor is likely to drive up anytime now to tell us we have a phone call."

"Did you get a person when you called the phone shanty Joshua mentioned?"

"Jah. One of their neighbors. They'd heard the phone ring earlier and didn't get down to tend to it before. They were going to get the word out about the accident to Joshua's parents, and to David's, as well. Of course, I didn't know about the wedding then." Gravel crunched in the driveway. Daed stood, and Annie followed his gaze out the window. A neighbor's car. He grunted. "As I expected."

Chapter 20

"Y ou should go back to bed," the male nurse urged Joshua.

Once he'd complied, climbing back into the hospital bed, the nurse snapped up the side rails, then called for another nurse, who wheeled him out the door, down the hall, and into another room. It was dark, but the other patient was watching television. The volume was turned down low, but Joshua could see the eerie blue light flashing on the other side of the curtain. Evidently, his new roommate wasn't quite ready to sleep.

But then, neither was Joshua, remembering how gray-blue David had looked. Was he dying? They'd just reconciled; the past was forgotten; a new friendship was forming. It seemed so wrong for him to lose a friend just when he'd made one. Joshua closed his eyes. *Lord, please spare David, if it is Your will. Guide the hands of the doctors and nurses. Help them to know what to do. David is a gut man, Lord. Take care of him....*

The volume of his roommate's television increased. Joshua opened his eyes and glanced up. The ten o'clock news. He was never up this late. Amish went to bed much earlier, so that they were well rested enough to get up around five or so. What time did they wake patients in the hospital?

Pictures of the accident flashed across the screen, while a male reporter recounted the event in an emotionless monotone. He said that two Amish men remained in the hospital in critical condition. Hmm. Joshua didn't think he was so critical. But David might be.

No "might" about it.

So much had changed for Joshua this Lord's Day. He'd kissed Annie—her very first kiss. Resolved a longtime feud with David. Gotten in a buggy wreck. And then found himself an engaged man. Certainly not the way he'd planned to spend the day. Well, maybe the first two. The fourth, in his wildest dreams. The third? It had been his worst nightmare come true.

Annie. If everything went according to the bishop's plan, tomorrow would be their first night as a married couple. And under such a situation…she must feel so ashamed. Yet it was his fault for asking her to come to him. Begging her to ask him to kiss her.

He groaned. If only he could be back at the Beilers' farmhaus, in bed. If only this were nothing more than a dream.

For a moment, he considered the possibility of this being a temporary illusion. He'd heard of drug-induced hallucinations. Casting a wary glance at the fluid bag hanging from his IV pole, he thought that perhaps the whole wedding thing had been a figment of his overactive imagination, fueled by his overtired body. Not that he minded marrying Annie. But he wanted to woo her. Win her. He didn't want her handed off to him in this manner.

He rolled over, turning his back on the television and his thoughts. He closed his eyes again. *Lord, please be with David.*

Annie tiptoed to the door of Cathy's room, opened it slightly, and peeked inside to see whether she was awake. She figured she ought to give her an update on David and his injuries. But when Annie touched her hand and whispered her name, she didn't budge. Mamm had said they'd given her some strong pain pills. She supposed she could tell her in the morning. So, she left the room, quietly shut the door behind her, and padded down the hall to her own bedroom.

Her *old* bedroom. She stopped and looked around at her dresses, hanging in the closet. Her ancient dresser, badly in need of refinishing, which housed her personal items. Her hope chest...she'd have the husband, unwilling though he may be, but not her own home. At least, not yet.

It crushed her spirit to think about how Joshua must resent her. The news was probably already spreading like wildfire around the community. The Amish grapevine was an efficient machine. Annie Beiler had been fired, and she and Joshua Esh were being forced to marry.

She wasn't sure which piece of news pained her more.

As soon as possible, she would go to the schoolhaus to collect her personal items. Would the students assemble for class tomorrow? Or would their education be put on hold until a new schoolteacher had been selected? Annie had already started preparations for the Christmas program the students performed, but the new teacher wouldn't know that. She'd have to pass along her notes, so that she'd know what had been done.

She opened a dresser drawer, lifted out her night-gown, and tossed it on the bed. Then, she pulled off her kapp and unpinned her hair, letting it fall to her waist. Reaching for her hairbrush, she sat down on the edge of the bed and began running the brush the length of it. One hundred strokes.

Would Joshua enjoy watching this ritual? Maybe he'd offer to do it for her.

Her face heated at the thought of marriage, and at the realization of the intimacy it would bring. Her stomach fluttered as she remembered the feel of Joshua's fingers trailing gently across her face, down her neck.

Beyond that, she had no experience. She would be found wanting. Was this fear normal? None of her close friends was married yet, though both Becky Troyer and Shanna Stoltzfus would be in December. Were they scared, too?

She would try to visit Becky sometime tomor-row, before Tony took Daed to the hospital to pick up Joshua. Surely, Becky would be able to offer some consolation—once she'd gotten past the shock at An-nie's announcement.

Or maybe Annie would be expected to go along to obtain the marriage license. Did she have to be there?

Tomorrow would be her wedding night, which meant that tonight would be her last evening spent alone. Soon, she'd be the frau of a man who'd been forced to marry her. She picked up her nightgown, clutched it to her chest, and then curled up in a ball on her bed to cry.

She must have fallen asleep, because the next time she checked the battery-operated clock on her bedside table, it read six o'clock. She'd overslept! The aroma of koffee wafted up from the kitchen, along with muted tones of conversation.

Her wrist was stiff, but she gritted her teeth and eased her way out of yesterday's clothes. After she'd put on a fresh dress and washed up, she hurried downstairs. Aaron sat at the kitchen table, holding a spoonful of oatmeal halfway to his mouth. When he saw Annie, he lowered his spoon and jumped up to enfold her in a hug. "Annie! Are you all right? Let me see." He gently raised her splinted wrist to study it. "Is it broken?"

"Nein. A moderately bad sprain, they said."

"Cathy is still in bed. I can't believe she broke her arm! I took her breakfast upstairs, as she won't even try to get out of bed. It's a miracle the four of you lived, and that the worst of the injuries were broken bones. Sorry about Penny. I'll keep an eye out for a gut horse for you. I've got one in mind, actually."

"Danki." Annie lowered her eyes. "But did they tell you the rest?"

Aaron cleared his throat nervously. "Jah. Never would have dreamed this one up. A forced marriage for kissing? Most of the teens in the district...well, some, at the very least...uh, never mind. Bishop Sol is outside with Daed right now, hopefully explaining things. Daed said he was going to talk with him about postponing the wedding." He paused. "I did your chores and Cathy's this morgen."

"Danki, Aaron."

"You just hurry up and get well."

"I want to run down to Becky's as soon as I've eaten breakfast." Annie picked up a clean bowl and dished herself some oatmeal. She topped it with a lump of brown sugar and a splash of cream, then sat down at the table. "But I expect Mamm will need me, with Cathy out of commission. There's laundry, and so much else to do...." And she had all the time in the world, now that she no longer had a classroom of scholars to teach.

Aaron shrugged. "I doubt if you'll need to go to Becky's. When Bishop Sol first arrived, he told Mamm that the women would help for a few days, so Becky will probably kum here. With Mamm's injuries, and now yours and Cathy's...I expect we'll be babied for a while."

Annie couldn't remember Aaron ever talking so much. He was a regular wealth of information this morning. She bowed her head for silent prayer, but her mind was still so jumbled, she couldn't formulate an articulate thought. Hopefully, God could decipher her groans, instead.

Joshua was dressed and fidgeting impatiently by the time Isaac strode into his room. The doctor had already been in to release him, but he hadn't been told a word about David's status, due to some patient privacy act.

Bishop Sol might know, or maybe David's host parents, but Joshua wasn't sure how that would work. Would they have to wait in ignorance until David's parents arrived from Pennsylvania? He walked down the hall to his old room, thankfully without the IV pole this time, but no one was there. Just two empty beds, waiting for a couple of new patients.

That didn't look good.

Isaac came into his room around seven thirty, carrying a clean change of clothes. He set them on the bed beside Joshua, then surveyed him, pulling at his beard. "So, the other room wasn't gut enough? You and David had to be separated?"

"David had trouble breathing. He passed out, and his skin turned a grayish color. A nurse moved me out. They won't tell me anything more."

"Hmm. Bishop Sol went to see where they moved David. But it isn't likely he'll be released today. My frau had to stay here awhile after her accident." He grunted. "Well, you ought to change clothes and get ready to go."

Joshua nodded. He wouldn't bring up the nightmare he'd had about being forced to marry Annie. If it had really happened, Isaac would have said something about it. And there was no point in embarrassing himself by talking about something that couldn't possibly be true. He was just glad to be off of whatever drug they'd pumped into him through the IV feed. Glad to be finished with those hallucinations. He shook his head, and the movement caused his head to ache even more. He lifted his hands and rubbed his temples.

"Still in a lot of pain?" Isaac sounded sympathetic.

"Jah. Moving doesn't help."

"It probably won't feel too gut riding in the van over the bumpy dirt roads."

Joshua sucked in a breath. It wouldn't. But he didn't have a choice. Nor could he choose another place to lay his head tonight, unless he opted for the porch just to avoid having to take the stairs.

His body hurt just thinking about them.

"I'll go get changed." Joshua gathered up the clothes Isaac had brought and headed for the bathroom.

Isaac nodded. "Annie is waiting in the car. The bishop will be going with us to the courthaus to apply for a marriage license. And, Joshua? You won't hurt Annie by refusing this."

Joshua froze in his tracks, then turned to look at Isaac. Met his steady gaze. Studied him in silence for a minute. So, it hadn't been a nightmare. Annie was in the car, ready to go get the marriage license that would seal their union. "I wouldn't dream of hurting her," he said, as reality continued to sink in. "But I thought I'd talk to Bishop Sol about waiting the usual two weeks."

Isaac shook his head. "I tried. He's insisting it be done immediately. Everyone's been notified...the word is out." He frowned and tugged at his beard. "I don't know."

Joshua cleared his throat and looked Isaac in the eyes again. "Well, then. I'd hoped to marry her, anyway."

Isaac crossed the room, grasped Joshua's hand, and squeezed it. "Tell her that. You must tell her that." He released him.

Joshua nodded. Then, he went into the bathroom, shut the door, and changed clothes before coming out again. "I'm ready to go." He took a step toward the hallway, then hesitated and looked back at Isaac. "How does Annie feel about this marriage? Did they force her to kum, or did she kum willingly?" He needed to know. Because, if she'd been forced, if she didn't want this, then he *would* back out.

Isaac sighed. "She came willingly. No one forced her. Maybe she feels hopeful. Probably scared. Confused. I know she desperately needs your reassurance."

Hopeful about what? He couldn't ask that. The scared part, he could relate to. "Terrified" was probably a more accurate description of his feelings. He'd do his best to reassure her.

When Joshua motioned toward the door, Isaac held up a hand. "Hospital policy. You have to be wheeled out in a chair."

Joshua huffed. "I can walk."

"The nurse is bringing a wheelchair. We'll wait." Isaac gestured toward the bed. "Have a seat."

Accustomed to obeying his elders without question, Joshua went back to the bed and perched on the edge. "I hope the nurse doesn't take long. I'm ready to get back to work. Back to real food."

Isaac chuckled. "With jalapeños?"

Joshua grinned. "Without, but danki."

"I talked to your daed last nacht." Isaac studied his fingernails. "He and your mamm are planning to kum out for Thanksgiving."

"Did you tell them about the accident?"

Isaac shrugged. "Jah. They needed to know. You may be a man, but they are still your parents. They are getting word to David's folks. Everyone is very concerned."

It looked like Isaac wanted to say more, but Bishop Sol came into the room. "Getting information from this place is like pulling teeth. I had to show a medical power of attorney for David to have a surgery on his arm yesterday because the injury wasn't life threatening. Gut thing I thought to ask the buwe in the swap to bring that. But then, I had to wait for them to verify they had a copy to get information about David. What's the holdup in here?"

"Waiting on a wheelchair," Isaac replied. "Hospital policy."

The bishop grunted.

"How is David? What was wrong?" Joshua got to his feet again.

"I forget the exact medical term, but there was an unexpected blood clot that started in his shattered arm and ended up in his heart or near it. Could have killed him. Actually, the doctor said he did die, technically, but they were able to revive him. Gut thing you were there paying attention to him, Joshua."

A nurse came into the room, wheeling a chair. "Here we go. Sorry that took so long. I thought we had one down at the end of the hall, but someone else must have used it. I had to hunt awhile." She pushed the footrests out of the way and smiled at Joshua. "Hop in and make yourself comfortable."

"Is this really necessary?" Joshua eyed the chair. "I can walk."

"Hospital policy," she chirped.

With a sigh, Joshua complied.

The nurse adjusted the footrests, then produced a white plastic bag and plopped it in his lap. "Gifts to remember your visit by."

Joshua peeked inside. A small box of Kleenex, the toothbrush and toothpaste they'd provided for him to use, a bottle of hand lotion, and a few other items. "Thank you."

As she wheeled him out of the room, Joshua looked over his shoulder. "Can I stop to see David real quick?"

Bishop Sol shook his head. "He was moved down to a more critical care section, where the nurses will pay closer attention to him until he's out of danger. When he's moved back to a regular room, you can kum visit."

❀

Annie returned home in shock. They'd obtained a marriage license. Now, all that was left was the marriage. And the ceremony would be over by noon. There'd be a big meal to get through, and then people would linger for most of the day, singing and visiting.

It'd been hard enough facing Joshua at the hospital. But then, going with him into the courthaus, applying for the license, her mind numb with resolve... he'd barely looked at her. Hadn't touched her. Hadn't spoken, except for a whispered "We must talk later." So different from what she'd imagined whenever she'd thought of applying for marriage. Instead of the joyful event it was supposed to be, it had been entirely somber. The wedding was supposed to be joyful, too. Of course, she hadn't been to many, seeing how they were held during school hours, and she'd always had to be with her scholars.

She shook her head. That wasn't an issue any longer.

How ever would she face Joshua when the time came to wed?

Then, she thought of Luke. Had he heard? There was at least one blessing to come from this: she wouldn't have to deal with his unwelcome attention anymore.

Aaron hadn't lied. The women of the district had descended upon the haus in droves. They carried casseroles, cakes, cookies, cold meats, canned goods, and cleaning supplies. Some of them openly studied Annie's waistline, making her cringe. She wouldn't be the first to marry due to the suspicion of pregnancy.

But she would probably be the first to marry in brown.

Becky was there, thank goodness. She put her eleven-month-old boppli, Emma, in a playpen in the kitchen. Then, she snagged a basket filled with cleaning supplies, along with a yellow plastic bag, and gently pulled Annie toward the stairs. "We need to talk."

Annie nodded. "I've got so much to tell you."

The two friends hurried upstairs, ducked inside Annie's old bedroom, and shut the door. "I heard you were fired," Becky whispered, "and that the bishop's granddaughter Ruth is the teacher now. What happened?"

Annie cast her friend a skeptical look. "I know that's not all you heard." Hadn't news of her imminent marriage gotten out? Daed knew. Her family knew. The community knew. The wedding was today, after all. She remembered the blatant stares at her waist. It was all too real.

Becky drew in a breath. "Jah. Not much that made sense, though. A buggy accident, I understand. Those are far too common. I heard some undercurrents that you were fired, but I didn't hear why. And that you and Joshua are getting married today. But why would you marry Joshua? You said you wouldn't agree to let him give you a ride. Ever. And yet, you were in the buggy with him when he got in the accident." She shook her head. "You two must have really been courting in secret. You could have told me."

"We're being forced to get married. I was in his hospital room, and...." She couldn't tell Becky they'd kissed. That was too private to share, even with a best friend. Her face heated. How would she ever get the answers she needed?

She had to tell Becky everything. She knew Becky would never have judged her if she'd been expecting— after all, Becky had gotten pregnant during her rumschpringe—and she wanted her to know the truth.

Annie took a deep breath and spilled the whole story. "And now, Daed says that I'm moving into Joshua's room. So, I guess that is where we start. Moving me."

Becky shook her head. "We'll start by making sure the other room—your parents' old bedroom—is clean."

An hour later, Joshua's room sparkled. Annie's dresses hung in his closet; her dresser had been emptied, everything having been transferred to the empty drawers in his bureau. She was moved. And just in time, too, because more buggies were pulling into the driveway. It would soon be time for the wedding, albeit a little later in the morning than usual, due to the last-minute nature of the preparations.

Annie turned away from the window in dismay. "Ach, Becky, I can't face him. I can't face the people downstairs. You saw how they looked at me when they came in. Daed tried to talk the bishop out of it. He said nein. Said it must be done. That word has already gotten out. But I can't do this." Her complaint ended in a whine. And she couldn't tolerate whiners.

Becky was quiet for a minute. Then, she shook her head. "Jah, you can. I know what you're going through. The speculations about you and Joshua will last only a little while, and then something else will get the gossips' attention, and you'll be old news. Hold your head up, and don't let the looks bother you."

"But what about Joshua? We're getting married. He's going to want...." Annie's face burned. "I'm scared."

Becky blushed. "Jah. That scares me, too, especially after that one terrible experience with that Englischer. But it can't be all that awful. No one talks about it, and everyone has so many children." She

204 ~ Laura V. Hilton

drew Annie into a hug. "You can reassure me on my wedding day. I want you and Shanna to stand up with me."

Annie pulled away and adjusted the shades in the window. Then, she walked over to the bed and smoothed the nine-patch quilt again, remembering when her wedding quilt had been in its place. How she'd hurriedly removed it while he'd been out of the room. Marrying Joshua had been a far-fetched dream when she'd first put her wedding quilt on his bed.

Now, it was all too real.

She heard footsteps in the hallway. The door opened, and Annie looked up into Joshua's eyes. He stopped, gazed at her for a moment, and then looked at Becky, at the hope chest at the foot of the bed, and at the open closet, filled with dresses.

She looked away shyly.

"You know, I thought it was a nightmare, until this morning," he said with a humorless laugh. "Then, I learned it was real. And here's the marriage license to prove it."

A nightmare?

Tears sprang to her eyes. Of course, he thought marrying her was a nightmare. He'd pursued her only because he'd wanted to follow through with his declaration to Luke that he'd steal her away from him. Because he was a player. Because, to him, she'd always been a trophy to be won. Never a potential frau.

A tear escaped and rolled down her cheek.

Guys like him didn't go for girls like her.

Chapter 21

J oshua took a deep breath and stepped further into the room, setting his bag of hospital "goodies" on the top of his dresser. He needed to talk to Annie. Tell her what he'd assured Isaac he would.

He also wanted to take a pain pill, followed by a brief nap. His head throbbed after the long ride from the hospital and then the courthaus, especially along the bumpy gravel roads outside of Seymour. It hadn't helped that he'd stood outside with Isaac, Aaron, and some other men, chatting about the accident. No one had mentioned the wedding that would happen in a matter of hours.

But, Annie. She needed to be first. Joshua looked at her. "Annie—"

She turned away from him, toward Becky, and then shoved past him, out the door and around the corner. A door slammed at the end of the hall.

Joshua scrambled to recall what had happened since he'd walked into the room. What could have sparked that reaction? Maybe she'd expected him to walk in with his arms open wide and say something quirky and funny, like, "Hi, honey! I'm home!"

He looked at Becky, who stood there, her eyes wide with shock. "Was it something I said?"

She hesitated a moment, then nodded her head. "You said it was a nightmare." Her hand reached up to cover her mouth, and then she ran from the room.

Joshua sighed, realizing how his comment must have sounded to Annie. And Isaac had emphasized how deep was her need for assurance. So much for helping in that regard. Joshua resolved to try again. After taking a pain pill. He'd have to go to Annie. As for what he would say or do, he had no idea. In fact, his bumbling attempts to comfort her—to reassure her—would probably backfire, as well.

If only he could take back the words he'd blurted out without any thought. He simply hadn't expected to find Annie and Becky in his room. He definitely hadn't anticipated Annie's having moved in already. They weren't even married yet. Mostly, his mind had been focused on the prospect of a nap, and the hope that he would wake up to find everything as right as it could be, given the situation.

Maybe he ought to go downstairs, find the bishop, and consult him about what to do in this predicament. He could demand to know the reasons behind this forced wedding, to understand why it had to be done immediately, rather than in two weeks, after the banns had been posted. So far, he hadn't taken that up with the bishop. He'd simply gone along on the ride to the courthaus and followed the necessary steps to be married to the woman he'd always wanted—even though he hadn't planned on making her his frau just yet. She didn't love him. Yet.

Plenty of Amish couples married without being in love, if they thought the other person would make a good spouse.

He rubbed his forehead, still throbbing in rhythm with the onslaught of harried thoughts. Time for a pain pill. He opened the top drawer of his dresser, expecting to find the bottle of Ibuprofen capsules he'd brought with him from Pennsylvania. It wasn't there. Even after digging around through each of the drawers, he didn't find it. So, he went to the bathroom and opened the medicine cabinet. There was his bottle of Ibuprofen, along with all of his other personal items— razor, toothbrush, comb, and so forth. He took inventory of them, noticing how neatly everything had been lined up. His medicines arranged in alphabetical order. His toothbrush in a special holder with the others, their colors forming a rainbow. He swallowed two tablets and headed for the room at the end of the hall, still barred by a closed door. *Lord, help me not to make things worse,* he prayed silently. *It'd be nice to have a pleasant wedding day. And nacht.*

Annie sniffed again, wiping her eyes on the Kleenex Becky handed her. At some point during her crying, Shanna Stoltzfus had slipped into the room. She sat on the other side of Annie, one arm holding snugly to her shoulders, and made soothing sounds as Becky talked, telling Shanna an abbreviated version of what had happened. The truth, not the exaggerated tales that were sure to be circulating downstairs, albeit out of earshot of Mamm.

"A nightmare…." Annie swallowed another sob. "He would think this was just a bad dream. Because it is, really. I should have known better. Why didn't he object when the bishop made us apply for a license? He could have. But he didn't say a word. He just acted like he wanted to go through with it." Annie pulled in a ragged breath. Her friends didn't know she'd fallen in love with Joshua Esh. They didn't know that she'd hoped he'd shared the same feelings for her. Touching her the way he did, kissing her...that'd been nice. More than nice. A surge of hope raced through her heart—hope that, once married, there would be more kisses and gentle touches. Or, maybe he would find her so repulsive that he wouldn't even be able to look at her. The woman who'd snared him by accident.

"I'm going to pray that you and Joshua fall deeply in love," Shanna said.

"Jah, for sure." Becky nodded, then clasped her hands and bent her head, as if she expected Shanna to pray out loud, then and there.

Annie blinked back the fresh flood of tears filling her eyes. She refused to cry anymore.

Someone knocked on the door. Aunt Sally peeked in. "Annie, honey, they need you downstairs. The wedding is fixing to begin. You need to change. Your friends will help you, jah?" After an affirmative nod from both Becky and Shanna, she backed out of the room and closed the door.

Seconds later, there was another knock on the door, and then it opened, just enough for Joshua to peek inside.

Becky jumped off the bed, hands on her hips. "You can't be in here."

Annie felt Shanna's arm tighten protectively around her shoulders.

No one spoke for what felt like a very long time. Then, a small grin lifted the corners of Joshua's mouth. He winked at Becky and then shifted his gaze to Shanna. "Do you ladies mind if I speak a moment with Annie...*my* Annie? We could talk out here in the hallway."

Becky lowered her hands and glanced at Annie. Then, she granted Joshua a sympathetic smile. "Of course not."

Shanna gave her a squeeze. "Everything will be okay," she whispered. Then, she stood and gave Joshua a pretend punch in the arm. "I'll be right inside the door. Listening." She grinned at him. There was nothing timid about Shanna. She came right out and said whatever was on her mind.

Still, her friends had betrayed her. Defected to the player and his charms.

Annie pushed herself off the bed with her good hand and followed Joshua out into the hall, trying to assume her schoolteacher posture. The one that helped keep the big *buwe* at school under control.

She couldn't quite locate it.

Not that Joshua needed to be controlled, anyway. She was the one struggling to find her emotional footing after being told that marriage to her would be a nightmare. She pulled the bedroom door most of the way shut and drew in a deep breath. "It's okay, Joshua. I can move my stuff back to my bedroom. I don't want to be married to you any more than you want to be married to me." She hoped her voice didn't sound as shaky as she felt it did. "We can tell the bishop *nein*."

Pain, along with an emotion she couldn't quite identify, showed in his eyes, but his grin never faltered. Instead, he took two big, confident steps toward her, stopping just a hairbreadth away. "Ach, Annie." He reached up and traced her cheek with his fingertips.

She willed herself not to lean into his touch.

"I never meant to imply that getting married to you would be a nightmare. I meant...I didn't want you handed to me against your will. I wanted to win you."

Of course, that's what he'd meant. Who wanted a trophy he hadn't earned? She stiffened.

His hand fell away, and he looked down. "That came out wrong. Let me try again. I will marry you. I want to marry you. I want to make this right—before God, before you, and before the community. I won't dishonor you by running away and turning my back on my responsibilities. And I don't want you to worry. I won't force myself on you in any way." He met her eyes briefly. Color crept up his neck. "And...I would be fine if you wanted to move back to your bedroom, except that we're expected to...well, to share a room."

They were expected to do a lot more than just share a room. But none of that would happen, based on what he'd said—basically, that theirs would be a marriage in name only.

That meant the gentle touches and tender kisses were a thing of the past. Enjoyed for mere minutes—more like seconds—on one short day.

It seemed her only concern was being married to a man she loved—a man who didn't love her.

Joshua tried to read Annie's expression. He thought he'd seen disappointment flash across her face when he'd said they ought to share a room. Should he back out, despite what Isaac had said? He couldn't. It would dishonor her not to marry her now. Her reputation would be forever tarnished, and he'd be sent back to Pennsylvania in shame. He was more than willing to make things right. And, if they didn't share a room, living as they were in her daed's haus, with her brother and sister right down the hall, and with his parents coming for Thanksgiving, it would invite a visit from Bishop Sol and an offer of marriage counseling. Forcing them to discuss things that

Joshua didn't want to talk about, especially in front of the bishop.

To be honest, they probably ought to consider counseling. After all, it wasn't typical for an Amish couple to enter into marriage with wrist splints, road rash, killer headaches, and a sense of obligation that might as well have been a loaded gun to their backs.

They'd figure this out.

Somehow.

She sighed, as if her thoughts echoed his, and her tongue crept out, moistening her lips. His breath caught as he watched it trail across their pink softness. He reached up to touch her again, his hand cupping the back of her neck.

When he started to lower his head, she gave a tiny, strangled cry and jumped back, out of reach.

He sighed, allowing his hand to fall back to his side. He had a lot of lost ground to recover. Her trust to win. If he could.

Not to mention her love.

With a nod, he stepped back, even though he wanted with all of his being to kiss her resistance away. Then, pivoting, he headed toward the stairs. "I'll see you down there," he said over his shoulder. "Bishop Sol and the preachers want to meet with us before they present us to everyone."

Chapter 22

Back in the room with Becky and Shanna, Annie slumped onto the bed, grabbed a pillow, and hugged it to her.

Shanna shut the door. "So sweet, what Joshua said about wanting to win you, ain't so? So romantic."

Annie sniffed. She still felt weepy, and she hadn't found his comment to be sweet at all. It had been... she didn't know what.

Becky nodded. "Jah, I thought it was really romantic, too." She picked up the yellow bag she'd carried upstairs and lifted out a garment of sky blue. "I know you didn't have time to make a dress, so I brought you the one I made for my wedding. I don't know why...I felt I needed to, I guess. I'll make myself another one. You know you can't get married in brown."

She could. She was still the same, brown Annie. But blue was a happier color than depressing brown. And, truthfully, she was tired of earth tones.

Shanna studied Annie, then Becky. "You're almost the same size. Let's get you ready."

Annie was tempted to run after Joshua, to talk about the whole marriage thing. To try to make things right, at least in her eyes, and declare that she loved him. Declare that she would marry him, regardless of the reason, but only if he wanted her. Only if he wasn't doing it out of a sense of obligation. For if he was marrying her just to make things right in the eyes of the bishop and their community, not because he loved her, then she'd rather remain a maidal and live with the disgrace than marry a man who would resent her forever.

But her own disgrace would affect her family, too. She couldn't dishonor herself and protect them at the same time.

And it would be even more shameful to back out now. They had the marriage license in hand. "No waiting period," the courthaus clerk had said with a smile. Their family, friends, and neighbors were already gathered downstairs, despite the short notice.

Reluctantly, she unpinned her brown dress and dropped it to the bed. Becky shook out the blue one and held it out to her.

Shanna openly studied her. "Too bad we don't have time to shop. You need sexier undergarments."

Annie's eyes widened in shock. "Shanna!"

Shanna shrugged. "I know what I'll get you for a gift." Then, grinning shamelessly, she handed Annie the pins to close the dress.

Heat crept up Annie's face as she considered what Joshua might think about.... But he'd said that he wanted to marry her. Just moments ago. Such beautiful words.

Maybe his love would come, eventually. And, if she married him, she'd have a chance to claim the kiss he'd tried to give her in the hallway. The one she'd declined because of his terms, or the way she'd interpreted them. She could hope for even more, someday.

On second thought, she should have allowed him to kiss her. That way, she would have had another one to remember, to relish, in the years of passionless marriage ahead.

She studied her reflection in the small handheld mirror.

"Annie, kum on downstairs," Becky urged her. "There's nothing left to do up here. You look beautiful."

Annie exhaled. "I need to check on Cathy."

"I'll do it," Shanna offered. "But I think you should redo your hair before you go down. It looks a little unkempt." She hurried from the room.

Annie yanked off her prayer kapp and unbound her hair. Becky grabbed a comb from the bathroom and helped her get a couple of snarls out, and then Annie redid it.

Shanna reappeared a minute later. "She's sleeping soundly, which is just what she needs. She's on some pretty strong pain medication—I peeked at the label to see what they'd prescribed—so I wouldn't try to rouse her for the wedding. In fact, I just tried to, and she slapped me. I'd say, leave sleeping Cathy lie."

"Okay." Annie motioned to her head. "Is this better?"

"Much. Kum on."

Annie felt a wave of panic. "But...but...some of the women looked at me with condemnation when they came in. And many of them were obviously checking out my waistline for any signs of change. Not that anything is really visible in these loose dresses, but they looked, anyway. Everyone probably thinks I'm expecting and figures that's why I was fired, why the bishop's forcing us to get married."

Shanna rolled her eyes. "Jah, and they're probably thanking the gut Lord that their own daughters haven't brought such disgrace upon themselves. But if what Becky told me is true, and I completely believe her, then there is nein boppli. It was merely a kiss." She grabbed Annie's hand. "Everyone gets gossiped about sooner or later. You've just been so perfect, no one's had anything to say about you until now." She laughed. "Unlike me. You know I've been a topic of conversation ever since I could walk."

"And I have been for over a year," Becky added quietly.

"I suppose," Annie conceded. Shanna had been in trouble almost constantly, so much so that her daed hadn't allowed Annie to play with her when they were children. And Becky's situation had been regrettable, although, with Jacob, she was starting a new life.

"Don't forget, some couples get married only a few days after being published," Shanna pointed out. "And weddings can happen on Mondays, as well as on Tuesdays or Thursdays. I recently attended a wedding in another district that was on a Monday. It doesn't matter so much anymore. There are so many weddings, sometimes, they just have to fit them in wherever they can. How many were announced for this week? I think four, at least." Shanna rolled her eyes again, and Becky nodded in agreement. "Some of the people probably figure they missed the announcement about your wedding in the service. My mind always wanders during announcements. Or, they might think the bishop forgot to announce it, with so many other weddings happening."

Shanna was so encouraging. Maybe Annie could convince herself that the accusatory looks and malicious whispers weren't what they seemed.

Shanna took a deep breath and went on. "Okay. You know there's nein boppli. Becky and I know this.

Joshua knows it. I'm sure your parents know it. So, you simply act and speak as if you believe what you know to be true. Soon, the ones who think there is a boppli will feel foolish when it's disproved."

Annie stared at her, her mind struggling to process everything she'd heard. Yet her stomach continued to roil with nausea. Seconds later, she darted into the hallway, dashed into the bathroom, and lost her breakfast.

When Annie raised her head, Shanna stood there, holding out a glass of water and her toothbrush, already prepared with toothpaste. "There now, don't you feel better? Brush your teeth, and then let's go downstairs."

"Have you nein sense of privacy? Following me into the bathroom?"

Shanna blushed. "Sorry. I didn't think. Besides, I deal with stuff like this all the time in my nursing rotations."

A few minutes later, Annie stood at the top of the stairs, wearing a color other than brown for the first time in what felt like forever.

What would Joshua think? Would he like her in blue?

He wanted to marry her.

She took a deep breath and grabbed Becky's hand. After another moment, she grabbed Shanna's. She needed their strength. Their courage.

As they headed downstairs, she prayed, *Lord, please help Joshua to love me. Sooner, rather than later.*

The wedding was over, and the noon meal had been served, with Annie and Joshua waited on first. Annie had picked at her food, probably still scared.

Now, the afternoon of singing was in full swing, but some people were leaving early. Deciding he wouldn't be missed—who was to know he wasn't simply stepping out to give someone a private good-bye?— he grabbed his cell phone from his pocket and went behind the barn. He needed to call home and tell his parents about the wedding before the news reached them via the gossip grapevine, assuming it hadn't already. It was uncanny how fast information spread. He did have some relatives who'd relocated to Missouri, and they'd been at the wedding. Not that he'd paid too much attention to the guests. Most of the faces had passed by in a blur. After all, his thoughts were mostly consumed with Annie. By her beauty. By how happy he was to have her as his frau. By how much he wanted to kiss her, until her knees buckled.

He had no idea how the bishop had gotten word of the wedding to spread so fast around the district, but, the truth was, it had probably been easy. Just a word in the ear of the right person yesterday, and it would have worked its way throughout the community before the supper dishes were cleared from the table.

He speed dialed the phone shanty back home. How he'd wished his daed would just give in and get a cell phone. A lot of Amish carried them now, not to chat casually, but for a purpose, such as ordering farm supplies, conducting business, calling in the case of an emergency. But Daed had decided to stick to the old ways.

Joshua sighed, listening to the phone ring once, twice, three times. And then, there was a click, followed by a voice saying "Hullo?"

"Uh, who is this?" Joshua had never before actually reached a person at the shanty.

There was a slight pause. "Samuel Miller. Who are you calling for?"

"Arthur Esh. Would you mind telling him to call his son, Joshua, in Missouri, as soon as he can?"

"Jah, I can do that. I'll go over that way right now."

"Danki." Joshua said good-bye, then ended the call. He pulled out his pocket watch and glanced at it. The evening meal, which would be a light supper, was still at least an hour off. Maybe he'd have time for a brief nap now. He glanced around at the remaining buggies. Where was Annie? Probably sitting with her friends in the singing, or chatting somewhere.

He went inside the barn, making a point to be seen where everyone was gathered for the singing, so that no one would think he had vanished, and found Annie sitting in one of the rows. She looked so pretty in blue. He'd have to encourage her to expand her wardrobe beyond basic brown. Bending down, he whispered in her ear, "I'm going to take a brief nap. My head is hurting still."

She nodded but didn't look at him.

He slipped outside and headed for the haus.

Annie kept up her conversation with one of her friends as she watched Joshua leave the barn. She stayed there for another ten minutes, so that no one would think she'd followed him, and then got up to go to the haus for a drink of water. This was not how she'd thought she'd spend her wedding. Sitting in the singing, alone, without her new husband. But he'd had a concussion, according to Daed. Those probably took a while to recover from.

Shanna followed her into the kitchen. "How long did they say you'd need to wear the splint? Six weeks?"

"The doctor at the hospital told me to see my primary care physician in two weeks. He probably didn't realize that my physician is the local vet. You know he usually makes the haus calls around here and tells people when they need to see an actual doctor."

Shanna chuckled. "Well, the vet should know how your hand is healing. He has plenty of experience treating sprains—but generally on horses."

Annie forced a smile. "I think I'll run my binder over to the schoolhaus so that Ruth will know what I'd planned for the Christmas program. Do you think they'll miss me?"

"They shouldn't. I'll go with you. Where's your binder?"

"In Joshua's room." She glanced toward the stairs. Her room.

Shanna grinned. "I'll wait for you down here."

Annie hesitated a moment, then turned and headed upstairs.

When she reached the door, she hesitated again. Should she knock? Maybe he was asleep already. He'd looked tired when he'd come to talk to her, with some wrinkles on his forehead and creases around his mouth, despite his smile, that had spoken of the pain he'd mentioned. She listened but didn't hear anything. Not even snores. Though he might not be a snorer. After another moment, she twisted the knob and opened the door.

Joshua stood at the open window, shirtless, and holding his cell phone in his hand. He turned and looked at her, his eyes narrowing. He pressed a button on the phone, laid it on the dresser, and took a step toward her as she shut the door behind her. No one should see him like this. She wasn't even sure she should. Still, she could't help but notice the muscles, the sprinkling of hair.... She forced her gaze up to his eyes, her face heating. "I...I just came in for my binder. I put it in the bottom drawer." She pointed at the dresser, trying to keep her eyes on his. "Shanna and I thought we'd slip away for a moment to run it up to the schoolhaus and leave it for the new teacher. They replaced me with Ruth King." She was babbling like a nervous schoolgirl.

"Giggly Ruth," Joshua said softly. He bent down and opened the bottom drawer, his arm muscles rippling, and retrieved the binder. Then, he straightened and adjusted the black notebook in his grip, his gaze lowering to her lips. "I don't know what they were thinking when they hired her. She's bu crazy."

Annie was beginning to feel a bit "bu crazy," too. A shiver worked its way up her spine, and she took a step back, but she found herself pressed up against the door. At least her craziness was directed toward one particular bu—man, rather. Her husband, no less.

"You drive me wild." Joshua's voice was low. Intimate. He took a few more steps toward her, closing the distance between them. "I've wanted to kiss you ever since I first saw you. Kissing you yesterday wasn't nearly enough." He stopped inches away from her.

Her stomach started doing funny flips. She stared up at him, afraid to look away, afraid to see something that wouldn't be proper. She'd never even seen Daed without a shirt. Her face heated.

"It was a church Sunday, my first one in Seymour. After church, you were reading to a whole bunch of kinner under an oak tree. I thought you were the prettiest girl I'd ever seen. I asked about you right then, who you were, so I could try to court you."

He remembered meeting her? He'd wanted to court her, even that long ago? She began to feel even funnier. The fluttering in her stomach made it hard to breathe.

He held the notebook to his chest, so close that she was afraid she might accidentally touch him if she tried to take it from him.

"I want to kiss you, Annie," he whispered. "That's all. Just a kiss. Then, you can take your binder and go."

Just a kiss. Something told her it'd be more than that. The way she was feeling right now, aching to wrap her arms around his neck.... She shivered so violently, she was afraid her back would freeze in a cramp. He'd offered to let her reclaim the kiss she'd so foolishly passed up just a little while ago. One she desperately wanted, with every breath. Suddenly, she was glad Shanna had decided to wait downstairs.

At least the two of them had a measure of privacy. If she could find the words to say, to let him know she'd welcome his kiss. His kisses. But it seemed as if her tongue had decided to render her speechless. All she could do was stand there.

He lifted his gaze. Looked into her eyes. "Ach, Annie," he groaned. He raised a hand, his fingers grazing her cheek.

Music blared, breaking the silence.

She jumped.

He pressed the binder into her hands and spun around. "I'm sorry. It's...it's my phone. My daed. I have to take this."

Annie released a shuddering breath, opened the door, and fled.

Chapter 23

The number displayed on the screen of Joshua's cell phone was for the phone shanty back home, where Joshua had left his messages. The caller had to be Daed. Joshua stared down at his phone for a moment before pushing the button to answer the call. Had Isaac told Daed about the forced marriage? Or had he left that bit of news unsaid? Joshua dreaded hearing Daed's reaction to this most recent escapade. He swallowed his fear. "Hello?"

"Joshua. Are you back at the Beilers' farm, then? Or still in the hospital?"

"The hospital released me this morgen." He watched out the window as Annie and Shanna walked side by side across the yard, headed in the direction of the schoolhaus. Annie carried the binder, and Shanna appeared to be talking. How had Annie managed to escape from the wedding festivities? Considering the nature of the ceremony, perhaps she felt she could come and go as she pleased. And maybe she felt that delivering the binder to the new schoolteacher was a higher priority than visiting with her guests.

In actuality, Joshua supposed he could be accused of being just as negligent of their guests. He had a splitting headache, to be sure, so severe that even his stomach felt a bit off. And he'd felt the need to contact Daed before the gossips had a chance to twist the incident into something unseemly. He'd thought taking a nap and making this phone call were both necessities. If he and Annie hadn't been forced to marry—if this had been a long-anticipated wedding they'd both wanted—neither of them would have left the festivities.

His chest hurt. He'd sent Annie the wrong message again. And, apparently, she'd received it loud and clear. She thought the wedding was unimportant to him. And she'd responded in kind.

He'd finish talking to Daed, take another pain pill, and then go find his bride.

Ach, Annie. He still tingled from their too-brief encounter.

Daed had picked a bad time to return Joshua's call. He could hear Daed's voice speaking, with the occasional pause, but his mind didn't register what was said. His thoughts were centered on Annie. He'd thought he'd seen a hint of desire in her eyes. Maybe, if he pressed hard enough, he would be rewarded with a kiss.

His stomach knotted when he turned away from the window and faced the bed. The bed where he and Annie would sleep that night. Together. For the first time. Without a chaperone.

He'd promised not to take advantage of her.

Ach, Lord. How much will I be expected to take?

"Joshua? Are you there? Hello? Hello?" Daed's voice finally broke into his thoughts. "I think I lost the connection."

"Ach, sorry, Daed. Jah, I'm here."

"Isaac Beiler said you weren't hurt bad?" It sounded like a question, as if Daed wanted to verify for himself that Joshua was fine. There was also a bit of annoyance in his voice. He must have repeated himself multiple times.

"I jumped out of the buggy when the horse bolted. I guess I hit my head on something, because I woke up in the hospital. But I'm fine. They say I've got a bad case of road rash." Joshua laughed, hoping his daed wouldn't realize it was forced. "Wasn't real sure what that was, until they pointed to the raw skin on the palms of my hands and my wrists. My knee-caps are pretty scraped up, too. I'm not sure how I managed that. But I guess whatever I hit ripped holes right through the knees of my pants."

"I'm just glad you're alive. Your mamm and I want you to kum home. Are you well enough to travel? Isaac Beiler seemed a bit hesitant when I mentioned buying a bus ticket for you. I was afraid you might be worse than he said. I told him we'd kum down for Thanksgiving." He hesitated. "But if it's just...'road rash,' did you say? I think you can kum home, instead."

So, Isaac hadn't told Daed about Annie. About their marriage. Joshua swallowed again. "Daed—"

"About David. His parents are making preparations to go to Missouri. He's bad off?"

"Jah, worse than I am. He broke a couple of bones...had to have some surgery. I'm not real sure about the details. He's still in the hospital."

"Isaac Beiler said something about a couple of girls?" There was a note in his daed's tone that Joshua couldn't decipher. Censure, maybe. As if the girls had been the cause of the accident. Or, as if he suspected that Joshua had been flirting with one of them and not looking out for traffic.

"Jah. David and I, we were going fishing. We had Isaac Beiler's two daughters with us, Annie and Cathy. Cathy broke something...her arm, I think. I haven't even seen her today. She was treated and released. And I shoved Annie out of the buggy, so she had only a sprained wrist."

"Gut, gut. Well, I told this Isaac that I appreciate him taking you in when that other family kicked you out. We got your letter, just Saturday, with your change of address. I guess I'll buy the bus ticket and send it along with your mamm's reply."

"Ach, Daed, there's something else you need to know. I, uh, I married Annie this morgen. Today." He hated saying it like that, but he couldn't think of a better way to deliver the news. Even if this type of news wasn't meant to be dumped without a warning.

The silence stretched on, and Joshua could only imagine the thoughts that were going through his daed's head. A slight gasp was the only indication that he was still on the line.

Joshua sighed. "I didn't mean to blurt it out like that, but—"

"Do I even want to know what you've gotten yourself into down there?" Daed's voice was tight, fierce, and hard, as if he feared the answer. "You and this... this Anne—"

"Nein, it's not what you think. The bishop here is just really strict, and he caught me kissing Annie. He forced us to marry. Annie and I, we haven't... well, we've hardly even kissed. Yesterday was the first time, really."

"That's ludicrous. We'll talk to him about this. If you and Annie haven't been together, there's.... Why didn't you refuse? You could have declined getting the marriage license."

"I couldn't leave her in shame. And I would have been sent home in disgrace. Besides, I...I love her, Daed. I wanted to marry her, anyway." There. He'd said it. Admitted his feelings to someone else, as well as to himself. Something he hadn't dared do before.

"You haven't been down there long enough to fall in love." Daed exhaled shakily. "I wasn't expecting this. You never mentioned her. I thought you'd marry a local girl. That you'd just gone to Missouri with your friends to see the different sights, like you said. And you wind up marrying some girl we've never even heard of? Your mamm and I will kum down, then, to meet our new daughter-in-law. I'll call you again to let you know when to expect us. And to discuss when you're returning home, son."

"I'm sure you'll love Annie. We look forward to seeing you." Both lies. The idea of his parents coming and meeting Annie scared him more than he cared to measure. What if they didn't like her? Joshua disconnected the call with a sigh. He didn't know how to tell Annie that they'd be moving to Pennsylvania— that he'd intended to return home all along—when she and her daed believed he'd intended to stay. After all, he'd technically agreed to remain in Seymour to build a family and start a farm when he'd signed up for the swap.

But he couldn't. His home was in Pennsylvania.

The lies were turning into a miry pit. He wasn't sure how he'd dig his way out.

✿

Annie climbed the porch steps and turned to stare at the barn. She could still hear the wedding guests singing inside. But she wasn't ready to face anybody again just yet. Shanna had gone back into the barn, probably to find Matthew. Had anyone even missed the bride and groom? Maybe they had, and assumed they were together somewhere. Her face heated.

"Annie."

Her breath caught, and she spun around. There was Joshua, sitting on the porch swing. Funny she hadn't seen him. But then, she hadn't been looking. "Feel better?"

He shrugged. "Passable. I took another pain pill. It's beginning to kick in." He patted the seat beside him. "Kum here. Just for a minute. Then, we'll go back to the barn."

"And pretend to be the picture of wedded bliss?" She hadn't meant to sound so sarcastic.

He winced. "I'm sorry. I didn't mean to give the impression I didn't care."

How could he confuse an impression for reality? She knew he didn't care. She frowned, took another glance at the barn, and then went to sit beside Joshua. Playing the part of the obedient little frau. After all, everyone would expect her to be submissive to her husband. He slid his arm behind her, resting it loosely on the back of the bench.

"I suppose I gave the same impression of not caring." Except that she did care. Too much. And it tore her up inside to know that the wedding being celebrated—their wedding—was a complete sham. That she and Joshua would probably never be truly married, in the full sense of the word.

His hand closed around her shoulders and tugged her tightly against him, which caused her to jump slightly. Her heart rate escalated.

He set the swing to swaying, while his thumb started making circles on the sleeve of her dress. Then, he looked at her. Really looked at her, in a serious way. "What I was saying upstairs, before my daed called? I want to court you, Annie. If you'll let me."

"Court me? We're married." Did her tone sound as flat to him as it did to her?

A smile flickered across his face. "Jah. But it doesn't change that I want to court you. I still want to woo you and win you."

"I don't know why you'd want to do that." Annie looked down. "We were forced...."

He reached out a hand and touched her chin, then gently turned her face toward his. "Because my ultimate goal was to marry you, regardless. I hadn't planned on its happening so soon, of course; that much is true. I thought maybe next wedding season, after we'd courted, because I wanted you to love me." His smile grew. "But I'm not going to complain too loudly."

"You wanted to marry *me*?" Her voice had squeaked, but she didn't care.

"Jah." His gaze dropped to her lips, and her breath hitched again. "And now, I want to kiss my bride."

Her eyes widened. "But we're in public! Someone might see us." Yet she wanted it as badly as he apparently did.

"Please? It's our wedding day. And no one is around right now." He glanced toward the barn. "No one will see." After her hesitant nod, he cupped her face with both hands, his thumbs gently sliding over her lips, with the effect of lightning bolts.

Gazing deeply into her eyes, he slowly lowered his lips to hers. One hand slid behind her neck, fingering the wisps of hair that had escaped from her kapp, while the other hand drew her nearer. He twisted to face her fully, angling his mouth to fit hers. Then, he groaned, deep in his throat, and pulled her tightly against him, pressing her body to his.

Annie's hands were crushed between them, flat against his chest, which was painful with her sprained wrist. She tugged them free, and then, not knowing what else to do with them, wrapped them around his neck, her fingers tangling in his hair. She heard herself make a little moan.

Then, his kisses changed, becoming a little harder, more desperate. Her knees turned to liquid; her toes curled uncontrollably in her shoes. His hands wandered down her back to her waist. "Annie," he sighed. She didn't expect him to wrench free as he did, moving away from her. "Ach, what you do to me." His voice was hoarse.

But she didn't want his kisses to end. She reached toward him, wanting, needing, to snuggle in his arms again.

"There you are. We were looking all over for you." The familiar voice was an unwelcome intrusion.

Annie dropped her hands to her sides and looked up. Becky, holding Emma, stood with Jacob on the bottom step of the porch. Jacob aimed a smirk at Joshua. "Think you two had better go back to the singing before someone else misses you."

Joshua stood. "Jah. Maybe so." He took Annie's hand and helped her to her feet.

"We're going," Becky said. "It's Emma's nap time." She handed Emma to Jacob, then reached out to give Annie a hug. "I'll be praying." She pulled back. "You'll still kum to my work frolic, ain't so? You can do some work with one hand."

"We'll be there," Joshua assured them. He draped an arm around Annie's waist and held her loosely as they stood there, watching Becky and Jacob head to their buggy. Then, Joshua dropped a quick kiss on Annie's lips. "They're right. We need to get back." He grinned at her. "It's our wedding day."

Annie nodded, feeling happier than she had in a long time. Maybe her wedding day would be joyful, after all.

Joshua held Annie's hand all the way back to the barn. He hoped no one would peek out and ruin the moment. The strict rules regarding public displays of affection banned even the simplest of touches, such as holding hands. And he'd broken every one of those rules with Annie.

He didn't care. Except that he didn't want to cause her any embarrassment. It was enough that she'd allowed his advances on the porch swing. He wouldn't force her to hold hands in view of their wedding guests.

He sighed, thinking of the Englisch wedding he'd attended. The groom had actually been encouraged to kiss the bride in front of everyone, and not just once. Often. In that case, it had made Joshua uncomfortable. But now, as the groom, he wished that the Amish allowed such behavior. Then, he'd feel free to act like a lovesick puppy around his frau. To kiss her with abandon, without having to worry who was watching.

As they neared the open doors of the barn, he released her hand with a smile.

She returned his gaze with the sweetest grin, one that almost melted him into a puddle of water, right there on the barn floor. He could have stood there and gazed into her chocolate-brown eyes all night. Grinning like a fool the entire time.

Jah, he was in love. Totally, deeply, forever.

And he seemed to be making strides toward winning her heart.

He found a place next to his cousin Matthew, sat down, and joined in the song, watching Annie as she sat down next to Shanna and began singing, too. Then, he looked away, scanning the faces of the guests who remained.

His gaze locked on a pair of angry brown eyes. He flinched when the redhead to whom they belonged made a rude gesture at him.

Luke.

Chapter 24

Heading up to bed with Joshua that night was more than awkward. No one said anything, of course, since they were married, but Annie felt weird. Uncomfortable. Scared. And excited.

The moment became more awkward still when Joshua shut the door behind them. She eyed the bed, her eyes widening. "I'm nervous."

Joshua glanced at the bed, too, then turned and trailed a finger down her cheek. "We can just kiss all nacht, if we want to. Nein rules against that."

Oh, she wanted to. Kisses, she could handle. She went willingly into his arms. Welcoming his kisses.

The next morning, Annie awoke to the feel of Joshua's fingers lightly tracing the skin of her arm. She stretched sleepily, then snuggled against him again.

"Ich liebe dich, Annie Esh," he whispered.

A thrill worked all the way through her. He'd never told her that before. She wrapped her arms around him and smiled. "Ich liebe dich, Joshua Esh."

His grin faded, and he lowered his head. She pressed against him, no longer feeling so awkward or embarrassed. She wasn't sure why she'd been so afraid.

A few minutes later, she rolled out of bed. It must have been later than five o'clock, since the sun was now up. She hurried to get dressed, wanting to get downstairs and take on the day—her first as a frau. Unlike most newly married couples, she and Joshua would not be traveling around to the homes of various relatives. With Mamm and Cathy injured and out of commission, they'd stay home, instead. Annie needed to work, sprained wrist or not.

When Annie entered the kitchen, she saw Mamm leaning on her walker with one hand, trying to carry the teakettle to the stove with the other. Annie hurried to take it from her. "Gut morgen, Mamm. So sorry I'm late."

"I think it's understandable." Mamm gave her a tender look. "I'll let you take over, if you don't mind. I'm a bit overtired from yesterday. Though it was beautiful. And, even if I might have changed the situation, I couldn't have picked a better son-in-law."

Joshua came into the room and kissed Mamm on her cheek. "And I couldn't pick a better mamm-in-law. Is Isaac out in the barn already?"

"Jah, starting the chores."

"I'll go straight there." He winked at Annie, then grabbed his shoes and went out the door.

Through the window, Annie watched him sit down on the porch swing to put on his shoes. "Did Cathy ever get up?" Annie turned to look at Mamm. Her sister hadn't made an appearance at the wedding celebration, as far as Annie knew. But she supposed that was understandable, if she was taking strong pain pills, as Shanna had suggested.

"Nein, she's still in bed. I think she's had quite a shock, with the accident and all. Some people don't handle them well."

Annie put the teakettle on the stove. "You have a seat. I'll be right back down to start breakfast, but I need to check on Cathy."

Upstairs, she tapped lightly on Cathy's door. She didn't hear a response, so she opened the door and entered the dark room. She walked over to the window and adjusted the blinds to let in a bit of sunlight. Then, turning, she faced the bed. Cathy's eyes were open, and also red, as if she'd cried all night. "Go away." Her voice was raw.

Annie was taken aback. "What's wrong?"

"What's wrong? You're really asking me what's wrong? I'll tell you what's wrong. *He* survived. And I'm so afraid David didn't. Nobody will tell me!" Fresh tears rolled down Cathy's bruised cheeks.

"Nein, Cathy. David's okay. He's alive, thanks to Joshua. He had some kind of blood clot in the hospital, after the surgery they did on his broken arm."

Cathy sat up. "Really? You aren't just making that up to make me feel better?"

Annie shook her head. "Why would I lie?"

"I don't know. How did Joshua save his life? He isn't a doctor."

"I don't know the details, but that's what Bishop Sol's wife said yesterday."

"What was Bertha King doing here? I dreamed that Shanna Stoltzfus came by, and that she was trying to wake me up and get me dressed." Cathy shook her head confusedly.

"It wasn't a dream. She tried to wake you up for... my wedding." Annie glanced at Cathy. She dreaded telling her who she'd married. But maybe the ensuing storm wouldn't be as bad as she feared.

Cathy snorted. "You're not serious. There is nein way you could have gotten married without my knowing about it."

"I know it seems unbelievable. In fact, I have trouble believing it myself." Annie smiled, remembering her evening with Joshua. "But I did."

Cathy frowned. "Luke? I heard he was bragging around that he'd be marrying you sooner rather than later. Saturday nacht, someone told me that."

Annie froze. "It wasn't Luke." *Danki, Lord.* "I married Joshua."

Cathy snorted again. "Joshua Esh."

"Jah."

"Now that, I don't believe. I'm sorry." Cathy shook her head and looked away. "David's okay? I'll see if Daed will let me call a driver to take me to visit him."

Annie shook her head. "He won't. The bishop would take issue with your being in a bu's hospital room." That was a serious understatement, of course.

Cathy frowned again as she pulled herself out of bed. She held up her arm with the cast. "Can you help me get dressed? If Daed lets me, I'll find some friends to go with me, so that we don't upset the bishop."

Annie went to the closet to pull out a dress for Cathy, her fingers sliding over the soft fabric of a green frock. Maybe it was time she bought some new material. Something other than drab brown. She'd have to plan a trip to the fabric store. She took the dress off the hanger and brought it to Cathy. It was kind of awkward to get Cathy dressed, with one of her arms in a cast, not to mention Annie's wrist in a splint. She finally had to rip the sleeve along one seam so that it would fit over the cast. "We can mend it after you get the cast removed," she said as she helped Cathy back into the sling, supporting the arm.

"What's for breakfast? I'm not going to be much help, but I can carry the jams and such to the table."

"One of the women brought by a breakfast casserole. I just need to put it in the oven to warm." She should have gotten it warming before she went upstairs.

"Do you have time? Before leaving for school, I mean? Or did they let you go, since you're *married* now?"

Annie nodded, wincing. "They let me go. Ruth King is the new teacher."

Cathy shook her head. "That won't last long."

"Well, be that as it may, she is. And we probably won't need to worry about cooking much. Aaron says that the bishop arranged for meals to be brought in for a while, along with women to kum help with the laundry and basic cleaning...whatever we can't handle. It'll all get done. We might just have to work together to lift a heavy casserole dish. With one good arm each, we should be able to manage."

After breakfast, Joshua followed Isaac out to the fields where the beehives were kept. At least Joshua felt well enough to work. His knees hurt worse than his hands, but he was functioning. The pain pill he'd taken before breakfast kept his headache under control.

There was one last task to do before they'd leave them alone for the winter, according to Isaac: inoculating the bees, whatever that meant. He pictured Isaac trying to capture individual bees and give them shots.

He soon found out that Isaac had added the medicine to some sugar water he'd prepared for the bees to feed on until they hunkered down for the winter. The purpose was to prevent any of a number of diseases that could wipe out an entire hive. Isaac stressed that now was the time to treat the bees because the honey that the humans would consume had already been extracted.

Bees interested him more than he'd ever imagined possible. They were fascinating to watch and learn about. But he had a long way to go before he could claim to be even remotely comfortable working with them.

If nothing else, Missouri had been a learning experience. An exercise in frustration, maybe, but a learning experience overall. He sighed as he remembered Luke's many threats, getting kicked out of that haus, Cathy's pranks, the buggy accident, and the forced marriage. Funny—he'd thought Missouri would be so much simpler. At least Annie had made the frustrations worthwhile.

They were finishing the last hive when the musical tones of Joshua's cell phone ringtone came blaring out of his pocket. He and Isaac both jumped. Then, he grabbed the phone and glanced at it. "I should get this. It's my daed." Walking away from Isaac, he pressed the button to answer the call and raised the phone to his ear. "Hello?"

"Joshua. I got the bus tickets. Your mamm and I will be arriving in Springfield on Thursday morgen at ten. Can you arrange a ride from there?"

"Jah. I can do that."

"Isaac Beiler, he'll have room for us, ain't so?"

"Jah. There's an extra bedroom." Annie's old one. His blood heated, and he glanced toward the haus, wondering what she was doing now. He really needed to find some way to tell her about his—their—upcoming return to Pennsylvania, before his parents arrived and mentioned it. He had only a couple of days to somehow find the words to tell her.

He hoped she wouldn't be too upset when she learned that marrying him meant she'd be leaving not only her position at the school, but her family and community, as well.

After lunch, Annie went outside to take down the laundry. The temperature was cooler, maybe in the low 60s, but breezy, so the clothes had dried quickly. The sky was taking on a rainy cast, but, not having heard a weather forecast, nor having seen an almanac, she wasn't sure what might be coming in. She hoped it was rain, and not a late, out-of-season tornado. Rather awkwardly, thanks to her wrist, she folded the dry clothes, dropped them into the basket, and then carried it inside, balanced against her waist with her good arm.

As she put the clothes away, she lingered over Joshua's, making sure they were folded neatly in the drawers where they belonged. When that task was complete, she didn't know what to do with herself. Mamm had the mending and sewing under control, for now, though Annie still planned to make a trip to Seymour as soon as she could to buy material for some new dresses.

She went to her old bedroom and retrieved the historical romance she'd borrowed from the library but hadn't had time to read. Then, she curled up on the bed, but only for a few seconds. This was no longer her room. She shouldn't be here.

She couldn't quite bring herself to go into the room she shared with Joshua to read, so she tiptoed out of the haus and scampered to her special place in the woods. No one would find her there. And, hopefully, the rain would hold off until later.

She didn't know how long she'd read—she'd gotten more than one hundred pages into the book, at least—when she heard rustling in the bushes. She looked up. Joshua emerged from the undergrowth, carrying a thermos and two mugs.

"Break time." He climbed onto the boulder, grinning at her. "I brought us some tea, and...." He fished into his pocket and brought out something encased in plastic wrap. "Cookies."

"How did you find me?"

"I went looking for you. You weren't in the haus, and all the horses are home except Aaron's. I figured you were either here or at Becky's." He lowered himself beside her, then looked at her. "You don't mind that I came, do you? I know this is your alone spot."

"I don't mind." She scooted closer to him and reached for the thermos. "You made the tea?"

"Jah. Cathy had put on water to heat, so I used that and then refilled the teakettle." He held the mugs while she poured the tea into them. "Cathy apologized to me just a few minutes ago. She said she heard that I saved David's life and that she appreciated it. That she hopes we can be friends. Especially since we're family now."

"That's gut." Annie screwed the thermos lid back on and then reached for the cookies. "Danki for thinking of this." Strangely, she felt nervous now in his presence, away from their bedroom. She hoped she wouldn't start babbling.

He shrugged. "Kind of like a picnic, jah? And we're newlyweds. Nein place I would rather be than with you." He smiled, slowly but broadly, and his gaze heated. He leaned closer to her.

Flustered, she took a mug from him, then took a sip from it. "Peach?"

"Jah."

"Joshua? Annie?" Daed's voice drifted through the trees. "Bishop Sol's here. He wants a word."

Chapter 25

Reluctantly, Joshua rose to his feet. One couldn't ignore the bishop's summons, but he sure wanted to. He reached out a hand to help Annie up, then grabbed his mug and the thermos. She picked up the cookies, still wrapped, and dropped them into her apron pocket. Then, taking up her mug and her book, she surveyed the sky. "It looks like rain."

"Jah." Joshua felt a raindrop on his skin. Probably good they'd been interrupted. Although he could think of more pleasant interruptions than visits from the bishop. He held several branches out of the way so that Annie could climb through. Then, they crossed the lawn as light rain dotted their skin with moisture.

Isaac and Bishop Sol waited in the kitchen, both of them seated at the table, sipping from steaming mugs. Joshua smelled koffee; Isaac must have made some for the bishop. The plate of cookies in the middle of the table had been replenished since he had packed a few for his "picnic" with Annie.

Joshua placed his mug and the thermos on the table and sat down, while Annie started to carry her tea and the book into the living room. She paused to smile at Bishop Sol. "Nice of you to kum by. Let me know if you need anything."

"This concerns you," the bishop said. "You may stay."

Joshua sucked in a surprised breath. He hadn't expected that. And, from the apprehensive glance Annie sent him, she hadn't, either. He looked at Isaac and saw his eyes widen.

Annie set her book and her mug on the kitchen counter and came over to the table, feet dragging. She sat down between Joshua and Isaac, folded her hands in her lap, and lowered her eyes, the picture of demure submission. The way she'd looked at the school board meeting while everyone was shouting accusations at her and demanding she defend herself and her decisions.

Joshua felt sick to his stomach. He hoped the bishop wouldn't say anything that would hurt her more. Hurt *them*. Or have another ruling that would throw their world into additional turmoil.

He would admit it—he was glad they'd been forced to get married. It had given him an unexpected excuse to kiss Annie—and more. And she'd said she loved him. He smiled, but it faded quickly. What was the bishop mad about now? Maybe Ruth King, the new schoolteacher, was floundering, and the bishop wanted Annie to help her adjust. Or, what if Luke had accused him of something he hadn't done?

He couldn't help but wish he could reach for Annie's hand and support her physically while the bishop brought down whatever judgment he was about to pronounce. And he thought Isaac felt the same inclination, judging by the way he slid his chair a bit closer to Annie's.

Bishop Sol was probably about to ask for a public confession of whatever sin they'd committed to make marriage necessary, but it hadn't been sinful. Jah, Annie had been on his hospital bed, but she'd been sitting up, not lying down. And her kiss hadn't been heated or passionate. It'd been tentative. Uncertain. With an undercurrent of fear. And just the tiniest hint of hope.

Of course, the potential for more had been there. Maybe that was the problem.

Still, Joshua could name a dozen couples who'd had closer encounters than Annie and he, at that point. And the bishop must have been aware of at least some of them.

Joshua forced himself to lean back in his chair, to try to relax, and to prepare himself mentally for confessing to kissing a girl he hadn't been courting.

Annie hadn't expected to be asked to stay at the meeting. Especially since, now, Daed and the bishop sat there, calmly conversing about the weather, the crops, the bees, and the machine shop, as if this were a purely social visit. She knew it wasn't. Otherwise, the bishop wouldn't have asked her to stay.

Wouldn't have forced her to sit there and listen to things that didn't concern her.

Why had they descended into small talk instead of getting on with it? Maybe what the bishop had to say was really that bad, and he felt he needed to soften it up with casual fluff first. She glanced over at Joshua to see his reaction. He reached for a cookie, met her eyes, and gave a slight shrug.

When Bishop Sol had asked her to stay, and she'd sat down, Daed had scooted closer to her. He must be concerned about what was going to be addressed, too. So, why was he indulging the bishop with idle chitchat?

That the bishop had asked her to stay could mean only one thing: he was about to confront her about her transgressions and demand that she confess and seek forgiveness. May as well get it over with. Then, she could escape and finish her book before it was due back to the library. She sucked in a breath and, instead of waiting for a break in the conversation, blurted out, "I need to confess."

All three men turned to look at her, their faces matching expressions of shock.

Okay, so maybe that approach had been wrong. She should have waited, abided her stomach's churning, until the bishop decided to address her.

Yet Bishop Sol's eyes were filled with compassion. She hadn't expected that. It about knocked her for a roll. "Go ahead."

She took another deep breath before beginning. "I went to Springfield with some Englischers, and I tried on Englisch clothes. And I went to the battlefield, and then to the Bass Pro Shop, but all I did there was order lunch. And some chai." She wouldn't mention Joshua's part in this. That would be between him and the Lord.

Blinking was Daed's only reaction. But then, he'd been aware of most of those details. Except maybe the clothing part. Joshua remained quiet.

"I was uncomfortable in the clothing, so I changed out of it right away." She studied her fingernails.

Bishop Sol nodded. "I expect you would have been." He lifted his koffee cup to his mouth and took a sip. Then, he downed the rest of the liquid in one long gulp and set the mug down. "You always did love history. Goes to reason you'd want to visit a historical site. I'd figured you'd be an excellent teacher due to that trait. Probably the best teacher we've ever had.

You didn't limit the scholars' education to Amish history; you taught them American history, the history of language, the history of writing, the history of mathematics…. I can't imagine we'll ever have another like you." He sighed. "I didn't want to let you go, and I even disliked having my granddaughter assigned to the position. She isn't the best choice. But she is only temporary. Hopefully, we'll have a new teacher in the spring. If not, maybe by next fall, if the Lord wills." He fell silent again, running his index finger up and down the handle of his cup.

Annie sat in stunned silence. She couldn't believe her ears. Surely, he was about to bring down his judgment.

But after a long, uncomfortable moment, he turned back to Joshua and started discussing horses. Should she offer him a refill? Probably. She stood, picked up the bishop's mug, filled it with koffee, and set it back down in front of him. Then, she settled in her seat again, waiting.

It wasn't long before Annie started to fidget. She wished he'd get to the point of his visit. No way had he interrupted their picnic and asked for a word with the sole purpose of sitting around the kitchen, talking about normal things. And, on the slight chance that his visit had no purpose, there wasn't any reason Annie should have been there with the men.

She glanced at Joshua. He met her eyes for a moment, then turned his attention back to his tea and the conversation at hand. If only she knew him well enough to understand anything he might have tried to communicate nonverbally.

Now, the bishop was questioning Joshua about his intentions to purchase a horse and buggy of his own. Why did Joshua's responses sound so noncommittal? It was as if he were beating around the bush instead of giving a straight answer. "Aaron said he'd look around" was just one example of his vagueness.

Annie furrowed her brow and looked at the bishop, but he had apparently accepted Joshua's answer, for he turned to Daed and asked about his latest honey harvest. Would this mundane discussion drag on forever? Annie wondered if she shouldn't get up and go check on Mamm, though she probably was napping, or see where Cathy had disappeared to. But she might have gone to visit a friend. Or to work. Could she still work as a cashier with a broken arm?

Finally, the topic of honey apparently exhausted, Bishop Sol turned back to Joshua and her. Studied them. And drew in a deep breath. "I'm not in the habit of explaining my decisions. And I'm not entirely comfortable doing it now, but I feel I must." He inhaled deeply once more and glanced at her daed. She looked that way, too. Daed was tugging at his beard. He must be just as nervous. "I had a gut reason for demanding that you two get married, and I must confess that what I witnessed in the hospital room had nothing to do with it. Well, next to nothing. The truth is that I witnessed something similar in my early years as a bishop, and I let it pass. It turned out the couple was actually expecting." He picked up his mug, studied it, then set it down and reached for the sugar bowl. "But, like I said, that is not the whole reason."

Joshua felt his stomach roil as the bishop's gaze settled on him. Had he somehow found out his secrets? Decided to force him to marry a woman whose family clearly needed her close by, so that he wouldn't be allowed to go home to Pennsylvania?

He should have told Annie of his plans right away. Instead, he'd put off telling the truth in favor of more pleasurable things—things that might not have happened, had she known his intentions.

And now, he faced a deadline. His parents were probably on the bus at this very minute, headed toward Missouri. Even if the bishop didn't bring it up, his parents would be sure to do so.

He clenched his fists under the table, determined to focus on the present. He would not act guilty. He would pretend he didn't have the slightest idea what was going on inside the bishop's head. After all, he wasn't a mind reader.

Joshua leaned forward a bit as the bishop picked up his mug again. It seemed that this man of God was a bit nervous, too.

"I heard some very disturbing news on Saturday nacht. My frau and I had decided to go down to the pond and look at the stars. Admire God's handiwork. Great way to grow close to the Lord and to spend time with my frau. But we weren't alone. There were some buwe on the other side of the pond, and I don't think they ever saw us. They were drinking, probably drunk, and talking loudly. I knew most of them, and they were in their rumschpringe. There isn't much I can do about it, other than make a few visits around to their homes." Bishop Sol glanced at Isaac, then set the koffee mug down once more and folded his hands on the table.

Isaac shifted his gaze to Joshua for a moment, then looked back at the bishop. Joshua's stomach threatened to revolt. He knew. He had to. But who among those drinking at the pond could have known his secret? Jacob and Matthew were the only other two who knew, and neither of them drank. They'd both joined the church. He opened his mouth to confess but quickly pressed it shut again. Maybe it'd be better to wait until he'd heard the bishop out.

"They were talking about Annie."

What? Joshua turned his attention to his frau of just one day. He couldn't stop himself from reaching for her hand, even if the one closest to him had the sprained wrist. It felt icy cold, despite the thick gauze wrapped around it.

"Annie?" Isaac sounded numb. "Why would they be talking about my Annie?"

The bishop exhaled. "Apparently, they felt 'that transplant' was trying to woo her away from someone who had a prior understanding with her. They were talking about some Englischers helping to kidnap her on her way home from school and forcing her...well, shall we say, dishonoring her."

That transplant. Joshua knew immediately who was involved. And so did Isaac, judging by the way his face turned a frightening shade of red.

Annie's face paled. "Nein. Nein."

Joshua tightened his grip on her hand. She winced, and so he released it, sliding his hand down to her fingers.

Bishop Sol looked at Annie. "That is why I had to get you away from the school. I had to get you married. I had to protect you, as fast and as best I could." He turned his eyes on Joshua. "I'm sorry. I puzzled and prayed over it all day Sunday, knowing I had to fire her to protect her, at least in part, and not quite sure how to shore up that protection. I'd planned to discuss it with Isaac on Monday, but...." He bowed his head briefly. "When I walked in and saw you two kissing, I saw the beginning of a relationship. I knew Annie would not kiss anyone unless her heart was committed. And it was then that I knew what I had to do."

"Jah, you did the right thing," Isaac said. "With Joshua and me both protecting her...." He leaned forward and reached for Annie's shoulder. His voice had broken with emotion and probably some suppressed rage.

"She mustn't go anywhere alone," the bishop insisted. "I'm not convinced those buwe won't still try something. Some of the young men were at the wedding, and I could tell they were angry."

Joshua had seen it, too. He winced at the memory of Luke's menacing gesture.

But then, he said a prayer of thanks. Because it looked as if he'd have a way out of his predicament, possibly without having to reveal that leaving Seymour had been his plan all along. "My parents are on their way to visit. Annie and I will go back to Pennsylvania with them."

Chapter 26

A nnie dropped her jaw and turned to stare at Joshua. "What?" She kept herself from adding, "We'll do nein such thing." A comment so lacking in submissiveness would be a big mistake. Especially in front of the bishop, though she'd forgiven him for firing her and for forcing her to wed.

She loved Joshua. Was glad to be his frau. But she would *not* leave Seymour. Period.

"Might be a gut idea." Daed's voice quaked with his words. He didn't want her to leave.

She didn't want to go.

"That might be best," the bishop agreed. "An extended honeymoon, of sorts."

"But I'm needed here." Annie spoke quietly, calmly, not wanting to reveal her indignation at Joshua's idea. "Mamm is still recovering from her buggy accident. She's getting better, but progress is slow." She looked at Daed for support, agreement, something. But he merely studied her with a concerned expression. "Cathy has a broken arm, so she can't do much," she went on. "And Aaron is planning on marrying. Besides, Daed needs Joshua here. We can't go."

"Lots of history in Pennsylvania." The bishop tossed the comment out there, just like Daed trying to tempt the wild bees with a bowl of sugar water. Of course, Daed had given up trying to capture the

bees for his hive and had ended up ordering a start-
er set, instead.

And, if she could frustrate the plan by balk-
ing, they would eventually give up on this ridicu-
lous idea.

"We can't go." To emphasize her position, she
rose to her feet, walked over to the counter, snatched
up her book, and left the room. The rain was falling
more heavily now, so she retreated upstairs rather
than back to the woods.

She wanted to slam the door to add further
emphasis to her statement, but that would disturb
Mamm and Cathy, and then Daed would have plenty
to say about her show of temper.

As if walking out on the bishop weren't enough
to get her into trouble.

Daed would definitely have something to say to
her about her attitude.

Or maybe he'd leave that up to Joshua, since she
was married now.

*Let's see them try to get me on a bus to Pennsyl-
vania.* She would not leave her home, her family, and
her friends. Besides, the Bible said that a man was to
leave his mother and father and cleave unto his frau.
It didn't say for the woman to leave and cleave.

As Joshua watched Annie bolt from the room,
he was tempted to run after her and offer comfort.
He rose from his seat, intent on doing just that, but
the bishop's voice stopped him. "Of course, you'd be
expected to return to Seymour."

Joshua hesitated in the doorway and turned
around. "What?" *Don't give yourself away.* He glanced

at Isaac, relieved to see no signs of suspicion. Then, he looked back at the bishop, awaiting an explanation.

"Once Annie's out of the way, I expect the bu will leave for gut. Either that or he'll find another girl to court and marry, and then he'll confess and join the church, ain't so? And, at that point, it would be safe for you to kum back."

Joshua could have sworn that Bishop Sol was smirking. He felt a wave of nausea rise in his throat. At least the bishop had waited until Annie had left the room to spill this part. Joshua went back to his chair and sat down again. *How did he figure it out?*

Maybe he hadn't. Maybe Joshua's guilt-ridden conscience was reading into his expression and the conversation meanings that weren't there.

Annie flung a pillow across Joshua's room—their room—and then went to retrieve it, ashamed of her show of anger. *Forgive me, Lord.* Still, she never wanted to leave home. It seemed unfair that they'd force her to, just because of some comments made by a few drunks. Okay, so one of them happened to be Luke, but what could he do now? She was married. No longer available. And wasn't kidnapping a crime?

Luke wouldn't do anything to her, now that she was married. The men downstairs were just overreacting.

Had to be.

Because she wouldn't leave. No way, no how.

Hadn't her dream been to marry Joshua and have him help with Daed's businesses? Like Jacob and Becky's story, only rewritten with different names. And Joshua would build her dream haus next door to Mamm and Daed's, or he'd construct a smaller dawdi-haus for her parents to inhabit, while Joshua and she took over this one. Especially when the babies started coming.

Aaron would probably get the haus, however. And the land. Which meant that Joshua would have to buy new property.

Still, she would not be ripped away from her family. Especially not now. Daed would never force her to go. Joshua would see things her way soon enough. He'd have to agree to stay. Hadn't he been prepared to do that when he'd signed up for the swap?

As for Bishop Sol...he might be the trickiest to convince, but one never knew exactly where he stood.

She peered out the window. The rain still came down in sheets. The bishop would be in no hurry to leave in the middle of a downpour. And Bertha King wouldn't be expecting him home anytime soon, either.

Annie had to convince him to abandon this foolish idea. She stood up, straightened her shoulders, opened the door, and started to march downstairs.

"Do you have anything you want to say, Joshua?" Something in Bishop Sol's voice froze her in her path on the staircase.

There was a long silence. Annie peeked around the corner and saw Daed, still tugging at his beard, staring at Joshua. He was going to pull his hair out by the roots if he kept that up.

Joshua stood by the table. He raked his fingers through his hair. "Uh, nein. Your reasoning sounds right."

What reasoning?

"You know, I asked for references on the buwe who signed up for the swap," the bishop said gently. "I know a lot of things—probably more than you think."

It fell quiet. The silence lasted one second, two, three.

"I know things about you, Joshua." The bishop's voice was intimidating.

What?

The silence stretched on again. Wasn't Joshua going to respond? What could the bishop possibly know that Joshua didn't want him to?

"Jah, I'm sure you do." Joshua sounded troubled.

Annie was beginning to feel guilty about eavesdropping. Whatever secrets Joshua was keeping couldn't be that bad. But then, they could be. They didn't know each other well enough to share their innermost thoughts. That kind of intimacy took time, and they'd been married for only a day.

"Do you want me to say it, or will you?"

She heard Joshua exhale. "Fine. I have nein intention to settle here."

She caught her breath. Did he have to sound so firm? Couldn't there be a measure of doubt in there? A willingness to compromise?

"What?" Daed sounded strangled.

Kind of the way she felt.

Tears rolled down her cheeks, while her heart landed somewhere around her toes.

"I planned to stay only until it was time to harvest the maple syrup back home."

"I thought you said you wanted to marry Annie," Daed choked out. "All this time, your plan was to marry her and take her away?"

Annie shoved her fist to her mouth, hoping no one had heard her pain-filled whimper. Then, she turned and fled back upstairs, to the safety of the bedroom. She wanted to go to her old room, but she didn't have that option anymore. It had been cleaned and prepared for Joshua's parents. She ran into the room she shared with him, closed the door, and shoved a solid wooden chair against the knob, since it didn't have a lock. She wasn't sure that would work, but it was her only hope of keeping Joshua out.

She'd told him she loved him. She'd given herself to him.

And he'd said he loved her.

Had it all been a lie?

Chapter 27

And Joshua had thought he'd get off without the truth coming out. At least Annie hadn't heard. It was bad enough that the bishop had known and had pretty much forced him to confess to Isaac.

"Be sure your sin will find you out." Numbers 32:23. He should have known better. Should have been truthful from the start.

His throat seemed to close, cutting off his air supply. He avoided Isaac, whose betrayed expression pained him, and focused instead on Bishop Sol. "Why did you approve me for the swap, then?"

"Because." His Adam's apple bobbed. "I prayed over it, and I felt the Lord impressing on me that you needed to kum. I guess I selfishly hoped you'd decide to stay."

"Annie won't take this well." Isaac rubbed his eyes. "She's my baby. The last one. The one I delivered."

Joshua nodded. Their unusual bond was undeniable. "I'm sorry." He really was. "I never meant to hurt you. And I did want to marry her. "

Isaac looked away. "Jah. I forgive you. You're like a son. And I always knew someone would kum and take my baby away. I just didn't expect it'd be so far."

"Danki for forgiving me." Relief flooded through Joshua. The last thing he'd wanted was to ruin his friendship with his father-in-law.

Isaac nodded.

Joshua didn't look forward to telling Annie. He didn't want to injure their fledgling relationship. Yet he didn't want her finding out from anyone but him.

And until everyone came to terms with this unpleasant reality, there would be a wedge between Joshua and Bishop Sol, Isaac, and Annie. Not to mention the rest of her family, when they found out. And her friends. And the community.

He raked his fingers through his hair. Why hadn't he weighed the inevitable consequences of his deception long ago?

It was because he'd arrived in Missouri a single man with no attachments, and he'd expected to leave Missouri that way.

Then, he saw Annie. And the more he saw her, the more he liked her. Wanted her. Loved her.

He sighed. Maybe, if he could warn his parents, they'd keep quiet, and she could go back to Pennsylvania under the impression that they'd return to Seymour before long. Would that be a lie, too? The sin of omission?

Joshua knew the answer. He also knew that taking Annie to Pennsylvania under false pretenses would only cause additional problems later.

He sighed. "I need to find Annie."

It was past time he started telling the truth.

Annie lay curled on the bed, hugging a pillow. Joshua was a player. She'd known it all along. But she'd foolishly decided to believe she was different. And she'd married him.

The Amish marry for good. She wouldn't have the option of divorce.

She gulped. Joshua could go back to Pennsylvania, if he wanted to. But she would never leave.

So, the bishop wanted to protect her from Luke. She'd still have Daed. She'd have the name of a man. *Joshua's Annie.* Her heart skipped a beat. It'd been so nice to be his Annie. She tried to squelch her traitorous emotions.

She'd have the shame of being unable to keep said man.

But no one would know the whole story, as long as no boppli resulted from their too-brief union....

She heard a floorboard creak outside her door, and she tensed, praying the chair she'd propped against the door would do its job.

Someone tapped. "Annie?" It was Joshua. She held her breath. "We need to talk."

Maybe, if she didn't answer, he'd go away.

"I know you're in there. May I kum in, please?"

How did he know she was there? She could be anywhere. She could have crawled out the window, climbed down, and gone to the barn to hide. She glanced at the window again. Still pouring down rain. Okay, that scenario was unlikely.

But she could still make a run for it. After all, the rain fit her mood.

"I'm coming in."

The doorknob rattled. She sat up and eyed her makeshift barricade of a chair, praying it would work.

It didn't. Joshua opened the door with ease, while the chair merely slid across the wood floor. He peeked at the piece of furniture, then looked up at her. "A chair? Ach, Annie."

Why did he have to sound so genuinely caring? He was good.

She wiped at her eyes.

"We need to talk."

"There's nothing to talk about." Annie straightened and swung her legs over the side of the bed.

Afraid she might try to make a run for it, he shut the door, slid the chair in front of it, and sat down. She'd have to go through him to get out. "There are. I have things I need to tell you."

Her chest rose and fell with her sigh. "I'm not going to Pennsylvania." She speared him with a glare. "And you are a player. You lied about loving me. You lied about wanting to settle in Missouri."

He cringed. She'd overheard. She must have come downstairs in the midst of their conversation and overheard the wrong part. And the anger, distrust, fear, and pain he heard in her voice about killed him.

She looked at the pillow she'd been holding, then flung it at him, hard. He caught it easily and kept it in his lap, his fingers curling around the edges. "Annie, it isn't what you think."

"It most certainly is! Don't you feel wunderbaar to know you won?"

He winced at her heavy sarcasm. *Won?* He'd won nothing. If anything, he'd lost—lost her love, her trust, and maybe their marriage. His friendship with Isaac had been wounded. The list could go on. Indefinitely. "Annie, please. Let me explain."

"You are never touching me again. Ever. And when your parents kum, I'll sleep with Cathy, because there is nein way I'm sharing a room with you."

He reacted as if he'd been slapped. Time to rein in this conversation.

He rose to his feet but still hovered near the door, to discourage Annie from bolting. His hands, still gripping the pillow, had begun to shake. Must be from nerves. He loosened his grasp a bit, but the quivering persisted.

He had to fix this. Right now. He couldn't allow things between them to remain so unsettled.

He closed his eyes briefly. *Lord, give me wisdom. Help me to know what to say.* When he opened his eyes again, he aimed a steady gaze at Annie. "First of all, we're married, and you will sleep with me. Nein other option there."

She fixed him with a rebellious glare, one that clearly conveyed the message "In your dreams." And her hands wrung the front of her apron as if she wished it were his neck.

He had to formulate his thoughts or their marriage would end up being only in his dreams. "Second, jah, I lied. And I'm sorry. But I lied only about intending to stay in Missouri. Not about loving you. Not about wanting to marry you. Nothing will change that. Ever."

Her face expressed a mixture of confusion and hope. At least, he thought it did. So, he plowed on. "Third, I'm not a player. You should know that by now. If I was, I wouldn't have married you. Absolutely no one could have made me. I would have been objecting loudly. Did you hear me refuse? Nein, Annie. I married you willingly. And there's no one else I would rather have married."

She opened her mouth, but he held up his hand to stall whatever she was about to say. "And, four, you are going to Pennsylvania with me." When her rebellious glare returned, he tried to soften his voice. "But whether we stay there or not is negotiable."

Okay, not really. But perhaps they could work something out. Whether he could handle two farms, one in Pennsylvania and one in Missouri, was questionable. He was very doubtful anyone could do it.

Better not to lead her on, get her hopes up. "Somewhat negotiable," he muttered.

"Somewhat?" She sounded broken. Skeptical.

At least she'd accepted the rest of his conditions without question. That was assuming he'd correctly interpreted her silence as consent.

He dared to take a step toward her, still holding the pillow. "I'm the only child. The only son. Daed is leaving the farm to me, and I want it. But my two best friends live here now, near your friends and family. There are going to be times when we're free to leave Pennsylvania. We can kum to Missouri then, for a month or two, to see your family and our friends. I know family is important, Annie. And you can write."

She stared up at him, tears glistening in her eyes.

He tossed the pillow onto the bed beside her.

She snatched it up and hugged it to her chest. "So, really not negotiable at all."

His mouth quirked. "Nein. I guess not." He crossed the room and fell to his knees in front of her, bowing his head. "I'm sorry I lied to you, Annie. More sorry than you'll ever know." Tears sprang to his eyes and quickly overflowed. He buried his head in her lap and cried, feeling the coarseness of the brown material against his skin.

Lord, I truly am sorry, he prayed silently. *Please forgive me. Help me to resist any temptation to lie from now on. And forgive me for my sins—all my sins. I'm so very sorry.*

Peace flooded through him.

Danki, Lord. Danki.

He pulled in a shuddering breath. "Ich liebe dich, Annie. I really do."

He felt the pillow brush against his head as Annie laid it aside. Then, her fingers filtered through his hair, tousling. Feathering. He was afraid to move. He managed only to inhale and exhale, feeling the dampness of his tears on her dress. *Lord, help me not to hurt her again. Let me know how to win my frau's love. Her trust. Her forgiveness.*

"But what about Mamm?" Annie asked quietly. "I can't go until she's healed. And Cathy...it'll be six weeks before she's out of the cast."

He didn't dare say anything. Her fingers caressing his scalp felt good, so good. Besides, he didn't know what to say. Her touch erased every thought from his head.

Finally, Annie spoke again. "I guess Daed could get someone to help. And Bishop Sol did say they'd be taken care of."

He swallowed. Hard.

"*'Whither thou goest, I will go; and where thou lodgest, I will lodge: thy people shall be my people, and thy God my God.'*" Her voice was barely above a whisper.

His breathing caught as he recognized the Scripture verse from the Bible. The book of Ruth. He wanted to ask if she meant it.

"I'm sorry I've been so immature. I think I have a lot of growing up to do."

"Me, too," he whispered, his voice thick.

They could grow up together. Grow old together. *Ach, Lord. Danki.*

"Ich liebe dich, Joshua."

A fresh round of tears filled his eyes, and he raised his head. "Annie?"

She wrapped her hand around the back of his neck and drew him to her. Pressed her lips to his.

She tasted of tears and spearmint. Of hopes and dreams.

Of forgiveness.

He moved into the kiss.

She welcomed him, her arms going around his neck.

She tasted of love.

Chapter 28

A t the sound of gravel crunching in the driveway, Annie looked out the kitchen window. She heard Mamm huff. "Ach, the therapist is early. Cathy, run back to my room, if you would, and get the folder he left the last time he was here." She wheeled into the living room, where she'd left her walker.

Cathy nodded and got up, while Daed went to greet their visitor.

But it wasn't the therapist's small hybrid car. It was Tony's minivan. Annie turned to Joshua. "Your parents are here." She wiped her suddenly sweaty hands on her apron, feeling not at all prepared to face them. Would they like her? And what did they think of her for snaring their only son barely four months after his arrival in Missouri?

If she were in their shoes, she wouldn't like her. She'd be upset. Angry. And probably suspicious, just like everyone else. Instinctively, she lifted a hand and smoothed the fabric over her flat stomach.

Well, whether they liked her or not, she would not allow them to see the haus a mess, no matter that they'd just finished lunch. She gathered up the dirty dishes from the table and piled them neatly in the sink.

If only the tension that had resulted from the exposure of Joshua's lies could be cleared away just as easily. Fortunately, Daed was still talking to him, but the easy camaraderie they'd established was gone. Daed no longer joked with Joshua. Annie prayed that their friendship would return, given time.

Joshua moved to the doorway and put on his shoes. Then, with a quick nod to her, he stepped outside. While she finished wiping the table, she watched through the window as he enfolded his mamm and then his daed in a hug. He favored his daed.

Swallowing her fear, she put down the dishrag, slipped on her garden clogs, and stepped onto the porch. It would be best to meet her new in-laws before they came inside. Otherwise, they might think she didn't want to meet them, or that she was standoffish. She was halfway to the van when they noticed her.

Joshua reached for her. "Annie, these are my parents. Mamm, Daed, this—"

With a cry, Joshua's mother engulfed her in her arms.

Annie tensed, feeling caught off guard. After a moment, though, she forced herself to relax and returned the embrace.

"I was so excited when Arthur told me Joshua had fallen in love. I always wanted a daughter. I'm sure we're going to be great friends."

Annie hoped so. "It's nice to meet you, Mrs. Esh."

"If you're comfortable, call me Mamm. If you're not, I answer to Lavina."

Annie glanced at Joshua. Maybe, once she got to know his mamm, she could do that. The woman had unusually kind eyes.

They drew apart, and Annie turned to face Joshua's daed.

He surveyed her in silence for a moment. Then, he smiled, nodded at Joshua, and stepped forward to pull her into his arms. She knew now how Joshua had come by his demonstrative tendencies. "Welkum to the family, Annie Esh."

Later that afternoon, Joshua sat on the dirt floor of the shop, reassembling another lawn mower, while his daed worked on winding up a string inside a weed eater someone had brought by. The two of them talked—well, Joshua did most of the talking, filling his daed in on why he and Annie had been forced to marry, as well as why they wanted to return to Pennsylvania sooner rather than later, due to the possibility that Luke might do something drastic.

Isaac was talking on the wall phone in the shed with another customer about a chainsaw when a shadow fell across the machine shop doorway. Someone cleared his throat.

Joshua looked up and froze when his eyes met those of Luke Schwartz. *Speak of the devil.* He pulled in a deep breath and stared, unblinking, at his rival—well, former rival. And maybe his current enemy.

For a moment, everything seemed suspended in time. Then, the phone receiver clicked back into its base, snapping Joshua out of his trance. He brushed off his hands and rose to his feet. Without turning around, he knew that Isaac had come to stand beside him.

Luke studied the floor. "Can we talk?"

Somehow, Joshua managed a curt nod.

"Bishop Sol came by my haus earlier." Luke looked from Joshua to Isaac to Joshua's daed. "Uh, can we talk privately?"

Joshua hesitated. He glanced at Isaac, then nodded. "Jah."

Luke stepped back outside, and Joshua followed him. He turned just in time to see Isaac shut the door, leaving it open a crack.

Luke scuffed his feet. "I'm sorry. For everything. Please forgive me. I was so wrong to treat you like I did. Wrong to talk about Annie the way I did, to discuss the horrible plans the bishop overheard." He bowed his head. "I just want you to know that I fell at the foot of the cross." His voice broke. When he looked up, Joshua saw tears brimming in his eyes.

Joshua swallowed hard. He could relate. He'd fallen there, himself, only two days earlier. There was no better place to land when you had to hit bottom. He stepped forward and wrapped Luke in a bear hug. "I fell there myself, and I forgive you, just as the Lord forgave me." He wasn't quite sure he completely meant it, but simply saying those words was freeing.

The barn door opened with a creak, and Isaac stepped outside. He came over and clapped Luke on the back. "I forgive you, too." And then, he turned to Joshua. "And you, son."

A wave of relief washed over Joshua, followed by a surge of hope that the strain between him and Isaac was going away for good.

After Luke left, Joshua turned to Isaac. "If it's okay with you, we'll stay."

His daed stepped out of the shop, and Joshua looked at him. "At least until it's almost time for the maple sugar harvest. Then, we'll go home, as planned."

He looked back at Isaac, who grinned. "That's more than fine with me, son. More than fine."

❧

Later that evening, Annie helped her in-laws get settled in her old bedroom, making sure they had everything they might need. She liked them already, especially since they seemed to be getting along so well with her parents. Daed and Arthur, in particular, had laughed and joked a lot that afternoon.

Then, she slipped down the hall to her new room. For a moment, she stood in the doorway, just gazing in at it.

Annie glanced at the bed, still covered with the faded blue nine-patch quilt. She yanked it off, folded it, and set it on the chair. Then, she marched over to her hope chest and pulled out the quilt she'd sewn for her marriage bed—the green one with the double wedding rings. She spread it over the mattress, smoothing out the wrinkles with her hand. As she did, she remembered the last time she'd put it on the bed, when Joshua had first come to stay with them. Only in her wildest dreams had she thought she would share it with him someday.

Cathy came into the room, carrying an armload of garments. "Mamm made you a couple of dresses as a wedding present." She dropped them onto the bed.

"These are beautiful!" Annie fingered a pretty pine-green dress, then a wine-colored one. "When did she find the time to sew? Or to buy new material?"

Cathy smiled. "She bought it before the accident and sewed while you were at school. She said she could tell that you were almost ready to move on from wearing only depressing brown. I hope she was right."

Annie nodded, her heart melting with love for Mamm. She'd miss her. "She was. I've been thinking about going into town to get some material. I need to go downstairs and thank her."

"She and Daed are already in bed. You can thank her in the morning." Her sister gave her a hug. "I know I've been a real pest, but I truly hope you and Joshua will be happy together. I'll miss you when you go to Pennsylvania."

Annie sighed. "Jah. I'll miss you, too." She released Cathy as Joshua came into the room. "When do we have to leave?" she asked him. She still didn't really want to go, but she was prepared to do whatever was necessary to be with him.

He hesitated, glanced at Cathy, and then looked at Annie. "Luke came by. And apologized, to both your daed and me. I figure we can stay here until it's almost time for sugar season. That should give both your mamm and Cathy time to heal."

"Really?" Annie could barely keep from squealing. "We don't have to leave yet?"

"Nein. Not yet." He walked over to the edge of the bed and fingered the quilt.

Cathy met Annie's gaze and smiled. "Well, I'm glad we have some time together yet." She turned and left the room, shutting the door behind her.

Annie removed her kapp and reached up to pull out the pins holding her hair in place. Then, she stopped and studied Joshua. Her husband. Her heart swelled with love for him. For a lingering moment, he looked down at the double wedding ring pattern on the quilt. She watched him trace the colorful rings with a forefinger. "Pretty. I missed this quilt when you replaced it. Aaron told me it came from your hope chest."

Her face heated. "Ach, silly thoughts."

"Not so silly. I had the same ones for you." He looked up, hesitated a moment, and then approached her. "Here, let me help. I've wanted to do this for you." Facing her, he slid his fingers through her hair, pausing to remove each pin they came upon. "I love your hair. So long, so pretty." Released from the restrictive kapp, her curls tumbled down her back. He walked around behind her, running his fingers down the length of her hair. Then, he pulled her against him, his arms across her chest, and nuzzled her neck, her ear. She shivered.

"I know I've said this before, but ich liebe dich, Annie Esh. And I will keep on loving you, forever and ever."

About the Author

L aura Hilton graduated with a business degree from Ozarka Technical College in Melbourne, Arkansas. A member of the American Christian Fiction Writers, she is a professional book reviewer for the Christian market, with more than a thousand reviews published on the Web.

Promised to Another concludes Laura's first series with Whitaker House, The Amish of Seymour, which also includes *Patchwork Dreams* and *A Harvest of Hearts*. Previously, she published two novels with Treble Heart Books, *Hot Chocolate* and *Shadows of the Past*, as well as several devotionals.

Laura and her husband, Steve, have five children, whom Laura homeschools. The family makes their home in Arkansas. To learn more about Laura, read her reviews, and find out about her upcoming releases, readers may visit her blog at http://lighthouse-academy.blogspot.com/.